# TOO CLOSE FOR COMFORT

"What in hell are you doing?" Reed asked.

"I'm shaving you."

"Who told you to shave me?"

"Dr. Carr said to clean you up."

His head was beginning to pound. "Get away from me."

"I'm not finished."

"Oh, you're finished, all right."

Reed felt a warning prickle up his spine as Chastity stepped back, responding coolly, "Anything you say."

Touching his clean-shaven cheek again, Reed then touched the other to find it still fully bearded. "Give me that razor."

"No."

Reaching out with a strength he did not realize he possessed, Reed grasped the slender wrist so close to his face. Catching her off balance, he pulled her abruptly toward him, knocking off her glasses and sprawling her across him as he rasped, "I want that razor."

The female warmth of her was pressed against him, the curve of her surprisingly round breasts tight against his chest. Her disturbingly sweet breath brushed his lips....

# DANGEROUS VIRTUES: CHASTITY

## ELAINE BARBIERI

LEISURE BOOKS     NEW YORK CITY

*To love, the purpose and meaning of life.*

A LEISURE BOOK®

January 1998

Published by

Dorchester Publishing Co., Inc.
276 Fifth Avenue
New York, NY 10001

ISBN 0-8439-4339-4

The name "Leisure Books" and the stylized "L" with design are trademarks of Dorchester Publishing Co., Inc.

Printed in the United States of America.

# DANGEROUS VIRTUES: CHASTITY

# CHASTITY

# Chapter One

*1882*

"How could you allow this man to get into such a condition?"

The doctor was tall, thin, and irate. His small eyes glared accusingly at Chastity Lawrence from a narrow face that was lined and leathery. When Chastity and her semi-conscious burden arrived at his door a few minutes earlier, the doctor had examined her companion briefly and had then turned on her.

Chastity protested, "I did the best I could for him! He refused to leave the train until we reached Sedalia."

"He's a sick man. He's burning up with fever. He wasn't responsible for what he was saying. You should've realized that!"

"I know, but—"

"But, but." The doctor's glare darkened. "Excuses won't help this man's condition!"

The doctor turned angrily back toward his patient. Noting the wounded man's dark clothing and clerical collar, he said respectfully, "My name is Dr. Carr. What's your name, Reverend?"

"My name's Reed Farrell," the wounded man replied.

"You're a sick man, Reed. It's your leg, isn't it?" Dr. Carr touched the parson's thigh. He frowned at the low groan the touch elicited. "I'm going to have a look at it."

When the parson did not reply, the doctor addressed Chastity gruffly. "You're going to have to help me. This man's in no condition to help himself, and he's too big for me to handle alone." Working at the parson's belt as he spoke, he loosened the buckle and began unbuttoning the closure beneath. Chastity caught her breath as the first patch of flesh was bared.

"What's wrong with you, woman?" Dr. Carr asked impatiently. "I'm going to lift him up, and when I do, I want you to pull his pants off."

His pants . . . ?

"Did you hear me?"

"But doctor, I—"

"Just do what I tell you!"

Chastity looked at the doctor, then at the parson, who had lapsed back into semiconsciousness. She hardly knew this man! But Dr. Carr was right. The parson couldn't help himself. She had no choice.

Swallowing, Chastity gripped the parson's loosened trousers. Her hands trembled as they brushed the taut, warm flesh of his hips, and her mind raced. If the maiden aunts who had raised her could see her now, they'd—

"Ready?"

She nodded.

"All right, pull!"

Closing her eyes, Chastity jerked the trousers down. She opened her eyes slowly, intensely grateful to see that the doctor was not looking her way and that the parson was unconscious of the part she had played in undressing him. She allowed her gaze to drop slowly downward past his tightly muscled midsection and was relieved to see that although the doctor had stripped the trousers from the parson's legs, his more intimate private parts were shielded from view by the brief shortclothes he wore underneath. But her relief was short-lived when she saw the bandage caked with blood that the doctor was removing from the parson's thigh. She gasped when he stripped it away to reveal a horrifying wound.

"Yes, you do well to gasp!" Dr. Carr continued his reprimand. "This wound is putrefying. The state that it's in, he'll be lucky if he doesn't lose his leg. How in the world did a parson get a bullet wound, anyhow?"

A *bullet* wound?

Chastity shook her head as Dr. Carr's question rebounded in her mind. Suddenly realizing that the doctor was waiting for her response, she offered, "I suppose you'll have to ask him."

Her response appeared to satisfy the irritable doctor no more than her previous offerings. "I'll take care of this," he said gruffly. "Go out in the kitchen and start some water boiling." He scowled. "You can do that, can't you?"

Chastity deliberately declined to reply. Were all Western men this rude?

"Then go into the cabinet in the back and take out some cloths. We're going to have to draw some of the infection from this wound with hot poultices. I hope you're ready for a long night."

Her only response was a wilting glance; then Chastity turned to do the doctor's bidding.

Heat . . . pain . . . a burning in his thigh that would not relent . . .

Reed groaned aloud. Then he saw her face. Jenny.

She was even more beautiful than he remembered, with brown hair shining gold in the sun and fair skin dusted with the freckles she despised. He remembered trailing his lips across the path of those freckles. He recalled that the path eventually led to her lips. And he remembered the taste of her lips . . . sweet and warm like honey.

But that vision of Jenny was fading. It was being replaced by another scene.

No! He didn't want to see Jenny that way again. He didn't want to see her devoid of life on the cold ground—her body broken and bloodied, lying like a discarded rag doll.

He fought the vision. He struggled to escape it. He called Jenny back as she had been before, smiling and glowing with life. He wanted to hold her again, to feel her close to him. He wanted to know that she was not gone from him forever.

He strained to open his eyes, to call her name. His heavy lids lifted and he saw her outline in the haze that enveloped him. He reached for her. He strained, battling the pain and the heat, knowing that if he could hold her again, all would be well at last.

But she held herself aloof from him.

Jenny, please . . .


"What the matter with you, woman?" They had been working for hours over the fevered parson with little progress, and Dr. Carr's patience was fading. He snapped, "Can't you see what that man wants?"

Frowning with consternation, Chastity bit back her reply. Her respect for the gray-haired physician's skill had held her silent under his unwarranted attacks as they worked side by side, but the overwhelming desire to snap back at him was almost beyond her control. Surely he realized that the parson's dangerous condition was not her fault. She had done the best she could for a man who was little more than a stranger to her. When she had met him on the train to Kansas City, she had seen that he was ill, and she'd tried to help him. She had delivered him to a doctor's door. She had remained to assist the doctor when there was no other nurse available. They had been working over him for three hours, with the Reverend Reed Farrell twisting and turning, fighting them every step of the way, and she was as exhausted as Dr. Carr was.

Chastity looked at the reverend's tortured expression, and her throat choked tight. That was the crux of it, she knew. Their efforts had had little effect on his condition. Dr. Carr was as tensely aware of that as she. Was it too late to save him?

"I asked you a question, woman!"

"My name isn't 'woman'." Her voice was shaking with the anger she had suppressed for so long. "It's Chastity, and I would appreciate it if you would address me by that name."

"Chastity, is it?" Dr. Carr's tone did not change. "Well, my question remains the same. Look at that man. Are you blind? He's reaching for you. He's trying to speak. He's in pain, and he needs your comfort. Forget the damned poultices! I can handle them. What I can't do is calm whatever agitation is tormenting him. You can." He stared at her when she did not move, then ordered, "Take the man's hand, damn it!"

Stunned by the doctor's scathing tirade, Chastity turned back to the reverend to see the intense blue of his eyes upon her. His lips were moving in an incoherent appeal that raised a lump in her throat. Suddenly trembling, she reached out to take his hand, only to be startled when he pulled her toward him with unexpected strength. She felt the heat of his body as his arms folded hungrily around her, as his unsteady hand twisted in her hair. She heard the soft, tender words he mumbled against her ear.

There was pain in his words. There was a longing and desolation, the depths of which she had never heard before. There was a yearning so intense that it brought tears to her eyes as she lifted her head to looked down into the parson's bearded countenance.

His eyes were also moist with tears, and Chastity ached inside. He was suffering and he was in need, but his debility was not only physical. She wanted to assuage his need . . . but how? She touched his bearded cheek, and his lips twitched with a smile. He rasped an unintelligible word, tightening his hand in her hair as he drew her mouth down to his. She caught her breath as their lips touched briefly.

"Jenny . . ."

Blocking out his rasping whisper, Chastity allowed him to hold her against a heart that was pounding as rapidly as her own. She felt the love that welled within him and she closed her eyes, aware that his thrashing had ceased.

"You're looking tired."

Chastity turned with surprise at the sympathetic tone of Dr. Carr's voice. He stood behind her in the Sedalia hotel room where the unconscious Reverend Reed Farrell had been carried a short time earlier. The glow of early morning filtered through the lone window overlooking the town's main street, which had not yet come to life with the new day. The slivers of light cast gray shadows against the bed where the parson lay sleeping quietly after a long and exhausting night. Clearly revealed by the pale luminescence were deep lines of fatigue marking the doctor's face as he awaited her reply, but she saw something else, as well.

Was he actually trying to smile?

"I'm sorry." Dr. Carr laid a heavy hand briefly on her shoulder. "I was hard on you last night. Any other woman would have given me back more of the same, but it occurs to me that you were too much of a lady to be as rude as I was. I'm afraid my concern for my patient affected my manners."

Chastity glanced toward the bed, not quite ready to accept his apology. "I was worried about him, too," she responded.

"I know. You were a great help."

"I've had some experience dealing with the infirm."

"I should've realized that was the reason for your coolheadedness when any other woman in your situation would've panicked. Reed is a lucky man to have you at his side." Dr. Carr turned briefly toward his patient. "That medicine I gave him will let him sleep for a while. I suggest that you get some sleep, too, while you can. I'll check back on him later."

The doctor's meaning filtered slowly through Chastity's exhaustion-dulled mind. He was expecting her to stay. No, she couldn't! She had to be on her way. She responded softly, "I think it would be best if you found someone to take over from here, doctor. I can't. You see, I—"

"You can't? Come now." Dr. Carr's surprise was obvious. "You aren't going to panic on me now, are you? I'm only a few steps down the street if there's a problem, and you've demonstrated that you're a capable woman."

"I'm not panicking." Chastity was suddenly at a loss for words. How could she explain that she was on her way to Caldwell, Kansas, on the first leg of a journey that she had waited all her life to undertake? And how could she make him understand that she feared further delay might weaken her already rapidly waning courage?

Chastity responded instead, "Isn't there someone else who can take care of him? I mean"—she searched for words that would not appear selfish—"someone more suited?"

"My dear woman," Dr. Carr said, sounding incredulous. "Someone more suited than you? You saw how Reed responded to you last night. Whatever demons were tormenting him, you were obviously the only one who could calm him. Surely you realize that if you hadn't, we might have lost the battle. He still isn't out of danger. I think that leaves you uniquely qualified for his care."

Her face heating with embarrassment, Chastity glanced again toward the bed. She remembered only too well the warmth of that man's strong arms around her, the loving words whispered against her hair. But those words weren't meant for her.

"He wasn't lucid. He didn't know what he was doing."

"My dear, he knew."

Unwilling to dispute the doctor's conviction, Charity blurted out, "But—but I have so many things to do! There are things I must take care of, people I must contact."

"I'm sure whatever those arrangements are, they are superseded by this emergency, my dear. You mustn't allow yourself to get upset about incidentals."

Incidentals? Chastity stared. Every stitch of clothing she owned was in the suitcase that she had abandoned when she'd left the train to help Reed Farrell. If she hadn't remembered Aunt Penelope's comment about always carrying money close to the flesh when traveling, she wouldn't even have a cent to her name!

Dr. Carr's expression softened. "Come, dear, why don't you rest? You'll feel differently about all this after a few hours' sleep. And Reed will be within your reach should he awaken."

Chastity was aghast. "You mean you expect me to sleep in this room?"

"Of course." Dr. Carr appeared puzzled. "It's a big room. That's why I told the hotel manager to send up those pillows and the extra blanket that're on the chair in the corner. The chair is well upholstered. You should be able to prop your feet on the ottoman and make yourself quite comfortable."

"But—"

"Please, no more talk. You need rest, and so do I."

Dr. Carr turned wearily toward the door. He looked back briefly, his hand on the knob. "I'll be back later this afternoon. You can send someone for me if you need me in the meantime. Reed's still very sick, but I think he'll be all right until then." Dr. Carr managed another smile as he drew the door closed behind him. "Try not to worry. Your husband is a strong man."

*Your husband . . . ?*

Chastity's response remained choked in her throat as the door clicked closed. She turned slowly to stare at the bed behind her, the import of the doctor's words rebounding in her mind. That was why he had been so angry with her that the reverend's wound had been neglected! That was why he had so casually ordered her to remove his patient's trousers and had become so annoyed at her hesitation! That was the reason he had so casually stripped away the parson's clothes in front of her and—and almost *ordered* her into the man's arms!

Oh, no . . .

Chastity's pale cheeks flamed with mortification! And she had followed the doctor's orders without protest, going so far as to help him remove the rest of the reverend's clothes, as if tending to a half-naked man was commonplace for her! What would the doctor think when he learned the truth? Her reputation would be ru-

2Elaine Barbieri

ined. She would never live it down. Gossip would follow her to Caldwell—wherever she went. She would be considered a scarlet woman!

Chastity unconsciously clutched her locket. No, she didn't want that, especially not now, when she was finally on her way *home*.

Chastity covered her face with her hands. Her head jerked up at a low moan from the bed. It was the first sound the parson had made since the doctor had given him the sleeping powder, and she was beside him in a minute. The high color of his fever had faded, leaving him startlingly pale. Deep circles ringed the blue eyes that fluttered briefly open as his bearded cheek twitched with pain. His lips separated with a grimace that displayed white, even teeth beneath, and a tremor moved down her spine. She remembered the warmth of those lips against hers. He had been tender and gentle, despite the yearning she had sensed inside him because he believed she was his dear Jenny.

She wondered where Jenny was now. And she wondered how it would feel to have this man love her that much.

The reverend's heavy lids fluttered open briefly, revealing another flash of brilliant blue. His lips twitched in a smile before his eyes again closed.

But that smile wasn't for her. She knew that instinctively, just as she knew that even while she stood beside him, in his mind, Chastity Lawrence didn't exist at all.

22

Weariness suddenly overwhelmed her, and Chastity turned to look at the chair in the corner. She was tired. She needed sleep. She'd straighten things out when she awoke, and then she'd be on her way. Just a few hours' rest was all she needed.

Sinking down into the chair moments later, Chastity pulled the blanket up over her shoulders, removed her glasses, and closed her eyes.

*Where am I?*

His head throbbing, Reed struggled to raise his heavy eyelids. Squinting, he looked at the unfamiliar room around him. A blur of mismatched furniture and faded wallpaper swam before him. How had he gotten here?

The pounding in his head increased as Reed strained to remember. He had been on the train going to Sedalia, and he was sick. His leg. He slid a hand under the blanket, suddenly realizing that he was naked except for his smallclothes and the bandage on his leg. He winced with pain when he touched his thigh. Yes, he remembered. The doctor had warned him that his wound had become infected and needed care, but he had been determined that Will Morgan would not escape him this time.

He felt hot. He pushed the blanket down to his waist, relieved when the damp skin of his chest was exposed to the cooling air. He had a fever. Yes . . . the train ride had become a nightmare that would not end. He recalled hearing the conductor call out that they were nearing

23

Sedalia, and he remembered standing up to get his bag.

Memory abruptly faded. Was that where he was, in Sedalia? He touched his leg gingerly. The bandage was dry. It had been changed.

Suddenly angry at his confusion, he lifted his head. Pain stabbed simultaneously in his temple and thigh, and he groaned aloud. The sound brought a woman to his bedside. He strained to identify her.

No, it couldn't be! Blinking his eyes, Reed struggled to clear his vision. The woman did not speak. Instead, she stood looking soberly down at him. Her hair glinted in the light filtering through the window. It glowed with a reddish cast. No, Jenny's hair was brown, and it glowed honey gold in the sun.

Hot . . . he was so hot.

Reed tried to uncover himself, to escape the heat. He was being consumed by the fire under his skin.

"No, don't do that."

The vision spoke and Reed froze into stillness. A slow joy began rising within. It *was* her! She was real. She was here. She had returned to him!

Choked laughter rose in his throat, emerging in a strange, croaking sound as he tried to throw the coverlet back.

"No, please. You're sick. Don't uncover yourself."

He caught her hand as she attempted to stop

24

him. He held it tightly, refusing to let go. He whispered, "Don't leave."

She went still, then responded softly, "You don't understand. I'm not who you think I am."

"Don't leave. . . ." The light was dimming. "Don't leave me again."

"Reverend . . . Reed, please try to understand."

Panic beset him at her tone. The heat within grew hotter. It consumed the light. She was fading away, and he begged with his last remaining breath, "Don't leave!"

The last spot of light dwindled as he heard her respond, her voice somehow sad.

"No, I won't leave you."

# *Chapter Two*

Sedalia's rutted main street was alive with traffic in the bright sunlight of early afternoon. Chastity walked along the board sidewalk, squinting against the glare. She turned at the sound of loud rumbling to see a large, dilapidated wagon loaded with hides lumbering past. A group of mounted men in travel-stained clothing turned onto the thoroughfare, their hats pulled down on their foreheads and their guns slung low on their hips. Loud music and shrill laughter came from the gaudily painted saloon across the street, while in front of her, women clad in unstylish clothing moved briskly along a line of wooden, false-fronted buildings that appeared hopelessly primitive to Chastity's eye. All contrasted acutely with the cobbled streets and graceful architecture of New York City, where she had been schooled and raised. She was struck with a momentary sense of unreality.

That feeling of unreality soared as Chastity glimpsed her reflection in a storefront window. The woman who stared back at her bore little resemblance to the meticulously groomed and soberly dressed Chastity Lawrence who had begun her journey West days earlier. Fiery hair formerly confined neatly under a modest bonnet glittered in the sun, the wanton tendrils at her hairline dancing in the warm breeze. Her discreet black dress, carefully chosen for its conservative style, was badly wrinkled and untidy, clearly revealing that she had slept in it. Adding to her dissolute appearance were two missing buttons on her bodice, lost somewhere during the previous night's struggles, which allowed her neckline to gap in a most improper way. The resulting effect was an appearance that gave a totally erroneous impression of the type of woman she was, and of the activities which had left her in such a tousled state.

Chastity suppressed an embarrassed groan. She had been so disoriented when she'd been awakened from an exhausted nap by Dr. Carr a few minutes earlier that she'd given no thought to her dishevelment when he dispatched her to "get herself a proper meal."

Chagrined, she could almost hear her aunts' anxious advice.

*"Chastity . . ."* Aunt Penelope would try to be

diplomatic. *"Your hair, dear . . . it is outland-ishly bright in color and far too unruly. You must make a better effort to control it if you wish to preserve a respectable appearance. A bonnet, dear . . . you must buy another one immediately. It's your only salvation!"*

Aunt Harriet, of course, would counter with a more direct reply. *"A bonnet! Penelope, really! Your eyesight must be failing! That's the least of Chastity's present concerns!"*

*"She needs a bonnet, I tell you . . . and her glasses! Where are your glasses, Chastity?"*

Yes, where were her glasses? For the life of her, she could not remember.

Incredulous at the turn her life had taken so unexpectedly, Chastity thought back to when it had all started a day earlier—when the Reverend Reed Farrell had boarded the train on which she was traveling west.

The truth was, he'd caught her attention the moment he walked through the doorway of the rail car. Bearded, wearing a cleric's collar and dark attire, his hat pulled down low on his forehead, he had seemed as out of place among the other Westerners filling the rail car as she. She had been able to discern little about him except that he walked laboriously and with a pronounced limp before he sat down, tilted his hat over his face, and fell asleep.

She remembered that her sense of disquiet had increased as the untamed countryside continued flashing past the windows of the rail car. Traveling alone, through unfamiliar country toward an uncertain destination, she had felt her courage failing her. She was increasingly drawn to the sleeping reverend, recalling the sage advice and encouragement she always received from the aging minister of the church she and her aunts had attended.

Dared she approach him?

An inner voice immediately responded. Of course not! The man was sleeping!

A more dogged inner voice nudged, but if he should awaken . . .

As if in answer to her thoughts, the parson stirred.

She approached him nervously, beginning hesitantly, "G—good afternoon, Reverend. My name is Chastity Lawrence. I saw you when you entered the car. I thought if you weren't busy . . . I mean, if you had a few minutes to spare . . ." Her train of thought faltered when she noted the parson's wavering stare and the unnatural flush of his skin. She asked, "Are you all right, sir?"

She did not expect his frown as he responded harshly, "What do you want?"

Uncertain, she took a backward step. "I—I didn't mean to disturb you. I thought if you weren't otherwise occupied, we might talk."

"I'm busy," he replied succinctly.

Shocked at his discourtesy, she managed, "Are all men of God in the Wild West *rude*?"

"I'm busy!" he repeated.

Had she not noted the telltale glaze to his eyes at that moment and the twinge of pain that

29

tensed his face, she supposed she would have
turned away on the spot. Instead, she reached
out instinctively to touch his forehead. He
jerked back from her touch, too late to hide the
burning heat there. She gasped, "You have a fever!"

Eyes that were incredibly blue held hers
coldly. "No, I don't."

She replied with equal firmness, "Yes, you
do."

The blue eyes turned to ice. "Go away."

Not quite believing her ears, she blinked and
adjusted her small, wire-rimmed spectacles. "I
beg your pardon."

She jumped as he snapped, "Go away!"

But she did not budge an inch.

Instead, she noted that he clenched his teeth,
then raised a shaky hand to his temple.

Unable to help herself, she pressed, "You're
in pain, aren't you?"

"That's none of your damned business!"

"Sir, your language ill befits a man of God!"

"Look . . ." His gaze grew ominous. ". . . let's
get something straight. My *language* is my business, too."

Chastity stiffened. "I just wanted to help."

"I don't need your help."

"You need a doctor."

"No, I don't."

"You do! You should see one at the next stop."
She glanced at the corner of the ticket visible in
his coat pocket. Sedalia. Aghast, she pressed,
"Surely you don't intend to wait until you reach

Sedalia to see a doctor. We won't arrive there until evening!"

The reverend's flushed face twitched. "Who are you, anyway?"

"My name is Chas—"

"Chastity Lawrence. But *who* are you?"

Her bafflement at his question was forgotten when she saw his face tighten. She whispered, "You *are* in pain."

Silence.

She saw his sudden pallor. "You're nauseated, too, aren't you?"

No response.

She noted his squint. "And your head is pounding."

His glare grew venomous.

She studied his fevered glower. She scanned the broad expanse of shoulders that filled his seat to overlapping and the muscular depth of chest beneath the dark jacket he wore. Refusing to acknowledge the peculiar tremor that moved down her spine when she glanced back up and met his unrelenting stare, she reasoned that he was neither old nor feeble, yet he had been stooped and limping when he'd entered the car. He had obviously injured himself and was more ill than he realized.

She spoke softly. "You're sick. You need help."

"Look . . ." His voice became a low growl. "It's none of your damned business if I'm sick. Go away and leave me alone."

Deciding it was better to indulge him, she

said, "All right, it isn't my business, but it's cooler in this part of the car, so if you don't mind, I'll sit here. You can sleep if you want. I won't bother you." When there was no reply beyond a deepening of his scowl, she urged, "But won't you at least tell me your name?"

"I thought you said you wouldn't bother me."

The poor man didn't know what he was saying.

Hours later she was holding a canteen to his lips, pleading with him to drink. His condition had deteriorated badly as the long afternoon, fraught with delays, had slipped into night. He had begun mumbling deliriously, remaining lucid enough only to insist that he would not leave the train until he reached Sedalia.

Chastity had looked around the darkened car, seeking a friendly face, a concerned glance, a helpful word. Despairing when there were none, she was not aware of the tear that trailed down her cheek until a gentle hand brushed it away. She turned, startled to see that the parson was suddenly awake and leaning toward her. His flushed face was tight with concern when he whispered, "No, please don't cry, darlin'."

Speechless, she had felt a strange fluttering within her as he trailed callused fingertips against the line of her jaw. His lips were only inches from hers when he rasped, "But you're beautiful even when you cry, Jenny."

*Jenny . . .*

Stiffening briefly with pain, he continued more fervently than before, "I missed you so much. We'll never be apart again. I promise. You'll always be—"

"Sedalia! Next stop, Sedalia!"

He jerked back abruptly at the sound of the conductor's voice and glanced around him. She saw his confusion when he stared at her briefly, then at the conductor as he approached. He was about to speak when the screech of the train's brakes stopped him and a dimly lit station came into view in the darkness. She watched tensely as he drew himself unsteadily to his feet in the rocking car and reached for his hat and bag on the rack above his head.

The conductor grasped his arm when he swayed. "Are you sure you can make it all right, Reverend?"

"I'm sure."

Chastity was sitting on the edge of her seat as the two men negotiated the few steps to the platform. She held her breath when the conductor released the parson's arm and he stood alone at last. She breathed again when the parson began limping painfully toward the street.

"All aboard!"

The familiar call sounded, followed by the deafening blast of the train's whistle, but she was somehow unable to look away as the parson hobbled slowly across the platform.

"Next stop, Kansas City!"

The train jerked forward at the same moment that the parson's step first faltered. Chastity sprang to her feet as he swayed and grasped for the support of the wooden column nearby. She dashed for the door of the car when he slid to his knees.

On the platform in a moment, she ran toward the reverend's slumped form and slipped her shoulder under his arm to raise him upright. His pale-eyed gaze locked with hers briefly as the train pulled from the station with another deafening blast of the whistle.

She turned back toward the sound, calling out, "Wait!"

She watched helplessly as the train pulled away, shouting frantically after it, "My bags!"

The parson sagged against her arm. Caught between anger and despair, she looked up at him and demanded, "Don't you think it's time you at least told me your name? And don't say it's none of my business!"

Ice-blue eyes . . . and silence.

Snapping back to the present, Chastity took a deep breath and surveyed the street around her with incredulity. Nineteen years old, conservatively raised and educated by maiden aunts who despised the "Wild West," she was now standing on a strange Sedalia, Missouri, street without a stitch to her name other than the clothing on her back, her reputation compromised by her attempt to help a sick, rude, arrogant parson who had not wanted her help in the first place!

How had this happened?

Taking a deep breath, Chastity raised her chin. However it had happened, her aunts were with her no longer, and the present situation was hers alone to salvage.

Holding that thought, Chastity steeled herself against further embarrassment and walked through the doorway of the mercantile store.

Grateful to see upon entering that she was presently the only customer, Chastity approached the counter, where a balding, rotund storekeeper stood waiting. She winced inwardly at his intimate sweep of her person. Uncertain how to delicately list the items of intimate feminine apparel she would need, she began hesitantly, "There are some things I need which I thought you might be able to help me with."

The fellow's smile became a leer. "Are there, now? And what might they be, darlin'?"

Chastity stiffened at the man's obvious intonation. Were all Western men boors?

She responded icily, "I arrived on the train last night without my bag. I need to purchase a change of clothing and some essentials."

"No bag, huh?" His leer broadened. "Does that mean no money, too?"

"I have money."

"Then, let's see it, darlin'. Otherwise"—he winked slyly—"we can make other arrangements."

Chastity's tone was frigid. "I said, I have money."

"And I said, let's see it, or you're not gettin' nowheres near them clothes."

Chastity's face flamed. "It's obvious you don't

35

want my patronage. I'll take my business elsewhere."

Turning away, she heard him reply, "You could do that. The only thing is, there ain't noplace else to go, not in this town, anyways."

Chastity's step slowed. If she weren't so desperate . . .

Humiliation pumping her color a bright red, Chastity changed direction abruptly and walked into an isolated corner of the store. Shielding herself from view, she reached down into the neckline of her dress to remove the small cloth bag where her money was secreted. Somehow she hadn't thought to remove it before she came into the store. The reason was simple, she supposed. She wasn't thinking clearly. In fact, she hadn't been thinking clearly since the first moment she had seen the Reverend Reed Farrell limp into that rail car and decided to approach him!

Her hand deep in the bodice of her dress, Chastity struggled with the fastener there. But to have that odious storekeeper look at her the way he did! To have her word doubted and to be insulted by his suggestive innuendos, as if she were a common . . . a common . . .

"What are you doin' there, darlin'?"

Taking a gasping step backward when the storekeeper appeared suddenly beside her, Chastity felt the wall at her back. A chill of revulsion crawled down her spine as he moved closer.

"You need any help with what you're doin'?

Hell, I'm real good at helpin' out with things like that."

Chastity strove to maintain her calm. "I realize that my appearance may be deceiving, sir, so I will repeat what I said before. I have money to buy the articles of clothing that I need. If you'll allow me a few minutes' privacy, I'll produce it for you."

"Play your cards right, and you won't need no money at all, darlin'."

"No, thank you! I'll pay for the things I want."

"I didn't say you wouldn't *pay.*"

A sudden fury rising within her, Chastity rasped, "I've had just about enough of you!"

"Sweetheart, you ain't had half of what you're goin' to get."

"I'm warning you . . ."

"You sure are a hot little tart, ain't you, darlin'!"

The storekeeper grasped her shoulder, and Chastity's breath caught in her throat. Reacting spontaneously to his touch, she clenched her fist and swung it with all her might.

Aghast, Chastity watched as if in a dream as her blow landed solidly on the storekeeper's jaw. Her eyes widened as he staggered backward, bouncing sharply against a counter before falling heavily to the floor.

The resounding thud of his body was interrupted by the unexpected sound of applause. Glancing up with a start, she saw a slender, dark-haired fellow who was standing nearby and smiling appreciatively.

"Seems like you put that fella in his place, all right." The stranger extended his hand. His smile broadened when she accepted it graciously. He continued, "My name's Will Jefferson and I'm pleased to know you, ma'am." Addressing the storekeeper, who was drawing himself shakily to his feet, he said, "Looks like you made a mistake here, mister. This lady wants to buy somethin', and I suggest you let her do it." He paused. "You do understand what I'm sayin', don't you?"

Allowing a few seconds for the import of his words to register, the stranger turned back to Chastity. "I'm thinkin' that we both got our points across here. Just in case we didn't, though, I want you to know that I'll be standin' outside the door for a little while, ma'am. If you have any more trouble with him, you just let me know and I'll come back in and settle it for you."

Aware of the debt she owed this smiling stranger, Chastity replied, "Thank you most sincerely, Mr. Jefferson."

Turning her attention back to the storekeeper, she paused a moment to regain her poise before requesting coolly, "If you'll show me where I may find the ready-to-wear dresses and women's essentials, please."

No longer leering, the storekeeper snapped, "They're on the other side of the store."

"Thank you."

Walking back out onto the boardwalk with her packages under her arm a short time later, Chastity scanned the street. Disappointed when she did not see the man who'd helped her, she heard a deep voice drawl from behind her, "I'm right here, ma'am."

Turning, Chastity looked up at Will Jefferson's friendly smile and even features. Smiling in return, she said, "I can't thank you enough, Mr. Jefferson. The storekeeper is not a gentleman, but to be totally fair, I suppose I can't blame him for jumping to conclusions. I'm afraid my appearance is deceiving."

"I disagree." Will Jefferson's engaging smile warmed her. "Any man with any sense at all can see that you're a lady. I think he understands that now."

The clatter of approaching hooves drew Chastity's attention to the street, where one of the two mounted men called out, "It's time to get goin', Will. It's gettin' late."

"All right." Looking back at Chastity, her rescuer raised his hand to the brim of his hat. "I have to be leavin', but I admit to feelin' real sorry that we don't have the time to get better acquainted." He paused. "What did you say your name was, ma'am?"

"It's Chastity Law—" Chastity hesitated, "My name's Chastity."

"Chastity. That's a real fine name. I'd be honored if you'd call me Will."

"Let's get goin', Will!"

Ignoring his friend's impatience, he added, "It's been a pleasure, Chastity. I hope we meet again."

Her response heartfelt, Chastity replied, "I'd be pleased if we did, too."

Watching as the three men rode down the street, Chastity unconsciously sighed. So, she had met a Western gentleman at last.

Still staring at their departing backs, Chastity could not hear Will Jefferson's companion snap, "What in hell was that all about?"

Nor could she see Jefferson's appealing smile vanish as he responded, "Since when do I have to report to you?"

"You're askin' for trouble messin' with one of them church types."

"Think so?"

"I'm sure of it."

Jefferson's dark eyes narrowed. "She's a damned good-lookin' woman."

"I told you—"

True viciousness abruptly surfacing, Jefferson snapped, "You don't tell me nothin'! You got that, Walker?"

Silence.

"I asked you a question!"

"Yeah, I got it."

"I don't hear you."

"I said, I got it!"

The three men disappeared from Chastity's view.

The open range glowed a brilliant gold in the sunlight, stretching out unobstructed to the horizon in all directions. There was no shade.

Reed's throat was parched. His mouth was dry.

He heard it then, the familiar thunder of pounding hooves. He heard the sound of gunfire. He heard gunshots bark again and again, driving the stampeding herd into a panicked frenzy as it came suddenly into view.

The herd was heading directly toward him! He knew what was coming next.

Oh, God . . . there she was! She was riding alongside the frenzied animals, leaning hard over the saddle, trying to turn them. She looked up and he saw her face. It was tight with anger as she shouted to him. He spurred his horse into the chase, shouting to her to let the herd go, that she wouldn't be able to stop it.

But she didn't hear him.

The terror returned. It squeezed tight inside him, stealing his breath as he pressed his mount to a faster pace, struggling to reach her. He saw her horse stumble, and his heart lurched. He watched her jerk back on the reins, fighting to hold her powerful gelding upright. He saw her struggle valiantly as the animal wavered amidst the battering of the panicked beeves. He saw . . . he saw her go down!

*No!*

The panicked herd disappeared into the distance. The shooting ceased.

Dismounting in the grainy mist, he dashed to her side. She lay motionless, her body broken and bloodied.

41

A frantic plea resounded in his mind. *Don't leave me, Jenny, please!*

"No, I won't leave you, Reed."

Reed went stock still. The soft voice in his ear was new to the dream.

"Lie back and rest, Reed." The voice had a familiar ring as it coaxed, "You're sick. Let Dr. Carr help you."

He strained to open his eyes, but his lids were so heavy. In the slim slit of light finally entering between them he saw her.

"That's right, rest. Your leg is infected. It won't heal if you don't."

He didn't care about his leg. He wanted to touch her.

"Reed, please . . ."

He heard another voice. It was gruff. "Here, give him this medicine. He won't take it from me. It'll make him sleep."

"Drink this, Reed."

No, he didn't want to sleep. If he did, he'd lose her again.

"Reed, please."

He caught her hand. It was warm and alive. He held it tightly.

"He's hurting me."

"It's the fever. It's rising again, and he's getting agitated. Talk to him. Calm him down."

"Drink this, Reed. It'll make you feel better."

*No.*

He felt her hand on his cheek, turning him toward her. She leaned closer, her voice a husky whisper. "Drink this . . . for me, Reed."

*For her.*

"Please."

He would do anything for her.

The liquid was bitter.

"That ought to do it." The gruff voice again. "We'd get ahead of that fever if he'd calm down. That wound doesn't look as bad as it did yesterday. How'd you say he got it?"

No response.

"He'll be asleep in a few minutes. That dose should hold him through the night. I suggest you get some sleep, too."

The voices were fading. He felt her hand slipping from his grasp and he gripped it more tightly.

"Reed, you're hurting me."

He didn't want to hurt her.

"Let me go."

"You're wasting your breath. He's not going to let go." The curt voice again. "Don't worry. He'll be asleep in a minute."

No! He struggled against the oblivion overwhelming him. He fought to open his eyes. He would not let her go again—not this time!

A disapproving grunt. "He must've heard me. He's panicking."

"No, Reed, don't struggle. I won't leave. I'll be right here beside you. I promise."

He felt the bed sink with her weight as she sat beside him. He heard her gentle voice. "Go to sleep, Reed. Please. I'll be right here when you wake up."

# Elaine Barbieri

She said she would stay beside him while he slept. She wouldn't lie to him.

He closed his eyes.

The darkened hotel room was lit by a single lamp on the nightstand. Outside the window, sounds of evening revelry echoed in the night. Inside, all was quiet.

Chastity sat on the edge of the bed, looking down at the man sleeping there. Dr. Carr had departed again, leaving her to tend this man who held her hand even as he slept.

Chastity closed her eyes. Surely she was dreaming! Surely she was not going to spend another night alone in a room with a man she had met only two days earlier. Surely she was not going to continue holding his hand and listening to garbled words of love meant for another woman. Surely she would awaken from this awful dream to find herself in her own familiar room, with the familiar sounds of her aunts bickering outside her door over the direction of her future:

*"What's the matter with you, Harriet? Are you insane, urging Chastity to devote her life to working among the Bowery poor? I never heard anything so ridiculous! It would be foolhardy for her to expose herself to an element of human society with which she is totally unequipped to deal!"*

*"Insane, Penelope? I suppose Chastity would've been better off marrying the 'respectable' Mr. Bertrand Bowles as you suggested?"*

*"Chastity made her thoughts adequately clear*

*on that subject. She doesn't intend to marry. That opportunity has passed by the board, in any case."*

*"A good thing, too! Mr. Bowles was old enough to be her father, and he was as singleminded a man as I ever knew! He wasn't looking for a wife! He was looking for a workhorse to care for his wild brood of children while he gallivanted nightly with dissolute women!"*

*"How was I supposed to know that the fellow had lascivious interests?"*

*"How could you not know?"*

*"Because I am not in the habit of exchanging idle gossip!"*

*"Are you intimating that I am?"*

*"If the shoe fits!"*

Seething silence.

*"I refuse to be baited by you, Penelope."*

*"I'm not 'baiting' you! I only—"*

*"Penelope, please! The point is, Chastity is far too intelligent and resourceful to squander her many attributes in the bondage of matrimony!"*

*"Oh, you're just saying that because no man ever asked you to be his wife! Although I am un-wed, my viewpoint is different because I had no lack of admirers in my youth."*

*"Surely you jest!"*

*"Bradford Dillon begged me to marry him!"*

*"The fool thought Father was rich! He beat a fast retreat when he learned your inheritance would be modest, at best!"*

*"He was devastated when I refused his suit!"*

*"Not true."*

*"He suffered terribly!"*

*"Hogwash!"*

*"Harriet, how crude!"*

Aunt Penelope had maintained to the end that marriage was the safest and best road for her to take. Aunt Harriet had urged with relentless zeal that she maintain her personal independence.

But she had cherished a dream of her own.

She had been very young when her aunts had assumed her care. It did not take her long, however, to discover the loving natures they found difficult to display. But those dear women were gone now—they had died within months of each other. She supposed she should have expected it to happen that way. One sister had never allowed the other to surpass her.

Her eyes still closed, Chastity reached up to clutch her locket. She had started out a week earlier to make her cherished dream come true, only to find herself involved in this distressing dream that showed no signs of ending.

Chastity slowly opened her eyes and looked down at the bed.

This was no dream.

Staring down into the parson's face, Chastity felt a familiar quiver in the pit of her stomach. The unanswered question returned. What was she doing here? This man with the clear blue eyes and irritable disposition had not spoken a civil word to her, yet she had put aside her own priorities in order to care for him. She had suffered insult and humiliation, and she had actually let her own integrity lapse by allowing the misconception to prevail that she was his *wife*.

Why?

That question joined the others as Chastity scrutinized her sleeping patient more closely. The parson's strong grip on her hand had loosened. The medicine had obviously taken effect and he was sleeping soundly at last.

Chastity glanced at the chair in the corner where the pillow and blanket lying there beckoned her to sleep. Cautiously sliding her hand from his palm, she jumped with a start when Reed's eyes snapped open abruptly. She saw the flash of panic there a moment before he began struggling anew.

"No, Reed!" Frightened by his sudden anxiety, Chastity grasped his hand and gripped it tight. His gaze met hers with startling intensity as she whispered, "See, I'm still here! I'm sitting on the bed beside you."

Reed went abruptly still. He blinked as he strained to identify her. Her relief knew no bounds when the tension left his body and his eyes closed.

Glancing again toward the chair in the corner, Chastity withheld a sigh. Her back was breaking and her eyelids were as heavy as lead. She was so tired. She looked at the unused portion of the bed beside her patient and gave a wistful sigh.

She was so, so tired.

# *Chapter Three*

It was morning. The night had been filled with confused dreams. His head hurt. His thoughts were muddled. Images of Jenny swam in his mind. He struggled to dismiss them and the familiar anguish they raised.

Reed opened his eyes slowly. He blinked at the bright glow of the rising sun. Every bone in his body ached. He tried to move, only to realize that the effort was somehow beyond him.

Where was he? Squinting past the throbbing in his temples, he observed faded wallpaper and mismatched furniture that were vaguely familiar. Yes, he remembered. Jenny was dead, killed in a rustler's raid, and he had made it his mission to see that someone paid for her death. He had received a wire saying that Morgan and his men had been seen in Sedalia. He had made arrangements to come to Sedalia to meet the fellow who had sent him the wire. But the infection in his leg had worsened, and his journey had become a nightmare. He had finally arrived in Sedalia, and that was where the nightmare had ended.

But . . . what was that noise?

A soft snoring snapped his head toward the bed beside him, and Reed was startled to see a woman in a wrinkled black dress sleeping there. She turned in her sleep, facing him, and memory stirred.

Her name was Chastity Lawrence. She had wanted to talk.

He didn't.

She had said he needed help.

He didn't want any.

She had said she wouldn't bother him.

She did anyway.

Reed stared harder, uncertain. Was she really lying beside him?

The woman's eyelids fluttered as if in response to his silent query. Her eyes opened and she met his gaze with a start. Gasping, she sprang to a seated position so quickly that the bed rocked with the force of her movement. He grabbed his leg as the motion started his wound throbbing anew. He groaned aloud as she jumped to her feet and reached for her glasses on the nightstand. They were affixed firmly in place when he managed to say at last, "What are *you* doing here?"

"What am I doing here?" Those annoyingly familiar, brownish-green eyes studied him intently through the hideous spectacles. "Do you remember who I am?"

He glared. "How could I forget?"

"Who am I?"

"Don't you know?"

"I asked a civil question."

He chose not to reply.

It occurred to Reed through his pain that Chastity Lawrence's gaze had turned deadly.

Oh, he really was an odious man. . . .

Breathing deeply, Chastity struggled for the control fast eluding her. It was almost beyond comprehension that this rude, insolent individual was the same man who had whispered so lovingly to her—to his Jenny—a few hours ago. It was even more difficult to remember that he was a man of the cloth!

Reed pushed his coverlet impatiently to his waist, revealing the broad, naked expanse of his shoulders and chest, and Chastity's discomfort increased. She reminded herself that he was ill, in considerable pain, and not fully responsible for his behavior. She attempted to assess him clinically. She saw that his hair, formerly dark with perspiration, was a soft, sunstreaked blond against his furrowed brow. His gaze, formerly disoriented and bright with fever, was clearer, and the skin of his cheeks, where visible above his ragged beard, appeared less flushed. He jerked back as she attempted to touch her palm to his forehead.

Chastity's lips twitched with annoyance. "I was merely trying to see if your temperature was normal."

"I'm fine."

"No, you aren't." Chastity forced a level tone. "Your leg is infected. Dr. Carr was worried that he might be forced to remove it."

The clear blue of his eyes frosted. "That would've been a mistake."

The sound of the door opening behind her prevented Chastity's reply. She turned toward Dr. Carr as he entered. Suddenly realizing that his misconception about their relationship was about to be humiliatingly revealed, she took an unsteady step back.

"Are you all right?" Immediately at her side, Dr. Carr assessed Chastity's lack of color and the shadows beneath her eyes. He patted her arm. "It's nothing a little rest wouldn't cure, is it, dear?"

Dr. Carr turned to face his patient without waiting for her reply. He smiled. "Well, well . . . lucid at last." He extended his hand. "My name is Dr. Carr. Most people call me Doc. If you don't mind, I'll continue to call you by your given name, Reed. You're not wearing your collar, and I'm more comfortable with things that way." Shaking Reed's hand firmly, he then touched his palm to Reed's forehead. "Your fever's down, too. So, let's take a look at that leg."

Throwing back the coverlet, exposing Reed's

semi-nakedness without warning, Dr. Carr began removing the bandage on his thigh. Reed's
gaze snapped to hers, and Chastity felt her color
rise. She was somehow unable to move as Dr.
Carr continued in a more serious tone, "I wonder if you're fully aware how dangerous your
condition was, Reed. I heard part of your conversation with Chastity as I entered. I can understand that you were disturbed at the thought
of possibly losing your leg, but I'm not pleased
by your attitude. Of course, since we were able
to draw much of the poison from the wound,
there's not much chance of such drastic mea-
sures being necessary now."

He paused, his gaze narrowing as he looked
up. "That is, unless you do something stupid,
like trying to be up and around before you're
ready." Dr. Carr's gray brows knit as he posed a
question he had asked several times before.
"How did a parson manage to get a bullet
wound, anyway?"

"I made the mistake of getting in the middle
of a gunfight."

Dr. Carr frowned. "You should've had more
sense." He turned toward Chastity. "Why did
you let him do such a crazy thing?"

Reed replied sharply in her stead. "What I did
had nothing to do with her."

"That's enough of that talk!" Chastity jumped
at the unexpected harshness of Dr. Carr's response. Her eyes widened as the gray-haired
doctor continued with no lessening of fervor, "I
won't have you talking to this woman that way!

You don't seem to realize what you owe her. To my mind, Chastity accomplished something just short of a miracle in managing to get you from the train station to Main Street all by herself. And I have no doubt at all that if Tom Wright and Jerry Potter hadn't helped her out, she would've gotten you the rest of the way to my office by herself, too."

Dr. Carr glanced back at Chastity where she still stood frozen to the spot. "I have to admit I wasn't too easy on her at first, blaming her the way I did for letting your wound fester. But she redeemed herself in my eyes that first night, and it's pretty obvious to me now that you're a hard case and probably not easy to live with, even if you do wear a parson's collar. A fact you might try to keep in mind while you're lying there is that I worked on you for three hours straight after Chastity got you into my office, and *she* worked right beside me. She took my orders without complaint until *I* was too tired to go on. After we brought you here, she stayed with you and watched over you while I went to get some rest. You couldn't ask much more than that from any woman! So, I expect you to keep a civil tongue in your mouth with Chastity while I'm present, or I just might forget how sick you are."

Appearing unfazed by the doctor's rebuke, Reed replied tersely, "I'm not sick."

"You are, too, dammit! *I'll* be the one to tell you when you're not! And don't you forget it!"

Uncovering the wound at last, Dr. Carr nod-

53

ded. "All right, take a look at that, and then tell me you didn't have a close call."

Chastity caught her breath. The exposed wound was red and swollen. Pus oozed from a small, round point of puncture made by a single bullet. Somehow more affected at that moment than she had been the first time she saw it, she felt herself sway. She caught herself as Reed glanced sharply in her direction.

Dr. Carr continued, "As bad as it still looks, it's much improved. But we're going to have to keep drawing out the poison." He looked at Chastity. "Your job isn't over yet, dear."

Dr. Carr looked back at his patient. When Reed stared emotionlessly at him, he stated flatly, "You're a strange fellow, for a parson. If I hadn't seen how you really feel about this woman when you were fevered and unable to hide it, I'd think you were as cold as ice. As it is, all I can say is that anybody but a fool would realize that you're a lucky man to have a woman like Chastity for a wife."

. . . *a wife* . . .

Dr. Carr had said it.

Chastity closed her eyes, silently groaning as she waited for Reed's explosive reaction.

It did not come.

Cautiously opening her eyes, Chastity saw Reed staring at her.

"I'm going to bandage your leg lightly for the time being." Apparently attributing the uneasy silence to his harsh reprimand, Dr. Carr continued, "No sense in doing anything else right now, since Chastity'll be applying hot compresses on it again as soon as you've had time for breakfast."

"I'm not hungry."

Ignoring Reed's curt reply, Dr. Carr turned toward Chastity. "Make sure he eats—and drinks a lot of water, too. If you're not too tired, you might help him wash up a bit afterward. He could use some freshening up."

Response beyond her, Chastity watched as Dr. Carr repacked his black bag, then walked toward the door. His hand on the knob, he turned back briefly and said, "I'll be back after I tend to some other patients. In the meantime, I'll tell Sally to bring up some food."

The door closed behind Dr. Carr, and Chastity waited. She did not have to wait long before Reed grated, "All right, what's this all about?"

"I don't really know how it all happened." Chastity Lawrence stared at him through those ridiculous spectacles. She looked tired and disheveled, and not as prim and proper as she had appeared when she first approached him on the train. He saw the uneasiness with which she continued, "I was experiencing some uncertainties about my journey. I saw your collar, and I thought you might be able to help me sort them out. And then when I approached you, you . . ."

Her words dwindled away and Reed felt impatience soar. He was beginning to feel weaker, and his stomach was beginning to turn. He had no time for this woman or the unexpected complications in his plans. For all he knew, Morgan had already left the territory. He needed to meet his contact before that fellow left town, too. The question was, how was he going to do it?

Chastity took a breath. "I thought you could help me." She paused. "Then, when I got closer, I saw you were sick."

"I told you I didn't want your help."

"You needed *someone's* help."

"I could've taken care of myself."

"You collapsed on the platform!" She shook her head. The amazingly bright spirals of hair that made a mockery of her formerly austere hairdo bobbed ridiculously against her neck. "I saw you go down!"

Chastity's final statement struck a raw nerve within him, increasing Reed's frown as he spat, "So you ran to my rescue."

He felt her wince. "That's right . . . fool that I was."

"Why?"

Chastity blinked at his question. He noted that she was momentarily at a loss for a reply. He sensed that her response came as much as a surprise to her as it did to him when she said, "I approached you thinking that I needed your help . . . and then I discovered that you needed mine, instead."

Reed's head was growing light as he pressed, "So, you came to my aid. You got me to the doctor's office, but then you stayed on. Why?"

Her reply was curt. "I've been asking myself that same question." Her look was pure disdain.

"It certainly wasn't because you have a pleasant nature. To the contrary, you are one of most *un*pleasant and *un*appreciative men I have ever met."

"You told Dr. Carr you were my wife."

"I did not!"

He returned her look of disdain.

Chastity's light skin flamed. "Dr. Carr *assumed* I was your wife when I brought you to his door. We didn't have much time for conversation and I didn't think to explain the situation. And then it was too late."

Reed's thinking was beginning to blur. He shook his head. "Too late? For what?"

"This situation . . . this whole affair is embarrassing! I was afraid my reputation would suffer if I tried to clarify it!"

He stared. "Your reputation?"

"An unmarried woman spending the night— two nights—in the same room with a man. Good heavens, what would people think?" She reached up to grasp the locket exposed in the open neck of her dress, and Reed's memory jogged at the strangely familiar gesture as she continued, "I couldn't let that happen."

"So, why did you stay?"

"How could I go? You begged me not to."

"I begged you . . ."

"You thought I was . . . Jenny."

Reed steeled himself against the sound of that name. "What else did I say?"

"Nothing much. You mumbled something

57

about your mission and that someone was waiting for you."

"My mission . . ."

"A man named Morgan."

Reed stiffened. He nodded. "Oh, yes."

Chastity took a step closer. The thought occurred to Reed through his growing confusion that the loss of the drab bonnet she had worn was an improvement on her appearance—even though the ugly spectacles remained in place and the morbid color of her dress still made her skin look like watered milk.

He knew something was coming the moment she raised her chin that almost indefinable notch. He inwardly nodded as she began, "Whether you're willing to admit it or not, I did you a service."

So, he was right. A strange disappointment nudged him. "You want something in return, right? What do you want? Money?"

"You *are* insufferable!"

He pressed, "What do you want?"

Her chin rose another notch. "I intend to leave Sedalia as soon as I can. It would save me considerable embarrassment if you would wait to explain the truth about this situation until after I go. I'll be happy to write a letter explaining everything to Jenny if you think she might not understand the situation."

"Jenny's dead."

"Oh. I'm sorry."

Reed closed his eyes. He wasn't feeling well at all. He felt a soft palm on his forehead and

58

jerked his head back, his eyes snapping open.

"You feel cool."

"Do I?"

"Too cool. You're feeling weaker, aren't you?"

Damn her . . .

"You need to eat."

Reed's stomach churned harder. "No, I don't."

"Dr. Carr said—"

"I don't care what Dr. Carr said." He closed his eyes. "Go away. I want to sleep."

He felt a glass against his lips. He opened his eyes to meet determined brown-green eyes staring into his.

"Drink this. Dr. Carr left it for you."

"What is it?"

"It'll make you sleep. He said to give it to you if you feel distressed."

"I'm not distressed."

"Yes, you are."

"No, I'm not!"

"Drink it!"

So, the soft-spoken little wren had a sharp edge. A strange satisfaction rising within him, Reed emptied the glass.

"Good." Chastity Lawrence paused. "We can continue our conversation when you wake up."

"As far as I'm concerned, I've made my feelings plain."

He saw the tenseness that entered Chastity's gaze as she waited expectantly for clarification of his words. That peculiar satisfaction expanded as he deliberately closed his eyes.

\*     \*     \*

Trembling with aggravation, Chastity drew back from the bed and stared down at the infuriating parson. All right, if that was the way he wanted it!

Chastity turned resolutely toward the chair in the corner where she had dropped her bundles. He said he wasn't sick. He said he didn't need her help. He had ended their conversation without even bothering to respond to her request. He *was* an odious man!

And she was a fool for maintaining that he needed her help when he so adamantly declared that he didn't! Well, she could remain a fool for only so long.

Snatching up her bundles, Chastity started toward the door, her head high. She reached up unconsciously to clutch her locket. Caldwell, Kansas, was her destination—her first step toward finding the sisters she had lost in a flooded river so long ago. They were alive, somewhere, she was certain of it. Unlike her courage, that conviction and her determination to be reunited with them had never faltered. This stop in Sedalia was an interruption in the path she had set toward that goal, and she would not allow it to stand in her way any longer!

Chastity looked back at the exasperating Reverend Reed Farrell. He would sleep until Dr. Carr returned later that afternoon. He had already gone totally limp, revealing that the sleeping powder had taken effect. She would leave it to him to tell the doctor the full story. It would doubtlessly give him great pleasure to tell the physician what a fool she was.

Chastity drew open the door, pausing with her hand on the knob as the sound of deep, even breathing filled the room. So what if Dr. Carr had been depending upon her to tend to this man's wound? So what if the fever returned to rage unchecked while she was gone? So what if the infection gained control again . . . if, because of her, the battle to save his leg was lost?

Oh, Lord!

Chastity clutched her packages tighter. She stared at the Reverend Reed Farrell's still face. That hideous brown beard hid his features as efficiently as a mask. She remembered its coarse texture when she had touched his cheek. She wondered if Jenny had approved of that beard. And she wondered if losing Jenny had turned him into the offensive person that he presently was.

Yes, despite his collar, he really was an odious man.

Her decision made, Chastity stepped out into the hallway and pulled the door closed behind her.

Reed winced, awakening slowly from a muddled dream to the sunlight of afternoon. He reached up to swat the mosquito nipping at his cheek, only to hear a soft protest in his ear. The mosquito nipped again, and he turned away from its annoying attack.

He heard a curt warning when he moved. He

recognized the female voice that issued it. He opened his eyes to see brown-green eyes only inches from his face . . . *and a razor at his throat*!

His spontaneous withdrawal was met with a sharp, "Don't move!"

Chastity Lawrence was staring at him through those grotesque glasses, her teeth locked together, her eyes narrowed. He could feel her breath on his lips as she tilted up his chin to expose his throat, then lowered the razor toward it.

He heard her mumbled words.

"Don't move, or I'll cut you again."

*Again . . . ?*

He raised a tentative hand to his cheek. It was cleanly shaven! The beard that had been as efficient a part of his disguise as the collar he had worn was gone! "What in hell are you doing?" he asked.

"I'm shaving you."

"Who told you to shave me?"

"Dr. Carr said to clean you up."

His head was beginning to pound. "Get away from me."

"I'm not finished."

"Oh, you're finished, all right."

Reed felt a warning prickle up his spine as she stepped back, responding coolly, "Anything you say."

He didn't like the way she said that.

Touching his clean-shaven cheek again, Reed

then touched the other to find it still fully bearded. "Give me that razor."

"No."

"I said, give me that razor!"

"And I said, no."

Oh, hell! Reed's head was beginning to spin. His stomach was empty and his throat was as dry as a desert, but he'd be damned before he'd let her near him with that razor again.

Reaching out with a strength he did not realize he possessed, Reed grasped the slender wrist so close to his face. Catching her off balance, he pulled her abruptly toward him, knocking off her glasses and sprawling her across him as he rasped, "I want that razor."

The female warmth of her was pressed against him, the curve of her surprisingly rounded breasts tight against his chest. Her disturbingly sweet breath brushed his lips—

A sharp knock on the door diverted Reed's attention the moment before it opened. Freezing in the doorway, Dr. Carr emitted a low growl of disapproval, then snapped, "That sort of thing is off limits for a while!"

Refusing to release Chastity even as her face flamed a beet red, Reed grated, "I want that razor."

Dr. Carr stepped farther into the room, stopping short again when he viewed his patient more fully.

"Good Lord, woman! What did you do to this man?"

Reed was actutely aware that Chastity was

still lying across his chest as she responded, "You told me to clean him up if I had the chance."

"That I did." The annoying physician struggled against a smile. "And you did a hell of a job! Seems to me I got here just in time before the jugular was endangered."

Reed did not bother to comment.

"Let her go, Reed."

"No."

Dr. Carr persisted, "Whatever you had in mind, I can tell you now, it's not going to happen. So you might just as well do as I say."

Uncertain if it was the subtle, feminine scent of the woman sprawled across him or his debility, Reed could feel himself weakening. Looking into the pale face so close to his, he said, "Don't ever try coming at me when I'm sleeping again. You won't get off this easily if there's a next time."

He saw Chastity's small features twitch with an anger held tightly in check as she whispered in a voice meant for him alone, "Don't worry. As soon as you let me go, I'm going to get as far away from you as I can!"

"That suits me fine!"

"Good!" Chastity snapped back awkwardly as Reed released her. Regaining her feet, she turned toward Dr. Carr and handed him the razor. "Here. You can finish. He slept all the while you were gone. I applied hot compresses to his leg and it's looking better, and I managed to get him to swallow some water. The rest is up to you. I'm leaving."

"Come now, dear"—Dr. Carr accepted the razor with a conciliatory smile—"you're exhausted and you need some time to yourself. I've arranged with Sally Greenwood for you to use the bathtub downstairs for a nominal fee. You'll feel much better after you've bathed and changed your clothes, I'm sure. I'll take care of your husband until you're done."

Reed saw determination flash in Chastity's eyes before she announced abruptly, "Dr. Carr, this man is not my—"

"Do as the doctor says!" Uncertain of his reason for interrupting her, Reed continued flatly, "He'll take care of things here."

"He'd better." Chastity's response held a caustic note. "Because I'm not coming back."

"Chastity, dear . . ." Dr. Carr smiled sympathetically. "You're tired. You don't mean what you're saying."

"Yes, I do." Chastity turned abruptly toward Reed. She challenged, "Tell him! Go ahead!"

Aware that his silence infuriated her even more, Reed watched, satisfaction burgeoning as Chastity drew her tall, slender, disheveled self up sharply, picked up her bundles, and turned toward Dr. Carr. "Thank you for arranging for my bath, and thank you for your competency. Good-bye, doctor."

Turning her back on Reed without another word, Chastity quietly pulled the door open and disappeared into the hallway.

Elaine Barbieri

Deep in thought, Reed did not realize he was still staring at the closed door until Dr. Carr snapped, "You really are a hard case! I don't know how she puts up with you. It would serve you right if she didn't come back!"

"She'll be back."

Dr. Carr glowered. "And you're damned arrogant for a man of the cloth!"

"It isn't arrogance." Reed frowned, cursing under his breath as a wave of weakness again assailed him. He stated flatly, "I need something to eat."

"Sally's making you up a tray now." Dr. Carr paused, then added, "I may be an old, small-town doctor, but I pride myself in knowing people. And something tells me you pushed that woman a step too far just now. She might not come back."

"She'll come back."

"Damned arrogant pup . . ."

Reed did not bother to reply as Dr. Carr turned toward his bag with a soft curse. Instead, he picked up the hideous, wire-rimmed spectacles that had fallen onto the bed beside him, and with great satisfaction, slid them under his pillow.

Oh, she had never felt so good.

Leaning back in the tub, Chastity recalled her incredulity when she first entered the primitive bathing facilities. She supposed her experiences of the past few days should have prepared her for the room that was nothing more than a shed added to the rear of the hotel, and a tub that was nothing more than a canvas sling attached to a frame that appeared too fragile to support even her weight. Still furious from her parting conversation with the Reverend Reed Farrell, she had momentarily considered abandoning the whole idea of bathing. But all her reservations were dismissed the first moment the warm water touched her bare skin.

Luxuriating in the steaming water for a few mindless moments longer, Chastity sighed aloud. She reached onto the stand beside her and picked up the washcloth and soap she had purchased from the loathsome storekeeper earlier. The fragrance of roses reached her nostrils as she worked up a lather, and Chastity sighed again. Aunt Harriet and Aunt Penelope had detested floral fragrances, but she had always loved the scent of roses. Somehow, it stirred blurred images of her mother and returned to mind more vivid pictures of bathing with her sisters in a common tub. She remembered that the aroma of roses had been strong as their mother had dutifully scrubbed them clean, and that the fragrance had often been accompanied by the sound of petulance in her sisters' voices. *"It isn't fair, Mama! Chastity's hair is prettier than ours!"*

*"That's not true."* Mama had been insistent. *"Chastity's hair is a more brilliant color, true, but Honesty's hair is as black as satin, just like your father's Irish great-grandmother, and Purity's*

*hair is the color of cornsilk, like mine. Your father is proud of you all. He says all his girls are beautiful."*

*"I know, but Chastity's hair is curly, like Papa's, and it's prettier."*

*"I wish I had hair like Papa's."*

*"It isn't fair."*

And later, when her sisters stroked her hair as they lay abed, *"You're so lucky, Chastity."*

A familiar sadness welled inside Chastity. She recalled so little about her sisters, but she remembered that Honesty had been the most beautiful of the three of them, and the most willful. She remembered that Purity was fair and angelic looking, but that she often tested Papa's patience with her mischievous nature. She recalled that she had been happiest when following in the footsteps of her two older sisters, and that she was proud to be the one who had inherited Papa's curly red hair and his brown eyes that danced with flecks of green. She recalled crawling up onto his lap and staring nose-to-nose into his face, so intently that he laughed aloud. She had loved to hear him laugh, and she had known no greater joy than to cuddle on his lap with his arms around her.

Chastity wiped away a straying tear. Her parents had perished when their wagon was swept away in the flooded river that day, she was certain. If they had not, they would have found her sisters and her and brought the family together again.

But her sisters were alive. She was certain she could feel their hearts beating when she clutched her locket—the same kind of locket her father had given to each of his girls—and she was just as certain that she would find her sisters if she had the courage to try.

Although they had never actually said the words, Chastity knew that Aunt Penelope and Aunt Harriet had not shared her belief—just as she knew that as conservative as they were, they had been uncomfortable with the bright shade of her hair and its persistent curl. She knew they felt the color was garish and that it stirred too much comment, because they encouraged her to conceal its unusual color as much as possible and to confine it tightly to control the curl. Knowing in her heart that her dear aunts had her best interests at heart, she had eventually put aside her childish pride and accepted their counseling.

"Are you ready for some more hot water, dearie?"

Chastity looked up with a start to see Sally Greenwood standing beside the tub, holding a steaming pot in her hand. The older woman's features were brightly painted, her hair color enhanced to a startling gold, and her matronly figure clothed in a dress obviously styled for a younger woman. It occurred to Chastity that Aunt Harriet's spontaneous comment would be that the woman's appearance was appalling, while Aunt Penelope would most likely disapprove of her outspokenness while silently agreeing with her sister. But Chastity had looked into Sally's heavily kohled eyes and seen only kindness.

She replied, "Yes, that would be nice, Sally."

Sally poured the water slowly. "Doc Carr told me that the parson was real sick. I just took a tray up to him, but Doc took it at the door, so I didn't get to see the parson at all. I hope he's feelin' better."

Chastity avoided the woman's gaze. She lathered the cloth again and rubbed it against her shoulder. "He's a little better. The infection will take a while to clear up."

Sally shook her head. "Doc says the reverend kept mumblin' about the mission and his delay in meetin' somebody. He says he seemed real worried. They're waitin' for him out there, you know."

Chastity looked up with surprise. "Oh . . . yes, I suppose they are."

"I know, because I worked for a while with the old parson when he went out convertin'."

Chastity could not hide her surprise.

Sally laughed. "I don't look much like the type to go out convertin', do I? Well, the truth is that I wasn't always." Sally settled back against the nearby stand, continuing, "I spent a good part of my life workin' in a saloon just like the Roundup across the street. I wasn't never as pretty as you are, but there was a time when the fellas really took to me. Of course, them days are long gone."

Chastity felt obliged to counter, "No, that's not completely true."

"Don't worry. It don't make me feel bad to speak the truth."

Sally smiled. "But the time came when I started feelin' empty inside. With you bein' a preacher's wife, you know the way I mean."

Chastity's conscience nagged at her, but she said nothing.

"That was when I took all the money I had saved up and bought this hotel. I made a good livin' at it, too, but I was still feelin' empty. Then I met old Reverend Stiles. Hell, he was so old that he needed somebody to take care of him or he never would've made it back from the wild country alive. So I put my hotel in the hands of a friend, and I started travelin' with the reverend. He died a year ago."

"Oh, I'm sorry!"

"The mission he started out in Injun Territory ain't had a preacher since. They heard a preacher was comin', though. A preacher and his wife, they said. But they're goin' to be real surprised to see a preacher with such a *young* wife."

"Oh, I'm not that young!"

Why had she said that?

"Anyways, I suppose it's my good fortune that the parson got sick and had to get off in Sedalia before goin' all the way to Baxter Springs, or I wouldn't have had the chance to meet you both."

"Reverend Farrell—I mean Reed—didn't intend going to Baxter Springs. Sedalia was his destination, and he was determined to get here at any cost."

"Really?" Sally shrugged. "I can't rightly understand that. Baxter Springs is right on the edge of the Injun Territory, but I guess a man has a right to make his way on the road he knows best."

Growing increasingly uncomfortable with the conversation, Chastity smiled. "I'm sure Reed is as anxious to reach the mission as they are to have him." She inquired politely in an effort to change the subject, "Could you tell me what time it is?"

"It was a little after three o'clock when I came in here." Sally smiled. "I suppose I'd better let you get on with your bath. You just call if you need anythin'. I'll hear you."

"Thank you, Sally."

Chastity silently groaned as the door closed behind her. Lies of omission . . . deliberate subterfuge. She could not take much more of it. She glanced toward the new clothing she had so carefully spread out nearby, knowing that in the pocket of the simple dress she had purchased was tucked the rail ticket that would take her on to Caldwell. She had already inquired when the train would leave. Two more hours and she would be away from here and back on track, in more ways than one.

Disturbed when that thought did not comfort her, Chastity submerged herself briefly beneath the water and then began soaping her hair. She would wash the last residue of Sedalia off her person, and she would strike these two difficult days from her mind if it was the last thing she ever did.

As for the Reverend Reed Farrell, she was done with him!

Drawing back to admire his handiwork, Dr. Carr grunted. "Well, seems to me that if I hadn't gone to medical school, I would've made a damned good barber!"

Reed ran his palm against his beardless cheek, irritation again rising. He had deliberately cultivated that beard, knowing that his face was becoming too familiar to too many outlaws in the area. He'd have to be damned careful now.

Dr. Carr frowned. "It also seems to me that no parson should be as unfamiliar with the words 'thank you' as you appear to be."

"Thanks."

"I can see that came from the heart." Dr. Carr squinted assessingly. "You did a good job on that meal Sally brought up. You should be feeling a lot better."

"As a matter of fact, I am."

"That's what I thought. And I can see what you're thinking, so let me set you straight right now. You're not *better* just because you're feeling a little better. You've got a long way to go until that leg is healed, and only a short way to go before falling back into the same shape you

were in when you got here. You're going to have
to take it easy for a while."

Those cold eyes stared back at him, and Dr.
Carr felt a familiar frustration inside him. Pulling out his pocket watch, he looked at it, his
frown deepening.

"Chastity's been gone for two hours. She
hasn't spent that much time away from you in
two days. You pushed her too far this time, I'm
telling you. And I'm going to tell you something
else, too. You'll only be getting what you deserve if she's already sitting on the train heading
east."

"She'll be back." Reed's icy gaze did not falter.

"You'd better hope that she does come back,
or you'll find yourself turned over to Sally for
the duration." Dr. Carr sniffed. "Don't get me
wrong. Sally's got a good heart, but she isn't half
as easy on the eyes as that young wife of yours,
and she won't let you get away with half of what
Chastity let you get away with, either."

Reed did not respond. The truth was that the
full scope of his temporary physical limitations
had become only too clear to him during the
past two hours. He had eaten and was feeling
stronger, but he had had the chance to get a
good look at his leg, and the truth in what the
doctor said was evident. He was also able to
think a little more clearly, and an idea that had
budded earlier in his foggy mind had come into
full bloom. Yes, he had a plan. It might be difficult for him to follow through with it, but he

had suffered through difficult circumstances before.

Looking up at the sound of a knock on the door, Reed prepared himself. The door opened to the sight of a short, middle-aged, heavily painted woman wearing a red dress so bright that he blinked from the glare of it. She assessed him in a manner so professional that he had no doubt, whatever her present occupation, that her past had been a full one. She continued her open scrutiny of him while addressing Dr. Carr.

"I came for the tray, Doc. Looks like the parson here did a pretty good job on it this time."

"Yes, he did." Dr. Carr squinted in the woman's direction, then turned toward Reed. "This is Sally Greenwood, the woman I was telling you about."

Sally gave a short laugh as she approached the bed and picked up the tray. "Pleased to meet you, Reverend. Whatever the doc said about me, I don't suppose it was too good from the look on your face when you saw me in the doorway."

"I didn't have anything to do with the look on the reverend's face when he saw you in the doorway, and neither did you." Dr. Carr raised his wiry brows. "The reverend's not the type to admit it, but he's been waiting for his wife to walk back through that doorway for the past hour."

"Can't say as I blame him." Sally balanced the tray with a practiced hand, obviously willing to linger. "I don't know what's holdin' her up. She got out of the bath a while ago, and then she walked up the street toward the train station. I figured the reverend sent her on some kind of errand or somethin'."

Reed spoke for the first time. "How long ago did you say that was?"

Sally gave him another appreciative sweep. "About an hour."

"An hour . . ." Reed frowned.

"She's a real nice young woman." Sally was watching him too closely for comfort as she continued, "I told her that there ain't been no preacher makin' regular trips out into Injun Territory since Reverend Stiles died over a year ago. They've been waitin' for the replacement they were promised at the mission ever since. They're goin' to be real happy to see you come, especially with such a young, pretty wife and all."

"At the mission . . ."

"Right. That's where you're goin', ain't it? I told your wife that I couldn't understand why you came to Sedalia when it would've been faster to take the train direct to Baxter Springs and start out by wagon from there."

"I had business here to take care of, first."

"That's what I figured. Of course, your wife didn't seem to know nothin' about it."

"It wasn't necessary for her to know."

"I suppose some men think that way." Sally allowed her gaze to linger a moment longer before she turned abruptly toward the door. "I'll bring you somethin' else to eat in an hour or so."

76

"That's a good idea, Sally." Dr. Carr nodded. "The reverend here needs to regain his strength."

Deep in thought, Reed was hardly aware of Sally's leaving as he considered the information she had imparted. A preacher and his wife were expected at a mission in Indian Territory. That was convenient. If he knew this country as well as he thought he did, the news had gotten around. Whatever direction he chose to go in, that story should provide him plenty of cover.

His thoughts interrupted when another bout of pain viciously stabbed his thigh, Reed silently cursed.

"I can give you a powder for the pain, if you like."

Reed shook his head. He couldn't afford to have his thinking impaired—not now. He would need his wits about him if he was going to turn things around when Chastity returned. But he'd handle her. He knew those church types. They were all the same.

Where in hell was she, anyway?

The train would depart for Kansas City in a scant half hour! She had to find them!

Her eyes on the ground as she retraced her steps toward the train station for the third time, Chastity felt the nudge of panic. Things were not going well.

Strangely, as she had reclined in her bath, she had begun to feel certain that the complicated morass of incidents that had deposited her in

Sedalia two days earlier would soon be settled. She had her ticket. The train was leaving in two hours, and she had finally made the decision to do exactly what the Reverend Reed Farrell had asked her to do from the first—leave him alone.

She remembered the sense of well-being with which she had emerged from the bathtub. She had felt clean and refreshed, and donning her new underclothes, she had forcibly ejected the hard-eyed parson from her mind and begun brushing her damp hair free of snarls.

That feeling of well-being had dropped the first notch when she had then donned the simple frock she had purchased earlier. Looking at herself in the mottled mirror Sally had provided, she had winced at the color. Aunt Penelope and Aunt Harriet had disliked light shades. They would have frowned their disapproval of the pale blue cotton, and of the square neckline that allowed a modest glimpse of the feminine flesh beneath. They would have called it undignified. As she struggled with the buttons on the back of the dress, however, she began to realize that the garment's color was not her only problem.

Chastity raised her chin defensively at the direction of her thoughts. She certainly was not to blame for the fact that she had grown to the towering mark of seven inches past five feet. Nor was she to blame that because of her height, the selection of clothing available to her in Sedalia's only store was limited. And she surely could not assume responsibility for the manner in which her womanly proportions, usually so carefully disguised, strained at the bodice of the dress, calling attention to rounded breasts which she had always considered too large for the otherwise slim line of her body.

Chastity inwardly groaned. She had then looked again at her black dress. She had picked it up, determined to put it back on—but it had reeked beyond redemption and she had tossed it aside in despair.

Reaching into the pocket of her simple frock, she had consoled herself by withdrawing the rail ticket she had put there, and by telling herself that she would soon be free of this disaster-laden situation into which she had somehow stumbled. It was when she had sought to confirm the departure time stamped on her ticket that she first missed her glasses. A few minutes of frantic searching had followed, after which she had quickly secured her damp hair at the back of her neck and started out onto the street to retrace her steps. She had been searching ever since.

Chastity looked up at the hotel entrance as she approached. She swallowed with discomfort. The train would soon be departing. She could not leave without her glasses, and there was only one other place they could be.

Chastity glanced toward the stairs as she entered the hotel lobby. She turned at the sound of Sally's voice beside her.

"The reverend's waitin' for you."

She doubted it.

"He ate real good. He's feelin' a bit better, but his mood ain't too fine."

It never was.

"He's goodlookin', that man of yours."

Chastity's smile was wan.

Sally took a confidential step closer. "But he ain't got the eyes of a preacher. I'd keep a close watch on him, if I was you."

Chastity paused at the foot of the stairs.


"I'm sorry. I have to leave." His lined face sober, Dr. Carr regarded Reed for a few silent moments before continuing, "She's been gone over two hours. I'll check around town to see what I can find out, if you like."

"That won't be necessary. She'll be back."

"You're sure of that, are you?"

"Yes, I am."

Dr. Carr regarded Reed for a silent moment longer. "Well, I hope you aren't disappointed. In any case, Sally will be bringing you something to eat again soon. If you need anything, you can let her know."

Remaining silent until Dr. Carr closed the door behind him, Reed cursed under his breath. He didn't like lying here, totally helpless. It was too dangerous. Nor did he enjoy the thought that his plans now depended on whether the annoying Chastity Lawrence possessed a spare pair of eyeglasses.

The minutes ticked past like hours.

Reed was suddenly furious. He'd be damned if he'd lie there waiting another second!

Gritting his teeth, Reed ignored the spasm of pain as he labored to draw himself to a seated position in bed. Finally sitting upright, he breathed deeply.

The absurdity of the situation suddenly striking him, Reed laughed. Reed Farrell—bounty hunter. If anyone had told him a few years ago that he'd be in this hotel room today, with a bullet wound rotting his leg, and with blood money in his pocket that he had earned by tracking wanted men like animals, he would've called that person a liar. But then, he wasn't the same man he was those few years ago.

He had loved Jenny from the moment he'd learned what the word could mean. He had held the world in his arms when he held Jenny. And when he lost her, he had been able to fill the void in only one way.

Actually, it had started out nobly enough. When the law was ineffective in finding the rustlers responsible for Jenny's death, he decided he would find them himself. He trailed the gang relentlessly. He recalled the incredible satisfaction of the moment when he finally delivered them to the law. And he remembered the bitter irony in discovering that the gang he had captured was not the same one that had driven Jenny under the hooves of her own cattle.

The reward offered for their capture was unexpected. With his funds running low, he accepted it, vowing to find the right men the next time . . . or the next. It had come to him during the dark hours of a lonely night years later that

81

he had not consciously chosen the path he had taken. Rather, it had chosen him.

The acknowledgement that that path had led him to the hotel room where he now lay helpless was suddenly more than Reed could stand. He took another fortifying breath. He was through waiting. He didn't need Chastity Lawrence. He didn't need anyone! He'd get up and take a few steps right now. He'd take a few more steps tomorrow, and in another day he'd be on his feet and able to make his own contacts.

A sound outside the door interrupted Reed's angry thoughts. He went still when he heard a soft knock.

*Well, well . . .*

Reed waited as the door slowly opened to reveal a tall, slender female outline held in dark relief in the doorway.

It was Chastity Lawrence, all right.

Chastity was momentarily at a loss. She had not expected to find the Reverend Reed Farrell sitting up in bed, his eyes clear and his gaze focused. Her stomach tightening in a way she had become familiar with when facing him head-on, Chastity realized that Sally had been correct. The reverend *was* a handsome man. Relieved of that hideous beard, the sunstreaked color of his hair appeared lighter and his eyes more blue. His even features, more clearly revealed, were indeed comely, and the line of his jaw was strong. Looking at him, Chastity realized in a surprising flash that although she had spent the last two days tending to this man in a manner far more intimate than she cared to acknowledge, she was truly seeing him for the first time. He was younger than she had realized. He had less the look of a fanatic and more the appeal of—

Chastity caught herself short on that thought. *Appeal*? This man who had the disposition of an adder?

Dr. Carr was right. She needed rest.

Holding that thought as she hesitated in the doorway, Chastity began, "You needn't concern yourself, Reverend. I don't intend to stay. I lost my glasses and I thought they might be somewhere in this room."

"Come in."

Chastity did not move.

"Come in, please."

*Please?*

"I don't blame you for looking surprised. A fever is no excuse for bad manners. I hope you'll forgive me."

Chastity was stunned into speechlessness. Was this truly the same man she had left in that bed a few hours earlier? Realizing that the light from the hallway allowed her the advantage by shadowing her startled expression, Chastity took a few tentative steps into the room. She scrutinized him more closely as he continued, "I don't remember the last few days too clearly, but I do remember some things. I remember you said you were embarrassed that the doctor assumed you were my wife. Don't worry about that. I'll be on my feet in a few hours, and then I'll—"

"What did you say?" Chastity interrupted, "Dr. Carr told you that you could get up *today*?"

"I didn't say that."

"You said—"

"I said I'll be getting up soon. As a matter of fact, I was about to get up when you knocked on the door."

Chastity gasped. "You mustn't do that! You've seen your wound! If it worsens, you could—"

"There are some things I need to do."

"Surely they can wait, whatever they are."

"It's a matter of priorities."

"Your health should be your first priority."

The reverend did not reply.

"What could be more important than your health?"

"I have to speak to someone here in Sedalia . . . about the mission."

"The mission . . ." The determination that had entered the reverend's expression was familiar. Chastity continued, "I can understand that you're anxious to get to the mission, but Sally said they've been waiting for Reverend Stiles's replacement for quite a while. Another week shouldn't make that much difference."

"Reverend Stiles . . . yes." Reed paused, then plunged ahead. "I was given some of his reports. I'm supposed to meet someone here in Sedalia who's connected with the Indian Agency. I need to talk to him about some special needs at the mission. He's on his way back to Washington, and if I miss him, I'll lose my chance."

"Oh . . ." Chastity looked deep into the reverend's clear eyes. His fervor was obvious. Seeing the dedication in his gaze, she walked a few steps closer to his bed. She paused, looking down at him soberly.

As Chastity Lawrence stepped out of the shadows toward him, Reed restrained a gasp of surprise. Gone was her severe hairstyle and hideous black dress. Instead, her hair was fastened loosely at the back of her neck in a mass of gleaming red-gold ringlets from which small, curling tendrils escaped to tease the fair skin of her cheeks. Without her glasses, the faultless line of her brows and the incredible length of her brown lashes were visible to him for the first time—and her features were smaller and more delicate than he remembered.

Reed swept her further with his gaze. The blue dress she was wearing complemented her delicate coloring and displayed surprising feminine curves. It was a vast improvement over her former attire, but he knew he could not blame his failure to react to Chastity's womanly appeal solely on the way she had been dressed. It was clear that he had been more ill than he had realized, and that his powers of observation—as well as his judgment—had been impaired. Also clear was the reality that under other circumstances, that deficiency could have proved fatal.

Aware of the importance of his next words, Reed said cautiously, "My meeting with the fellow from the Indian Agency is important." He paused for effect. "The children at the mission are suffering . . ."

Chastity blinked revealingly. Reed could almost see the images of needy children flickering across her mind as he continued, "I hoped to be able to put an end to some of the hardships at the mission with his help."

Chastity broke her silence at last, protesting, "But surely you understand that all your effort will be for naught if your wound should worsen."

"That could happen, I suppose."

"It *will* happen if you don't follow Dr. Carr's advice."

"I have to try."

"But . . . but . . ." Green flecks stirred deep in the soft brown of Chastity's eyes. "Surely someone else can locate this man for you and tell him to come here to meet with you."

"If he hasn't already left Sedalia."

"Oh, I'm sure he hasn't. He couldn't if he understood the importance of your work."

Reed felt victory within his reach. "He understands, but his time is valuable."

"Perhaps Sally could help you."

No, he didn't want that. Sally was too wise to be taken in by a story he was inventing moment by moment. He responded with a shake of the head and an apologetic grimace. "No, I don't think so. Sally's a nice person, but her appearance is misleading."

"Oh." He could see that Chastity silently concurred, and he could see the struggle that waged behind her sympathetic gaze when she glanced at the clock on the nearby dresser and then shook her head. "I wish I could help, but my train is leaving in fifteen minutes."

Startled by her response, Reed repeated, "Your train?"

"Yes. I'm on my way to Caldwell, Kansas. It's important. I . . . there's someone waiting. I mean . . ." She glanced at the clock again.

So, there was someone waiting for Chastity Lawrence in Caldwell. He wondered why he hadn't realized there would be. He replied, "You came back for your glasses."

"Yes."

"I haven't seen them."

Discomfort flashed in Chastity's eyes. "Do you mind if I look for them?"

"No."

Growing increasingly weaker, Reed closed his eyes. He listened to the sounds of Chastity's movement around the room. He opened his eyes again when the sounds ceased.

"They're not here." Chastity paused. "So, I suppose I'll be saying good-bye."

He couldn't let that happen. He responded, "I have a favor to ask of you before you do. If you could get my clothes"—He motioned toward the pants and shirt hanging on a hook in the corner—"and put them on the end of the bed for me."

"Your clothes? You don't intend to get up . . ." Reed did not respond.

"You can't get up until Dr. Carr says it's safe."

"Chastity . . ." He paused, deliberately evoking a sense of friendly intimacy by using her given name for the first time. "Don't worry about me. Your train is leaving."

"But—"

"I'll take care of what has to be done."

"Dr. Carr can find someone to help you."

"Your train is leaving. . . ." He looked at the clock. "In ten minutes."

"Dr. Carr knows everybody in town. He's sure to know where to find the fellow you're looking for."

"Finding him isn't the problem. There should be a message at the telegraph office telling me where to meet him. I'm feeling much better. I can make it."

"At the telegraph office? You intend to walk there? Do you realize how far that is from here?"

"I'll make it."

"No, you won't."

"Yes, I will."

"No, you won't!"

He saw the moment of capitulation coming. His satisfaction diminished as a new bout of weakness assailed him, Reed closed his eyes. He felt a soft palm on his forehead and opened his eyes again to see Chastity leaning toward him, her smooth brow knit with concern. He smelled the scent of roses.

"You're too weak to meet him. Surely you see that."

"I have to *try.*"

Chastity hesitated only a moment longer before replying, "I'll go for you."

"But your train . . ."

"There'll be another train tomorrow. I can't leave without my glasses, anyway. What's the name of the man you're supposed to meet?"

"I can't let you—"

"What's his name?"

"Edward Jenkins."

Chastity nodded.

As she turned toward the door Reed added, "A word of warning—some people around here have strong feelings about the Indians. For that reason, Mr. Jenkins travels incognito. He doesn't know you, so he might not acknowledge who he is. It might be best if you just went along with anything he says."

Chastity nodded again.

Incredulous, Reed stared at the door as Chastity pulled it closed behind her. The ease with which he had manipulated her astounded him. He had never met a more gullible woman! Whatever had that fellow in Caldwell been thinking when he allowed her to travel alone?

Suddenly annoyed by the strange discomfort stirred by that thought, Reed closed his eyes. What difference did it make to him, anyway?

# *Chapter Four*

He didn't like this one bit.

Leaning casually against the side of a building, Ed Jenkins squinted against the glare of the late afternoon sun as the red-haired woman left the telegraph office and made her way back up the street. He tipped his hat down low on his forehead, his gaze intent. Something was wrong. He had been waiting for two days for Farrell to make contact with him. He had just about given up when the red-haired woman showed up at the telegraph office asking for any messages left for Reverend Reed Farrell.

*Reverend* Reed Farrell?

Jenkins unconsciously sneered. He had heard plenty about Reed Farrell, and from all that he'd heard, the fellow was more adept at planting outlaws than converting them. He had also heard that Farrell worked alone.

Observing the red-haired woman more closely, Jenkins straightened up slowly and started after her. For all he knew, Will Morgan had figured out that he was in town and was using this woman to lay a trap for him. That would be just the kind of thing Morgan did. He was good at fooling people, at making them believe in him just like Sonny had believed in him. There was nothing he had been able to say to Sonny to make him see through the promises Morgan had made to him before it was too late.

The red-haired woman turned out of sight on the street, and Jenkins walked faster. He turned the corner in time to see her walk through the entrance of the Biltmore Hotel. He paused to survey the street. He wouldn't put anything past Morgan.

The red-haired woman disappeared around the curve of the staircase as Jenkins entered the lobby. He scrutinized the area carefully, then started up behind her, only to feel a hand on his arm stay him.

"She's a good-lookin' woman, ain't she?"

Jenkins turned toward the middle-aged woman in the bright red dress standing beside him. He leered purposefully. "She sure is. She gave me the eye out on the street, and then she turned in here. I ain't never had a clearer invitation."

"You're dreamin', fella." The woman laughed,

then extended her hand. "My name's Sally. I own this place, and I'm tellin' you that whatever you think you saw . . . you didn't. That lady you just saw walkin' up them steps is a *lady*. And she's married."

"Married, huh?" Jenkins shook his head. "You sure?"

"Couldn't be no more sure. Her husband's the Reverend Reed Farrell, so don't go gettin' any ideas."

"A preacher! She don't look like no preacher's wife to me!"

"And that preacher don't look like no preacher, either, so I guess that makes them a good pair. She's been takin' real good care of him, too."

"Takin' care of him?"

"He's sick. Doc Carr's been visitin' real regular."

"That right?"

"It took three men to get him up the stairs the first night they came. Good thing Room One was empty, too. As big as he is, I don't think them men could've carried him a step farther."

"So, you think I'd be wastin' my time if I introduced myself to the lady. . . ."

"Let me tell you somethin'." Sally's expression abruptly sobered. "If you know what's good for you, you'll stay as far away from that lady as you can, 'cause I'm tellin' you—preacher or not—there's somethin' about the look in that man's eyes that says, 'Don't mess with me'."

"That right?"

"That's right."

"What did you say his name was?"

"Reverend Reed Farrell."

"I think I saw him once. He's a short fella, with black hair . . . kinda fat."

"Hell, no!" Sally gave a sharp laugh. "That parson's a big fella with light hair and blue eyes as cold as ice . . . and from what I could see, there ain't an ounce of fat on him."

"Must have the wrong man." Jenkins tipped his hat. "Thanks for the advice, ma'am."

Smiling, Jenkins turned toward the door. His smile dropped away as he stepped out onto the boardwalk and cursed under his breath. He had the right man, all right, but something was wrong.

He didn't like this at all.

Chastity knocked on the hotel room door. She waited with her hand on the knob for a response from within, unconsciously grimacing at the sound of a train whistle disappearing into the distance. It had happened again. She had fallen another day behind on her journey to Caldwell. An hour ago she had steadfastly determined to put the past two days behind her, only to again put that resolution aside for a man she hardly knew.

Chastity reviewed her conversation with the Reverend Reed Farrell a few minutes earlier. She remembered that those incredibly direct blue eyes were no longer cold when she approached his bed. An undefinable emotion had flickered in them, sending a peculiar tremor down her spine. When weakness temporarily overcame him, something inside her had reached out to him, and she had been lost.

Still waiting for a response to her knock, Chastity took a nervous breath. Surely he wouldn't have tried to get up without help in her absence. Surely she realized the risk in doing so.

Chastity knocked more sharply. Her heart began a new pounding when there was no reply, and she pushed the door open to see Reed lying motionless in bed. Beside him in an instant, she touched her hand to his forehead, only to gasp aloud when his eyes snapped open and his hand grabbed her wrist. True menace lingered in his tone as he grated, "I told you not to come at me when I'm sleeping."

"I didn't come at you! I knocked twice. When you didn't answer, I thought—" Halting abruptly, annoyed at herself for her defensive tone, she continued, "Never mind what I thought. Just let go of me."

Releasing her abruptly, making a visible effort to shake off the last vestiges of sleep, Reed muttered softly, "I'm sorry. I must've fallen asleep. You startled me." He did not wait for her response as he pressed, "What did you find out at the telegraph office?"

Chastity's resentment lingered. "Nothing."

"What do you mean?"

"I mean exactly that. I did what you said. I asked if there were any messages for Reverend

94

Reed Farrell, and the clerk said no one came in asking for you."

"You're sure?"

"Of course I'm sure! It wasn't that difficult, you know. I made certain to—"

The sound of soft shuffling in the hallway outside the door did not prepare Chastity for Reed's sudden spring to a seated position, or for the force with which he swung out his arm and thrust her aside, hissing, "Get back!"

Chastity's spontaneous protest froze on her lips when the door snapped open, revealing a man standing with gun drawn. She swallowed convulsively as he said, "I'm lookin' for Reed Farrell."

Reed's response was equally harsh. "What do you want with him?"

The stranger's eyes narrowed. "You're Farrell, ain't you?" He paused. "Did you send this woman lookin' for me?"

"I did if your name is Ed Jenkins."

"We were supposed to meet two days ago."

"I wasn't in shape to do anything until today."

The gunman glanced at Chastity. "Who's she?"

"A messenger . . . that's all." Reed turned toward Chastity. "Mr. Jenkins wants to talk to me privately."

Chastity did not move.

"Chastity . . ."

Chastity turned incredulously toward him. "You want me to leave you alone with him?"

"Mr. Jenkins and I have business to discuss."

"But he has a gun!"

"He's just being cautious."

"But what if he—"

"Just go."

"No, you don't." Jenkins interrupted tightly. "She's not goin' nowhere!"

"If you don't let her go, we have nothing to talk about!"

Chastity watched Jenkins's reaction to Reed's sharp declaration. She saw his small eyes dart cautiously between them before he slowly lowered his gun. And she saw the satisfaction that registered in Reed's expression as he instructed, "You can leave, Chastity. Don't worry. Mr. Jenkins and I will be done here soon."

Aware that she was shaking, Chastity pulled the door closed behind her. She paused uncertainly, noting the sound of soft conversation as soon as the door clicked shut. Reassured when the tone was free of menace, she started down the hallway. Her ignorance about conditions in the West amazed her. She had not realized resentment against the Indians ran so high that a government agent was forced into a clandestine meeting with a man who wanted to help them. As for Mr. Jenkins's drawn gun . . .

*Barbaric, that's what the "Wild West" is. . . .*

Perhaps there was more truth to Aunt Penelope's words than she had realized.

But another truth was that Reed had shown no trace of fear when he faced Mr. Jenkins's gun. Somehow she hadn't expected that he would.

Puzzled at that thought, Chastity continued on down the stairs.

Reed eyed Ed Jenkins coldly. The fellow looked to be in his mid-forties. He was short and wiry, with the leathery, lined skin and callused hands of a cowman who had spent long years on the range. There was a look about him of unyielding resolution that he recognized. He had worn that same expression before the hatred inside him had turned to ice. He knew there was no compromise with the feelings behind that look.

Aware of his physical limitations as he battled another abrupt bout of weakness, Reed asked, "You wired that Morgan and his gang were seen around Sedalia. What I want to know is why you didn't go after him yourself if you're lookin' to get the reward—or why you got in touch with me instead of the law."

Jenkins gave a harsh laugh. "The law? You know the law ain't been able to touch Morgan. They're so caught up in their rules and regulations that he don't have no trouble at all keepin' a step ahead of them."

"He didn't keep a step ahead of you."

Jenkins's expression hardened. "No, he didn't. But I don't fool myself that I'd be able to take on Morgan and his gang. He's smart and he's fast—and I ain't no gunfighter. It ain't my life I'm carin' about, but I'll be damned if I'll take the chance of him gettin' away again."

"I'm not a gunfighter, either."

Elaine Barbieri

"The hell you ain't!"

"I said . . . I'm not a gunfighter."

Jenkins regarded him for a cautious moment. "No, maybe you ain't, but people talk. They say you got a personal grudge against men like Morgan. And they say a lot more, too."

"Like what?"

"They say you don't give up when you're after somebody . . . and that you've been after Morgan for a long time. And they say you ain't afraid of nothin'."

His patience stretching thin when his leg began a new throbbing, Reed asked, "What are you looking to get out of this?"

"Morgan's hide nailed to the wall."

"Oh, that's all?"

Reed's sarcasm was not lost on the wiry cowman. "Yeah, that's all!" he snapped.

"Why?"

"That's my business."

"No, it isn't. It's mine."

"I had a son, once," Jenkins said, his lean face tight, "and now I ain't got a son no more. I've got Morgan to thank for that. I want to see him pay."

Jenkins's words twisted tightly in Reed's gut. "Where's Morgan now?"

"He left town. I couldn't follow him because I was waitin' for you, but I know where he went. He's got a hideout in Indian Territory where the law ain't got no authority. He's keepin' a herd he rustled there, and he's takin' his sweet time puttin' his brand on it. Hell, he's so cocky, he ain't even botherin' to look behind him."

Reaching into his pocket, Jenkins withdrew a paper. He spread it out on the bed beside Reed, a tight smile on his face. "I drew you a map. You won't have no trouble findin' him." He paused. "There's only one thing I'm askin' from you."

Reed looked up at him sharply.

"Just a wire, tellin' me you got him, is all I want. I wrote where you can send it on the back of the map."

The look in Jenkins's eyes tightened the knot within Reed. Jenkins's son . . . and Jenny.

"All right." Reed took a shaky breath. "Get out of here and don't come back. I don't need anybody getting suspicious. I'll be on my feet in a few days. It won't take me too long after that, one way or another."

Jenkins straightened up slowly. Reed saw the telltale tic in his cheek before Jenkins extended his hand toward him. "Much obliged, Farrell."

Folding up the map as Jenkins left the room, Reed shoved it under his pillow. His hand grazed the spectacles lying there when he did, and he frowned. So, Morgan was in Indian Territory . . . where a parson and his wife were expected at the mission. It couldn't have worked out better. And if a parson and his wife were what they were expecting, that was what they'd get.

Reed leaned back against the pillow and closed his eyes.

\*   \*   \*

Elaine Barbieri

"The news isn't good."

Reed spoke softly. Chastity waited for him to continue, her gaze intent on his face. She had been searching again for her spectacles on the street when Edward Jenkins came out of the hotel and started toward the livery stable. Somehow anxious, she had headed directly back toward the hotel. One look at Reed and it was obvious that things hadn't gone well.

Reed's clear blue eyes were troubled as he continued, "Jenkins said there's a problem at the mission."

"A problem?"

"The children . . ." Reed paused, frowning as he began again, "Reverend Stiles started a school at the mission. He brought a teacher in who was good with the Indian children. Something happened to her—Jenkins wasn't sure what—but she left."

Reed paused, his gaze narrowing. "The mission's in real trouble. When Reverend Stiles died, the Indians felt abandoned. They turned to the teacher for guidance and she was able to handle things for a while, but with her gone, Reverend Stiles's converts began leaving the mission."

"But . . . but now that you're on the way . . ."

"They were promised more than a year ago that a new preacher and his wife were on the way. In the meantime, they lost their teacher, too. Jenkins said that the Indians think that no one cares about them or their children anymore. He says the only thing for me to do if I

100

want to get them back is to go out to the villages, one by one, and talk to them. The only trouble is that in the meantime I'll probably lose more of the converts who still bring their children to the mission."

"Can't you go to the mission and explain the situation—tell them that you'll come back as soon as you can and school will be resumed?"

"They've been given so many promises that haven't been kept. Jenkins said the only way to keep the Indians who still come to the mission would be to start the school again immediately."

"Well, you can't do both!"

"I know."

"Didn't anyone realize that when you were sent here?"

"The situation wasn't clear. The wife of the preacher they originally intended to send was a good teacher who could've handled the children while her husband was out at the villages, but she got sick and they weren't able to come. I was sent instead."

"Oh . . ."

Reed frowned. "No one expected the complications that held me up, including me. Now it looks like I'll be arriving to do too little, too late."

"You mustn't feel that way."

"The worst part of it all is that Jenkins said the government was looking into financing part of the school, but if the Indians appear to be losing interest, that'll probably be the end of it."

"Isn't there someone you can wire to have them send out a teacher temporarily—at least until you get back from the villages and can take over the school yourself?"

"I suppose they would send someone eventually, but I couldn't make Jenkins any promises."

"But—"

"It's the children that bother me most. . . ." Reed's gaze flickered. "I hate to lose them."

Reed's tone touched Chastity's heart. His eyes, so blue and direct, were filled with resolution. His face, so pale and drawn, reflected true intensity. She sensed that intensity ran deeper than he would admit. It tugged at her relentlessly in ways she could not quite comprehend, and there was a quiver in her voice as she responded, "Surely there's someone who can help. Perhaps Sally—"

Reed's brows immediately furrowed. "I don't think Sally's the right person."

Chastity stiffened defensively. "Sally's a nice woman. She worked with Reverend Stiles."

"She didn't teach school. I don't think she'd be able to handle it."

"Maybe she knows someone who could take the position."

"I can't afford to let the situation at the mission become general knowledge."

"You can't do this alone. You need help."

"I'll manage."

"I wish I could help you."

"I understand. You're on your way to Caldwell."

"It's important for me to get there. I've already sent a wire. I'm expected."

"Don't worry about it. I'll be on my feet in another day or so."

Chastity scrutinized Reed intently, her stomach tightening. The intensity in his gaze remained. He would do what he must . . . but she also saw the weariness behind his eyes.

"I can see you're committed to this."

"I'm committed, all right."

"You're going to do it with or without help."

It wasn't necessary for him to reply.

"I'll help if I can." The words emerged from Chastity's lips as if of their own accord. They reverberated in her mind even as she hastened to add, "But only for a few weeks—until you or someone else can take over the school."

She thought she saw a flash of satisfaction in his eyes. "That's very generous of you. I know you're worried about the effect this might have on your reputation."

Her reputation? A slow flush heated Chastity's skin. Somehow she had forgotten.

"Everyone in Sedalia thinks you're my wife. That misunderstanding hasn't hurt anybody, and nobody has to know anything different. As a matter of fact, it would probably make things easier all the way around."

Chastity nodded.

"As for Sally, her intentions are good, but

she's talkative. I don't think it would be smart to tell her too much."

*Right.*

"Thank you, Chastity."

*Thank you?* Would wonders never cease?

"You're welcome, Reverend."

The weariness behind Reed's eyes broadened. "I think it would be better if you call me Reed."

Exhaustion once again claiming him, Reed slid down against the pillow before she could reply. He mumbled, "I'm going to rest for a while."

He was sleeping within minutes.

Chastity backed away from the bed slowly. Her legs bumped the chair behind her and she sat down abruptly. Clasping her locket in her fist, she stared at the confounding man lying in the bed a few feet away. An hour earlier, she had been ready to board the train and turn her back on him without another thought, and now she had committed herself to traveling with him into Indian Territory. She had also agreed to teach school at an Indian mission—when the truth was that she had never even *seen* a real Indian!

*"Chastity needs to learn not to be ruled by her emotions! She must learn to consider the consequences before she acts!"*

*"Oh, pooh, Penelope! Chastity is an intelligent woman and she'll make intelligent decisions. I have complete faith in her!"*

Was she?

Did she?

Aunt Penelope's and Aunt Harriet's voices warred in her mind, as the answers continued to elude her.

"Well, this is a pleasant domestic scene."

Reed awoke with a start to see Dr. Carr smiling down at him. He glanced toward the window to see that the light of day had faded, then at the chair in the corner of the room where Chastity hurriedly rose to her feet. They had both been sleeping. It frustrated him that someone had again been able to enter the room and approach the bed without his awakening. The full extent of his vulnerability had never been clearer.

"That frown looks familiar." Dr. Carr touched Reed's forehead lightly. "No fever tonight. How's the pain?"

Still annoyed with himself, Reed said, "I'm all right."

"That tone sounds familiar, too." Dr. Carr turned toward Chastity as she approached the bed. "Has this fellow been behaving himself while I was gone?"

She nodded.

"Sally says you haven't been out of this room for supper, so she's bringing up a tray for both of you in a few minutes."

Chastity protested, "Oh, she doesn't have to do that."

"She doesn't have to do it, but she's pleased to help a nice young couple like you."

Chastity's eyes darted toward him, guilt

flashing bright and clear in her gaze. Annoyed, Reed was grateful that Dr. Carr was not looking her way. As guileless and naive as Chastity was, it was a mystery to him how she had made it this far without a major disaster befalling her.

The sudden thought occurred to him that Chastity's journey with him into Indian Territory was a disaster in the making, but Reed hardened himself against the thought. It was a matter of priorities, and he had set his.

"Now, let's take a look at that leg."

Dr. Carr threw back the coverlet without warning, and Reed could feel Charity's chagrin. Her color darkened as Dr. Carr unwrapped his leg and addressed her casually.

"Get over here and look at this, Chastity." When she hesitated he said, "Come closer, woman! You're partly responsible for this and you should see it." Not bothering to look down at his wound, Reed kept his gaze trained on Chastity's face as she came to stand beside the bed.

"Well, what do you think?"

"It looks fine."

"It looks better than fine!" Dr. Carr addressed Reed. "Either that collar you wear gave you some special help from On High, or Chastity and I just make a damned good team, because that wound of yours looks to be almost free of infection! At this rate, you'll be on your feet in a week."

"A week!"

"A week?"

Dr. Carr looked at Reed, then at Chastity. He frowned. "What's wrong with you two? I'd say you should be pretty damned satisfied to see things going so smoothly."

Chastity smiled weakly. "I'm satisfied."

Reed grated, "I'm not. I'm getting up now."

Dr. Carr gave a short laugh. "You're not serious."

"I'm serious, all right." Reed boosted himself to a seated position. A week was out of the question. He needed to be on his feet now—and no one was going to hold him back.

"Don't be a fool! Stay where you are."

Reacting sharply to Dr. Carr's order, Reed grated, "This is the way it is, Doc. I'll get up now, while you're here to help me, or I'll get up by myself, after you're gone."

"You're not ready to start walking, yet."

"I'm ready to get on my feet, and that's what I'm going to do."

"Reed, Dr. Carr knows what's best for you."

Dr. Carr exploded, "Don't waste your breath, Chastity! You should know this man by now, because I surely do! He wants to get up, and he's not going to let it go until he does! Well, we'll give him what he wants, and he'll be flat on his back again in a minute."

Not speaking again until he had rubbed a foul-smelling salve into the wound, Dr. Carr rewrapped the bandage, then addressed Chastity abruptly.

"All right, I'll take one arm. You can take the other."

Chastity glanced down at Reed's unclothed state, her skin flushing hotly. "But . . . shouldn't he at least put on his pants?"

Dr. Carr glared. "What's the matter with you, woman? He's only going to be on his feet for a few minutes!"

"But—

"But, but. Just take his arm when I tell you to!"

Chastity's gaze met Reed's with true panic.

Reed's intense stare held hers, and Chastity could feel perspiration bead on her brow and upper lip. It was bad enough to tend to an only partially clothed man when he was lying help-less and needy in bed, but . . .

Reed slid his legs down onto the floor and the quivering within Chastity turned to quaking. Somehow, seated upright, poised to stand, he looked bigger and broader. His hair looked more blond. His eyes looked more blue. His body looked more . . . *naked*.

"Grab his arm!"

Chastity jumped to Reed's side at Dr. Carr's command. Her heart fluttered in her chest as Reed slid his arm across her shoulders. His arm was heavy and warm. His callused palm brushed the flesh of her upper arm, and a tremor moved down her spine. The pure male scent of him increased that tremor to an inner shuddering as she moved supportively closer.

Pain twitched across Reed's face, and Chastity asked instinctively, "Are you all right?" She was unprepared for his sudden glance toward her—for the moment when his incredible blue eyes linked with hers. The shock of the contact jolted through her, as did the abrupt realization that Reed needed her at that moment more than anyone had ever needed her before.

Reed took one step, then another. His weight gradually shifted, and Chastity saw Dr. Carr's surprise when Reed began effectively supporting himself. She saw his surprise turn to incredulity when Reed began walking virtually unaided.

"You were bound and determined to prove me wrong, weren't you?" Grasping Reed's arm, Dr. Carr continued gruffly, "All right, so you did. You can walk, but you've had enough for the first time out. Don't be pigheaded or you'll find yourself right back where you started."

When he was again abed, Chastity pulled the coverlet up over Reed with trembling hands. Somehow unwilling to meet his gaze, she turned toward Dr. Carr as he addressed Reed sharply.

"I'm leaving. Just make sure you keep taking that medicine I gave Chastity for you. I'll be back tomorrow morning." He paused. "Remember, whatever you might be thinking now, you're not well enough to resume any *other* normal activities yet . . . if you get my drift."

Chastity stared a silent moment at Dr. Carr. She didn't get his drift.

Oh, dear . . . or did she?

Chastity glanced at Reed, relieved to see that he showed no reaction at all to the doctor's comments.

Dr. Carr paused at the door. "Behave yourself, Reed. I don't want to see all my hard work go for naught. Give yourself a week. No matter what you think, you need it."

Dr. Carr pulled the door closed behind him, and Reed stated flatly, "We'll be on our way in two days."

Music, shouted conversations, female laughter blending with loud male guffaws—sounds from the brightly lit street below echoed in the silence of the hotel room. Somehow unable to sleep after Dr. Carr left, Reed had listened to the voices as they grew gradually louder, the music more bawdy, the laughter more shrill. He had no need to look at the clock now to know that the midnight hour had passed. He had been a part of scenes similar to the one below too many times not to be familiar with its progress.

Another shriek of female laughter interrupted his thoughts, and Reed grimaced. That would be Trixie . . . or Pearl . . . or Ruby. Their names really didn't matter. They were a necessary lot on the frontier . . . or anywhere, he supposed. He had made use of their particular talents when the need pressed. The exchanges had been mutually beneficial . . . and mutually satisfying if he were to believe the smiles that had followed him out the door.

The sound of restless movement turned Reed, frowning, toward the chair in the corner of the room. Chastity moved again. Her face was shadowed. He recalled the warmth of her body pressed against his side when he had attempted to walk earlier. He remembered the softness of her flesh when his palm brushed her upper arm, and he recalled that when she looked up at him—

Reed halted that thought abruptly. The women below were soft on the outside and hard on the inside. A man knew they could take care of themselves when he walked away. Chastity Lawrence wasn't one of their breed. He had no time for her kind, but she would be immensely useful to him. She was made to order for this particular situation. There wasn't a man alive who would suspect they had entered Indian Territory with devious intent when they saw the innocence in her eyes. She was so inexperienced with the wilderness that he would be able to take as circuitous a route as he pleased in scouting the country where Morgan was hiding. And she was so trusting that she would not suspect for a moment that he was anything but the man he had told her he was.

The truth be said, Chastity Lawrence needed a keeper. The thought that there was a man waiting for her in Caldwell who was willing to assume that responsibility somehow lent him little comfort, and Reed tossed impatiently. He stiffened at the resulting pain that stabbed his thigh, and Chastity sat up abruptly. He could see the tension in her shadowed posture as she asked, "Is anything wrong?"

"No." Regretting his clipped response, Reed cursed under his breath, continuing more graciously, "I'm all right. It was just a twinge. I didn't mean to wake you up."

"I wasn't sleeping."

"I suppose not. It's a lively night at the Roundup."

"Yes."

"That's not unusual."

"I suppose it isn't."

"It's not what you're used to."

"Well . . ."

There was no need for elaboration.

Silence stretched between them for a long moment before Chastity asked hesitantly, "Do you mind if I ask you a question?"

Wariness prickled up Reed's spine. "No, I suppose not."

"When Mr. Jenkins came to see you earlier . . . how did you know he was outside the door with a gun?"

"I didn't."

"I don't understand."

"I didn't know it was Jenkins . . . but I knew someone was there with a gun."

"How?"

"I heard the click of the hammer when he drew it back."

"Oh . . ."

He could sense her surprise and the new questions that were raised in her mind. But he had questions of his own. "You said someone is expecting you in Caldwell."

"Yes."

Annoyed when Chastity didn't offer more, he nudged, "You should wire him that you'll be delayed."

"I will."

He didn't like her hesitation. "Will he be angry?"

"I hope not."

"He sounds understanding."

"Oh, yes. He's a wonderful man."

"Is he a rancher?"

"No, he's a banker."

*A banker . . .*

"Are you visiting, or do you expect to stay?"

"If all goes well, I hope to stay."

"Does he want you to stay?"

"I don't know."

Reed was suddenly angry. "Any man worth his salt would know better than to let a woman like you travel alone in this country."

He heard the edge that entered her voice. "A woman like me?"

Reed replied more cautiously, "A stranger to this country."

"I can take care of myself."

Sure.

"I know exactly where I'm headed and what

I'm going to do. I've been planning this journey for a long time."

He remained silent.

"It's very important to me."

"It sounds like *he's* very important to you."

"I'm depending on him."

The touch of desperation in her reply clenched Reed's stomach. "You don't have anyone else?"

"No . . . yes . . . ." She hesitated, then said simply, "He's all I need right now."

Reed strained to see Chastity more clearly in the semi-light, but her features were as vague as her responses. Vague . . . but truthful. He was sure of that. She didn't know how to lie.

It occurred to Reed that meeting him was the beginning of her education in that direction.

A light flickered outside the window, momentarily illuminating Chastity's face. She was leaning back against the pillow again, clenching her locket in her fist. That habit of hers had become familiar to him. It tugged strangely at his memory.

Reed spoke abruptly. "I'll make sure you get to Caldwell when everything is straightened out."

"That isn't necessary."

"Yes, it is."

He wondered why he had said that.

The answer was suddenly clear. The balmy night air filtering through the window, a soft feminine voice in the darkness, the remembered scent of roses that still teased his senses—

no, he wasn't going to fall into that trap!

He concluded their conversation abruptly.

"We'll be starting out in two days."

"But Dr. Carr said—"

"Two days. No longer."

# *Chapter Five*

The two days were up.

The sun shone brilliantly on the light traffic of early morning as Reed glanced out the window of the hotel room to the street below. Chastity had awakened earlier. He had allowed her to leave believing he was still asleep because it suited his purpose to do so. She had been using the early mornings to make use of Sally's bathtub, if he were to judge from the fragrance of roses taunting him when she returned. He knew she would be gone for a while and he needed the time.

Sliding his feet over the edge of the bed, Reed winced against the pain in his thigh. He drew himself purposefully to his full height and limped toward the washstand in the corner.

Two days had been shorter than he had originally anticipated when he'd made his adamant statement to Dr. Carr, but the situation forcing that decision had not changed. For all he knew, Morgan was even now preparing to leave Indian Territory. He couldn't let him get away again.

That thought foremost in his mind, Reed did not take time to assess his appearance in the washstand mirror. Instead, he poured water into the bowl, then picked up the soap and worked it into a brisk lather. He breathed deeply against the last remaining vestiges of weakness as he rubbed the lather against his face, chest, and arms, cleansing his body and his mind as he went over his plans for the days ahead. Relieved and refreshed minutes later, he wiped the excess water from his skin with slow, circular motions, rubbing broad shoulders stiffened by days of inactivity, and flexing powerful chest and arm muscles that ached for action. He felt strength rapidly returning as he reached for the razor nearby.

Standing fully dressed a short time later, Reed assessed his appearance at last. His dark clothing and collar in place, he saw a light-haired, hard-eyed, clean-shaven parson staring back at him. His skin was pale and his eyes were still shadowed, but he stood with apparent ease, with no hint of the pain that throbbed dully in his thigh, or of the lingering fatigue that lent an irritating tremor to his hand.

Satisfied, Reed picked up the carpetbag on the floor beside him. Glancing cautiously toward the door, he dug down deep into the bag, withdrew a small derringer from the lining at the bottom, and secreted it in the sling inside his boot. Ready at last, he turned toward the door.

Annoyed when his step was still a trifle unsteady, Reed softly cursed. A little fresh air was all he needed, and he'd be himself again. Holding that thought in mind, he walked slowly down the staircase toward the first floor.

"Oh, no, this can't be!"

Chastity held up the faded black dress that had been her carefully selected traveling attire when she'd started out on her journey. She assessed it with true distress. She had risen early that morning, indulged herself with another bath in Sally's tub, and then made her way directly to the small laundry shack where she had left her dress to be laundered two days earlier. Standing in the ramshackle structure now, she could feel tears welling in her eyes.

Chastity turned sharply toward the bewhiskered proprietor, who stared at her coldly. Unable to restrain her accusing tone, she rasped, "What happened to this dress? It's at least two sizes smaller than it was when I brought it in, and the color . . . there isn't any!"

"I didn't do nothin' to it! My girls washed and ironed it, like you wanted."

"But . . . but . . ."

"They wash all the clothes that come in here the same way. They don't treat none of them no

118

different than any other. Alkali soap gets everythin' clean."

"Alkali soap?" Chastity shook her head, incredulous.

"And boilin' water. There ain't no dirt in this country that my girls can't boil out."

"Boil out . . ." Chastity felt herself go limp. Aware that further protest was useless, she replied, "All right. Keep the dress. Maybe you know somebody who can use it."

"There ain't nobody in mournin' in this town that I know of."

"In mourning?"

"Don't know nobody who'd wear a dress like that if they wasn't." He paused to consider that statement. "Maybe old Ma Gillis might be able to use it, though. She ain't got much, and she ain't too particular what she looks like."

Chastity's lips twitched in a weak smile. "Fine."

The old man's expression tightened when Chastity started to turn away. "Wait a minute, there! Who's goin' to pay for the launderin'?"

"Pay for the laundering? My dress is ruined and you want me to pay?"

The old man bit down hard on toothless gums. Squinting in her direction, he spat, "Look lady, I don't know how they handle things where you come from back East, but out here, we pay what we owe, or we pay the price, if you get what I mean."

Aghast, Chastity stared at the small rooster of a man. "Sir, are you threatening me?"

"No, I ain't. I'm just tellin' you what's goin' to happen if I don't get what's owed me!"

*. . . barbaric country . . .*

Chastity forced back the persistent echo of Aunt Penelope's voice as she slapped a coin down on the counter and left the glowering old man behind her.

Emerging onto the street, Chastity glanced toward the mercantile store at the far end. She picked unconsciously at the skirt of the pale blue cotton dress she wore. She should never have trusted the delicate fabric of her traveling dress to the hands of frontier laundresses. She should have known better.

Chastity inwardly groaned. What was she going to do now? Reed had recuperated rapidly during the past two days. It was almost as if he had *willed* himself better, so swift had been the improvement in his condition. Whatever the cause of his remarkable recovery, she was certain they would start out soon on the journey into Indian Territory—a journey to which she had committed herself in a weak, sympathetic moment.

Chastity breathed a frustrated sigh. This wild, undisciplined country had affected her in ways she had not anticipated. She had never considered herself an emotional person and had always believed her decisions were based on logic, but she had been subjected to too many of those weak, sympathetic lapses since meeting the Reverend Reed Farrell. She had finally determined, during the silence of the previous night, that however great his need was in the future, she would not allow her own objectives to be relegated to secondary importance again. And if the realization had also nudged her that she was far too susceptible to the intensity of the blue-eyed gaze dwelling on her with increasing frequency of late, she had chosen to ignore it.

A sudden warm gust raised her skirt, interrupting Chastity's thoughts and returning her mind to her quandary. The fact remained that she could not undertake a journey of a few weeks without a change of clothing. She had no choice.

Chastity started up the street.

Reed walked slowly along the boardwalk. The sun felt warm on his shoulders and the pleasant breeze felt fresh on his face, but his mind was far from the balmy weather of mid-morning. He made a positive effort to ignore the twinging in his thigh as he continued toward the telegraph office at the end of the street. His keen observance of the street and the attitude of those he encountered was belied by his casual manner as he tipped his hat politely at a passing matron. He had been making his way systematically through town for almost an hour, and he was pleased with what he had seen so far.

At Sedalia's finest and only restaurant, he had been greeted warmly with inquiries as to his health. Casual questions had followed about the Indian mission, to which he had responded

Elaine Barbieri

vaguely and to the apparent satisfaction of all. Next had come a visit to the post office, where he had again been immediately recognized as the injured parson on his way to Indian Territory. Covert inquiries had confirmed Jenkins's story that men meeting the descriptions of Morgan and two of his cohorts had been in town for more than a week.

He had deliberately avoided the sheriff's office, where he feared inquiries might raise suspicion and he might be recognized. He had learned the hard way that bounty hunters were not popular with lawmen and were unlikely to get their support. He had decided instead to make his way casually toward the telegraph office, where a few carefully posed questions might net him some answers he was seeking.

"Good mornin', Reverend!"

His thoughts interrupted by the warm greeting of a balding, muscular fellow nearby, Reed responded, "Good morning, sir."

"My name's Archie Willard." The fellow extended his hand. "I'm the town blacksmith, and I'm glad to see that you're feelin' better. I admire a man who's not afraid to take a hard road like the one you're goin' to be takin'. If I can do anythin' for you, you just let me know, you hear?"

Accepting the fellow's hand with a firm shake, Reed replied, "Thank you, sir."

Continuing on down the walk, Reed inwardly smiled. He had no doubt where the town had obtained its information about his injury *and* his destination. Sally knew everybody and

122

everybody knew her. By the time he reached Indian Territory, his entry there would be old news and no one would give him a second thought.

Thank you, Sally.

Reed momentarily paused. Speak of the devil . . . Sally was standing in front of the saloon a few yards ahead. A buxom blond was standing beside her. One quick sweep of the younger woman's painted features and tight gold dress was sufficient. Pretty, experienced, *and willing . . .*

It occurred to him that it had been a long time since he had spent some time with a woman. He knew the danger in extended abstinence. Physical need was a complication that he preferred not to face during the long days and nights he would soon be spending in Indian Territory with a red-haired young woman who put too much faith in the restrictions of a parson's collar. He had already spent too many uncomfortable hours during the last two nights with the scent of roses plaguing him.

He considered the thought further. He had a few hours yet before he would be leaving Sedalia. . . .

"He sure is a good-lookin' man, ain't he?"

Observing Reed's slow progress along the street, Sally turned with a wink toward the brassy blond woman beside her. Opal Carter was young and one of the most sought-after girls at the Roundup. Opal put her in mind of herself years ago, when she was young and carefree and enjoying life as best she could. She liked Opal. She had even tried converting Opal at one time. That effort had failed, but it hadn't affected their friendship, and she was glad of it. She had every intention of trying to convert her again in a few years, when Opal would most likely have grown more jaded, but until then . . .

"He sure is." Opal's response to Sally's comment was deep and sultry. "Them fire-and-brimstone types usually ain't my cup of tea, but I wouldn't mind havin' that fella try convertin' me. As a matter of fact, I just might consider it for a while if it suits my purpose."

"You might just as well try to scratch your ear with your elbow, honey." Sally gave a short laugh. "That woman of his ain't lackin' in nothin'. And I should know, since I've seen her in the altogether more times than he has in the past few days."

Opal raised her well-tended brows and Sally laughed again. "That woman's got a fondness for my bathtub, and all I can say is, however close he came to losin' his leg, he's still a mighty lucky man."

"Lookin' at him, I'd say his wife's lucky, too."

Sally's expression grew thoughtful. "Yeah . . . maybe. But maybe not as much as you think. There's somethin' about that man—behind them bright blue eyes, and underneath all that hard muscle—and it ain't necessarily good."

"Meanin'?"

"Meanin' I have a feelin' that there's a side of

him that ain't too pretty. Despite that collar he wears, he's as hard and tough as they come."

Opal gave a husky growl. "That's just the way I like them."

"I'm tellin' you, you're wastin' your time even thinkin' about it for a minute. There's a look in his eyes when he looks at that woman of his . . ." She paused. "I can't put my finger on it, but ain't never seen a man look at his wife like that before."

"Sally, as far as a man's concerned, the grass is always greener."

"They're goin' to be leavin' Sedalia as soon as he's fit, anyway."

Opal winked. "I only need a few hours, honey."

Sally gave a low snort. "Here he is now. Just wait and see."

"Good morning, Sally."

Sally paused in response to the reverend's greeting as he stopped beside them. He towered over her, and she suddenly realized that she had never been this close to him when he was standing up. An appreciative quiver moved down her spine. She'd be damned if he wasn't all man and muscle, despite his collar. His lips stretched wide over his fine, white teeth when he looked at Opal, and Sally realized she'd never seen him smile before, either. The glow in those bright blue eyes as he assessed Opal's obvious attributes made it even clearer that his thoughts were originating from a part of his body far removed from his brain.

Sally suppressed a sneer. Opal was right. The grass was always greener. She must be getting old.

"Good mornin', *Reverend*." Aware that her smile was little more than a grimace, Sally continued, "This here is Opal, a friend of mine."

"I'm pleased to meet you, Opal."

Yeah . . . he sure was.

"I'm pleased to meet you, too, Reverend." Opal moved closer with open interest. She placed a hand on his arm. It was smooth and white and warm as she leaned toward him, allowing a deeper glimpse of her ample breasts as she looked up at him with eyes that gleamed as black as ebony. "Sally was tellin' me that you were sick." She swept him appreciatively with her gaze. "But you look real good and healthy to me."

Reed allowed his own gaze to linger. Opal was younger than she appeared at a distance. Her features were small, her skin clear where it could be seen underneath the heavy face paint she wore, and her body was slim and ripe. He suspected that she wasn't much older than Chastity in years, although her eyes told another story.

Taken by surprise at the unexpected sadness that thought evoked, Reed responded, "I'm feeling much better."

"Glad to hear that, Reverend." Opal played the game well, adding with a flutter of heavily darkened lashes, "Sally's been tellin' me how you're goin' to be leavin' Sedalia to go out convertin'.

126

I have a few hours off from the Roundup right now, and I was thinkin' that maybe you might like to practice some of your convertin' on me. I sure am in need. As a matter of fact, there are things I didn't even realize I've been needin' until you walked up here beside me. I ain't got no doubt you could handle them real well."

Opal moved closer. The casual brush of her breasts against his arm was not really so casual. Nor was it casual the way her tongue stroked her lower lip before she whispered, "You look to me like you'd be real good at what you do, Reverend, and I'll tell you a secret. I'm real good at what I do, too. We just might be able to come together with real benefit for the both of us." Her gaze dropped to his mouth. "I got a room in the back where we could be alone and have a good heart-to-heart talk. I could meet you there in a few minutes, if you like."

All female flesh, hot and sweet as honey . . .

Reed's gaze lingered on the open invitation in Opal's dark eyes. It moved to her parted lips, then to the warm breasts pressing more earnestly against his arm. The musky scent of her enveloped him in its seductive allure—and the sadness within Reed inexplicably expanded. He wondered if she had ever been innocent and trusting like Chastity. Or if she had ever smelled like roses.

Reed halted his thoughts abruptly. What in hell was wrong with him?

The answer to that question was growing uncomfortably clear.

Determined to eliminate that discomfort, Reed glanced at Sally. It was obvious that she wasn't entirely surprised by the direction Opal's conversation had taken. She was an old hand at this sort of thing. She would keep her silence. And if she didn't, it didn't matter. A half hour with Opal would cure all his ills. Then Chastity and he would be out of town on the afternoon train, leaving Opal behind him, smiling and a little richer for the time they spent together.

His decision made, Reed covered Opal's hand warmly with his own. He heard her short intake of breath and felt her responsive heat. He was about to speak when a flash of red hair at the end of the street caught his eye.

Sally's gaze followed his, and she muttered something under her breath. Something in her tone turned him sharply toward her.

"What did you say?"

"Nothin'."

Reed glanced up the street. "That was Chastity going into the mercantile store, wasn't it?"

"It looked like her."

He waited for her to continue.

"You don't have to worry about her in there. From what I hear, Chastity packs quite a wallop."

"A wallop . . ."

Sally's brows rose with surprise. "She didn't tell you about what happened, huh? I suppose she figured there wasn't no use to it since you was laid up and she took care of it herself, but it sure gave everybody in town a good laugh."

Reed slowly stiffened. "A laugh?"

"Yeah. Seems like Charlie Dobbs, the store-keeper, got the wrong impression of Chastity when she went in there to buy some things the day after you got here. From what I hear, she tried to tell him he was makin' a mistake, but he wasn't listenin'. He tried puttin' his hands on her, and the story is that she hauled off and knocked him flat on his back."

"He put his hands on her."

That thought struck all else from Reed's mind.

"They say the look on Charlie's face was somethin' to see when he got up. Some fella walked in then and backed Chastity up, so's Charlie didn't get any more ideas."

*"He put his hands on her. . . ."* The trembling that slowly beset Reed had no relation to weakness. He said, "Well, I'm not laid up anymore."

"Wait a minute, Reverend!"

Deaf to Opal's protest, Reed started up the street, a blood-red rage suddenly burning inside him.


Chastity walked cautiously along the crowded aisles of the mercantile store. She glanced around her, frowning. Mr. Dobbs was nowhere to be seen, and she appeared to be the only customer in the store.

Determined to make her purchases and a quick exit before the animosity of her former visit could be renewed, Chastity walked toward the corner of the store where the women's essentials were kept. She reached unconsciously into her pocket and closed her hand around the small cloth purse pinned there. She had ample funds and she had made certain to fasten the purse in a more convenient spot that would not put her in the same embarrassing position as before if she needed it.

Chastity surveyed the small rack of ready-made dresses with growing despair. If she were not so desperate . . .

"I knew you'd be back."

Chastity jumped at the sound of the store-keeper's voice behind her. She turned toward him as he continued with growing malice, "You and me got unfinished business to settle between us. You didn't think I was goin' to let you get away with makin' me the laughin' stock of the town, did you?"

"Sir," Chastity began, then stepped back, unconsciously noting as she did that the wall was again flush against her. "I came in here to make a purchase, nothing more. I would appreciate it if you would allow me to conduct my business and leave."

"It ain't goin' to be so easy this time." Dobbs's puffy face glinted in the light, and his small eyes were hot with anger. The sight of him advancing slowly toward her set Chastity's flesh crawling as he continued more softly than before, "You ain't got nobody to fight your battles for you this time, and you can be sure you ain't goin' to catch me by surprise like you did last time, neither."

His gaze raked her with an intimacy that flushed her face with heat. "A preacher's wife, are you?" He gave a harsh laugh. "There ain't no preacher's wife alive that looked like you did that day, with that dress you was wearin' hangin' open at the neck like a trollop's, and your eyes all hot and hungry like they were."

"Hot and hungry!" Chastity gasped. "Get out of my way! I won't stand for any more of your insults!"

"No, sweetheart. You ain't goin' nowhere. Not yet."

Chastity's chest began a slow heaving, and her fists clenched tightly. "Are you threatening me, sir?"

"No, I ain't threatenin' you. I'm *tellin'* you—you ain't goin' to hide behind your husband's collar—not when you come back in here as bold as brass, beggin' for what I got gypped of when that nosey cowpoke stuck his two cents in last time."

"Nosey cowpoke . . . What *you* got gypped of . . ." Disgust rank in her voice, Chastity grated, "I'm leaving! Get out of my way!"

The storekeeper continued his gradual approach and Chastity felt fury rise inside her as she rasped, "I'm warning you . . ."

"So you're warnin' me. What are you goin' to do if I don't let you go?"

A deep voice responded from behind in Chastity's stead, "It's not what *she's* going to do. It's what *I'm* going to do."

Startled, Chastity turned to see Reed suddenly beside them. Immaculately dressed and clean-shaven, he was standing erect, without a sign of distress, the sheer height and breadth of his muscular frame shrinking the space of the narrow corner where they stood. His collar was firmly affixed, but his eyes reflected little of the temperance of his calling and he looked more intimidating than she had ever expected he could be.

Dobbs froze in his tracks. "Wh—who are you?"

Chastity saw the sneer that pulled at Reed's lips. She saw his hands twitch into fists as he said, "I think you know who I am."

"I thought you was sick. Everybody in town said you was at death's door!"

"Well, they were wrong."

Dobbs's small eyes narrowed assessingly. "No . . . you ain't no preacher!" He shook his head with a scoffing laugh. "You may be wearin' a collar, but I ain't never seen no preacher that looks like you!"

Reed's lips spread in a cutting smile. "You're right. I'm not a preacher—not now. Right now, I'm just a man who's goin' to listen real close while you apologize for insulting a lady."

"A lady . . . You mean *her?*" Dobbs swept Chastity with a demeaning gaze. "She don't fool me with her airs, and I ain't apologizin'! She got what she had comin' when she came in here the way she did that day, lookin' like she just tumbled out of bed with one man and was ready to tumble right back with another."

Anticipating Reed's reaction, Chastity slipped between the two men in a quick step that halted Reed's furious advance. Brought up suddenly against his chest, she could feel the heat of him as his heart pounded against her breast. She could feel the fury that shuddered through him as she whispered, "No, please, Reed. He's not worth the trouble. Let's just get out of here."

"No."

Moving her aside in a motion so smooth and swift that she hardly realized what had happened, Reed was past her in a moment. Paralyzed by the visible power of his wrath, she was unable to speak as he grasped the terrified Dobbs by his shirt, holding him inches off the floor as he said in a deadly tone, "You owe this woman an apology, and I want to hear it . . . now."

"I'm sorry!" His arrogance abruptly vanishing in the face of Reed's barely controlled menace, Dobbs nodded, eyes bulging. "I'm sorry, I'm sorry!"

"You beg her forgiveness . . ."

Dobbs gulped. His voice emerged in a frightened squeak. "I beg her forgiveness!"

"Reed—"

Ignoring her attempt at intervention, Reed shook Dobbs roughly, eliciting a sound of pure terror as he hissed, "You're lucky I'm wearing this collar, because if I wasn't . . ."

Allowing that thought to go unfinished, Reed dropped the man abruptly back on his feet. Dismissing his presence just as abruptly, he turned back toward Chastity. He assessed her pale face for a long moment, then raised his hand to brush a straying wisp back from her cheek as he said, "I'll wait until you're done making your purchases."

Shaken, Chastity whispered, "No, Reed, please. I just want to get out of here."

His hand slipped to her shoulder where it lingered briefly. The touch was disturbingly gentle, but his gaze was cold. "Mr. Dobbs apologized. We should give him the opportunity to make amends for his behavior." It occurred to her belatedly that Dobbs had not moved an inch when Reed looked at him and prompted, "Isn't that right?"

"Right . . . right."

Reed replied with obvious restraint, "Chastity will let you know when she's done."

Disturbed and somehow uncertain as Dobbs disappeared from sight between the aisles, Chastity frowned. "You didn't have to do that, Reed. I—I could've handled the situation."

Reed's expression hardened. "Like you did the last time."

"Yes."

"I'll wait until you're finished."

The abrupt realization that no amount of protest would budge him from the spot, Chastity turned back to the rack in front of her and withdrew a plain dark skirt, then a simple cotton shirtwaist.

"All right, I'm done."

Outside on the board walk minutes later,

Chastity attempted to clear from her mind the scene at the counter when Reed thrust her hand aside and paid the price of her purchases. She was certain she would never forget the hatred mixed with fear in Dobbs's eyes. She preferred not to think of the pure menace in Reed's gaze when he looked at the fellow for the last time . . . for she was certain that no part of that look was feigned.

She was unprepared when Reed took her hand and slid it through the crook of his arm, pulling her close against his side as they started back toward the hotel. The anger in his voice was totally unexpected when he demanded, "Why didn't you tell me what happened the first time you went in there?"

"Because . . ." She drew back, suddenly as angry as he. "It wasn't any of your concern."

"Yes, it was." Those incredibly blue eyes linked with hers, sending a tremor of inexplicable emotion down her spine. "You're my wife, remember?"

The puzzling tremor caused her to return defensively, "What I remember is that this is just a pretense maintained for convenience!"

His gaze moved slowly over her face. "Don't ever do that to me again, Chastity."

"Do what again?"

"Don't ever put yourself in that kind of a position again."

Startled, Chastity was momentarily without reply. She blinked as he demanded, "Promise me."

Chastity stared at him in silence.

"Chastity . . ."

"No."

"Why won't you make that promise?"

"Because you don't have the right to ask!"

"I have the right if I'm responsible for you!"

Chastity's eyes widened. "Whatever gave you the impression that you were?"

"We'll be traveling as man and wife!"

"It's only a charade, and a temporary one, at that."

"Why are you so damned hard-headed!"

"Your language—"

"My language is my business!"

"And *my business* is my business!"

"Not while our 'temporary charade' is in place."

"You're determined to argue with me, aren't you?"

Reed's eyes hardened. "No, I'm not. We're leaving on the afternoon train."

Chastity gasped. "*This* afternoon?"

Reed's silence and his stiff expression was her only reply.

Furious and bewildered by his unreasonable anger, Chastity turned away to see Sally and a young, blond woman in a gold dress staring in their direction. Embarrassed that they had doubtlessly witnessed the sharp exchange between Reed and her, she forced a smile. Looking up at Reed, she grated from between clenched teeth, "Sally's across the street with a friend. She's looking at us."

Reed looked in their direction, his gaze cold.

"They're waving. Wave back at them." And when he refused, she said, "What will they think?"

His gaze so intense that she felt it to her toes, Reed rasped, "If you think I care what either of them thinks, you're wrong."

Solemnly, Reed repeated, "Don't ever do that to me again, Chastity. I let that slimy little weasel off easy, but I won't be responsible for what happens if there's a next time."

Somehow, Chastity had no reply.

"Well, I guess that proves my point." Sally turned toward Opal with raised brows. The handsome preacher ignored their attempt to get his attention, further emphasizing his total absorption in Chastity when he whispered softly to her with a gaze so intimate, it excluded the whole world even though they were in plain view. "You thought you had him just where you wanted him, but you were wrong."

"I didn't *think* I had him." Opal's youthful face drew into an unaccustomed scowl as Reed continued along the boardwalk with his wife's arm tucked possessively under his. "I *did* have him . . . for a few minutes."

"Until he saw Chastity up the street."

"Hell, she was the last thing on his mind when he was holdin' my hand and thinkin' how sweet it could be!"

Sally laughed aloud. "You might've tickled his fancy for a few minutes, but he sure forgot how sweet it could be when he heard somebody tried to put hands on his wife."

"That don't prove nothin'. The minute a man hears a woman repeat her vows, he thinks he owns her, is all."

Unwilling to let it go, Sally looked back at the two as they exchanged a few whispered words. "Look at them. Look at *him*. I'm tellin' you, I ain't never seen a man look at his wife the way that man looks at her. It's like he looks right down deep inside her, hungerin' real hard for what's there. But it don't take much of a brain to see that he's madder than a hornet that she went back in that store without him, and I'd bet my bottom dollar that Charlie Dobbs is standin' behind that counter right now needin' a change of longjohns. Look at that man." Sally shook her head, unconsciously sighing. "He ain't about to let go of that woman of his, come hell or high water."

"Yeah . . . but I'd like just one more chance."

"Like I told you, you'd just be wastin' your time."

Opal was momentarily silent. "What does it take, Sally?"

"What does what take?"

"What does it take to make that kind of a man look at a woman the way he's lookin' at her?"

True sadness suddenly overcoming her, Sally stared at Opal in silence. When she spoke, her voice was touched with a melancholy that came from the heart.

"Honey . . . I wish I knew."

\*     \*     \*

He was still angry, and he wasn't sure of the reason.

The monotonous click of the rails continued as Reed sat silently in the darkened railcar. The passage of time since the incident in the mercantile store earlier in the day had done little to ease his agitation.

Reed glanced at the seat beside him. Chastity's eyes were closed, but he knew she wasn't sleeping. The sharp exchange between Chastity and him outside the mercantile store earlier had set the tone for the remainder of the day. Dr. Carr had visited shortly before they were to leave for the station. When accepting payment for the care given, the outspoken physician did not hesitate to let Reed know that he thought he was a fool to start out before his leg was completely healed.

Chastity agreed. Reed didn't.

His discomfort when Sally came to the room to say good-bye emerged as a scowl. Chastity said his behavior was "inappropriate." He felt it was appropriate all right.

The fact that Chastity miraculously found her spectacles in the hotel room, in a place she was certain she had searched several times before, only added to his agitation.

The situation deteriorated further when they arrived at the station to discover that the train had been delayed. It did not arrive until darkness was falling and his leg had stiffened to the extent that he was hardly able to hide his discomfort when they boarded the train at last.

Reed allowed his gaze to linger on Chastity's still face. Why had he reacted so furiously to Sally's story? The answer had become abundantly clear. Chastity was a menace to herself—a babe in the woods who allowed good intentions to override good sense as she strode confidently forward, totally ignorant of the danger awaiting her behind every tree.

Reed's clear eyes narrowed. Jenny had believed in good intentions. She had been honest and loving and full of life—life that had been snuffed out so quickly that there were times he still awoke in the middle of the night expecting to find her lying beside him.

But truth was ruthless and reality was relentless. Jenny had needed him. She had called for his help, and despite all the love in his heart, he had been too late.

But Chastity did not ask for help. Instead, she gave it—without thought to the possible consequences.

Who in hell was the damned fool who had turned her loose on the world alone?

The question needed to be answered.

"Chastity . . . are you awake?"

Chastity moved restlessly. Her eyes opened, revealing angry flecks of green.

"You're still angry."

No response.

Reed spoke words that came from the heart. "That storekeeper deserved everything he got, but I was wrong to take my anger out on you."

"You didn't need to get involved."

Reed refused to argue.

"I could've handled the situation. I handled it before!"

A smile tugged briefly at Reed's mouth. "Is it true you knocked Dobbs flat on his back?"

Chastity's face flamed. "I didn't mean to hit him. He just made me so angry—then all of a sudden he was staggering backward. I couldn't believe the thud when he hit the floor."

"I'd say he got what he had coming."

"No, I shouldn't—" Chastity halted. "Yes, he did. He's a nasty little man."

"Did you really think he'd let you get away with that a second time?"

"I didn't expect there would be a second time."

"You expected he'd forget what happened?"

"A decent man would admit he made a mistake!"

"If he was decent, nothing would have happened in the first place."

Chastity remained silent.

"You're not back East now, Chastity. There are too many men out here willing to take advantage of your . . . inexperience." The hypocrisy of his words never more clear, he continued, "I wasn't willing to wait and see how it all turned out."

"Oh."

Those clear eyes, full of innocence, stared back at him.

"Tell me about your banker."

"My banker?"

"The man in Caldwell."

"He isn't *my* banker. He's my friend. Well, he's not exactly a friend. . . ."

Reed was starting to get uneasy. "If he's not a friend—"

"I've never met him, so I guess I can't actually—"

"You've never met him?" The uneasiness hardened into incredulity as Reed continued, "You're traveling hundreds of miles—*alone*—trusting that a man you've never met will be waiting for you when you get to your destination, just on the strength of his word?"

"Well, he didn't exactly say he'd be waiting. I wrote and said I was on my way, but I didn't wait for his reply."

Reed stared.

Chastity's fair skin colored revealingly. "You think I'm foolish, but I believe deep inside that I'm doing the right thing. You're concerned, I know, but don't be. You see"—Chastity paused, her voice choking—"I'm going *home*."

Home . . . a destination that couldn't be denied. Reed's own throat was suddenly thick as Chastity struggled to control tears close to the surface.

Somehow incapable of further inquiry, Reed slid his arm around her and drew her against his shoulder. Her warmth was a consolation that he could not quite define as he rested his cheek against her hair and spoke in a voice he hardly recognized as his own.

"It's too late to talk anymore. You're tired. Go to sleep, Chastity."

Chastity rested in the comfortable curve of Reed's arm. His shoulder was soft against her cheek and the echo of his steady heartbeat was warm solace in the darkness. He had told her that in this new world of the West, there were few she could trust. Perhaps that was so, but she could trust him. She was somehow certain of that now.

Chastity closed her eyes.

# *Chapter Six*

Will Morgan stared out the window of the cabin. His deceptively youthful features and dark eyes tense, he surveyed the dusty road that cut northward through the thin, sparse grass of Indian Territory. He moved his slender, tightly knit frame stiffly. It was hot, but the bright sunlight of early morning was fading. It was going to rain.

Irritated, he glanced toward the hastily constructed corrals nearby where his men moved lackadaisically with branding irons in hand. Rustling cattle was the easy part. He enjoyed the excitement, the danger, and the knowledge that with a simple twitch of his finger, he held life in his hands. But he had little patience for what followed until the cattle could be safely sold.

Morgan turned irritably toward the bucket in the corner. One taste from the ladle proved the water to be warm, and he spat it back with disgust. He had returned a few days earlier expecting to find the cattle ready for shipping, but he should have known better. His men weren't inclined toward the hard work of rebranding. The lazy bastards were worthless unless he was standing over them, and he had been forced to spend the greater part of the morning doing just that. He was sick of it! Causing him even more agitation was the realization that their laziness prevented him from following through with a plan of a more personal nature.

Red hair that shone like fire in the sunlight . . . brown eyes shot with green . . . cool, white skin . . . She had said her name was Chastity. He had told her his name was Jefferson. He hadn't been able to stop thinking about her. She was a lady, but he had seen the fire that simmered just below her calm surface. He had felt her inner heat when she looked at him . . . when she smiled. He had the feeling that she didn't give herself easily, but in the time since he had tipped his hat and ridden away, the feeling had grown rapidly stronger that, had he not been forced to leave town when he did, he would have gotten far more from her than a smile.

Fantasies of moist, white skin and hungry lips had allowed him no rest in the time since. So intense had his thoughts of her grown that he had pushed his men to the limit in returning to their hideout, hoping to follow the same trail back as soon as possible. It frustrated him no end that he needed to remain to ensure that the work was done. He had never felt so intense a desire as he did for that woman he had met so briefly. The thought of her was a knot tightening within him to the point of pain.

Suddenly realizing that he was all but salivating, Morgan halted his thoughts. He turned sharply at the sound of movement behind him, seeing the young, dark-haired woman who worked beside the fireplace. Sensing his gaze, she turned toward him. He had found Conchita in a border-town cantina several months earlier. A few smiles and the right soft words had been all that was needed. It had been easy . . . too easy. She worshipped him. She'd do anything to please him.

Morgan inwardly sneered. That didn't surprise him. Women were crazy about him. The charm that so effectively hid the true man beneath his boyish good looks drew them like magnets. He knew part of the reason for that charm was the education he had received from his father, who had taught him to be courteous and respectful, and who had impressed upon him the value of a smile. The only problem was that his father had beaten those attributes into him, using religion as an excuse for brutality, and courtesy as a means to an end.

His mother had died when he was ten, but he had felt little sense of loss. She had been a weak woman, who had bowed to his father's every demand, observing every beating as she prayed loudly for his salvation. Some said she died of pneumonia, but Morgan knew that she had been harried to death. He had decided then and there that he wouldn't let himself suffer her fate when he grew up, and that if anybody was going to do the harrying, it was going to be him.

Morgan's inner sneer became a smile. His father had remarried when he was fourteen. It pleased him no end that he had been so successful at emulating his father's talents that his new wife, Jessica had ended up panting after him like a bitch in heat. And the day he left them both behind, he made sure his father knew it. That had been one of the greatest satisfactions of his life.

On his own in the time since, he had quickly learned that the only true friend a man had was the one settled snugly in the holster on his hip, and that the only difference between one woman and another was how quickly he tired of her.

And if he saw signs of his father's brutal nature in himself, he dismissed them. Using his gun came as naturally to him as using women, and the truth was, the only person he cared about pleasing was himself.

Morgan glanced out the window to check the location of the men, then turned back to see Conchita already approaching him. Beside him in a moment, Conchita pressed herself against him. Her dark eyes glowed with emotion as she whispered, "You love me, Morgan?"

Love her? Conchita moved herself against him, and Morgan felt a familiar heat rise in his groin. It occurred to him that it might be amusing to tell her that she had been the furthest thought from his mind since he'd returned from Sedalia, that he already had plans to replace her, and that the pleasure she afforded him bore not even the slightest connection to love. But he wouldn't—not yet. And he'd tell her he loved her, if that was what she wanted.

Morgan looked down at Conchita's mouth. Satisfaction stirred when her lips parted. Her low gasp when he slid his hand up to caress her breast was the reaction he wanted. Grasping her hand, he could feel her trembling as he turned abruptly, drawing her along behind him as he walked rapidly toward the bedroom in the rear.

Morgan slammed the bedroom door behind them, and as Conchita turned into his arms, the fleeting thought struck him that he hadn't even needed to say the words.

She didn't like this.

The sky grew more threatening by the moment. The balmy air had turned heavier, and the trill of songbirds along the trail had gone silent. In their stead, thunder rumbled in the distance and occasional bursts of lightning were visible on the horizon.

A chill shivered down Chastity's spine as the wild terrain of Indian Territory enveloped their wagon more completely with every passing mile. Reed and she had arrived in Baxter Springs in the early hours of the morning. Reed had wasted no time in securing a wagon and filling it with supplies, apparently intent on getting immediately onto the trail. The few words she had been able to exchange with the townsfolk had reinforced what Reed had told her about the resentment and downright hatred some felt for the Indians, as well as the dire state of Reverend Stiles's mission. She had understood Reed's desire to get immediately under way, but . . .

Chastity glanced covertly at Reed as he sat silently on the driver's seat beside her. His features were sober and still as the afternoon waned, his gaze coldly intent as he scrutinized the passing countryside, and his hands strong and adept on the reins as he kept the team moving forward. Yet questions she could no longer avoid plagued her as she studied him in silence. The change in his appearance since she first saw him enter the railcar that day less than a week earlier had never been more glaring. Sitting erect and clean-shaven, his fair hair trimmed to lie neatly against his neck, his light eyes clear, he exuded a strength and masculinity that bore little resemblance to the stooped and bearded parson whom she had approached for help. His eyes were too sharp, his gaze too unyielding, the resolution that drove him too keenly displayed.

Yet the change was not only physical. Complete silence had reigned between them since they had begun their journey. There had been no talk of the mission or the needy Indian children there. Reed had made no attempt to discuss the part she would play in reestablishing the school or the supplies she would need. Instead, it was almost as if he had dedicated himself to a new cause from which she was purposely excluded. She could almost believe that the concerned, protective man who had rescued her from the loathsome storekeeper's unwanted attentions and the softspoken, sympathetic man whose arm had encircled her on the train the previous night were figments of her imagination, for those men had disappeared the moment they had stepped onto the soil of Baxter Springs. In fact, she could not be sure which of the many sides of the Reverend Reed Farrell was the true man.

It had become discomfitingly clear that *none* of them might prove true.

And it suddenly seemed plausible that in agreeing to accompany him, she may have made the biggest mistake of her life.

As they rode more deeply into the unsettled wilderness, the question again rose in Chastity's mind. What was she doing here?

The wagon slipped into a rut in the road, jolting Chastity from her thoughts, and another chill moved down her spine. She recalled her first glimpse of their large wagon, with its bleached canvas cover supported by a strong frame that allowed a grown man to stand almost upright inside it. The sight of it had stirred disturbing memories.

The steady, lumbering roll of the wagon as the journey progressed struck another uneasy chord, stimulating bittersweet images of the life, love, and family—her world as she had known it—that she had lost so many years ago in a wagon just like this.

*"The girls are worse, aren't they, Justine?"*

*"They need a doctor soon. Something's wrong, isn't it? You're frightening me, Clay. Please answer me."*

*"We've reached the river crossing, but it's flooded. It isn't safe. If we don't find another one, we'll have to wait until the river goes down."*

*"Until it goes down? It's still raining. How long will that take? The girls need a doctor now."*

*"It isn't safe to cross, Justine."*

*"Clay . . ."*

*"There's nothing I can do."*

The pain of remembrance suddenly overwhelming her, Chastity reached unconsciously for the locket at her throat and clutched it tightly.

Soft grunts of pleasure broke the silence of the darkened room as the heat within it grew more intense. Perspiration beaded Morgan's skin as he turned abruptly, pinning the naked woman beneath him to the bed with his weight.

Separating her thighs with his knee, he paused as she whispered, "No, not yet, *querido.*"

The longing in Conchita's dark eyes bespoke emotions that went past the stimulation of the moment. "It's too soon."

Too soon . . .

Morgan surveyed the heated golden tint of Conchita's skin, the loving hunger that glowed in her dark eyes. He allowed his gaze to sweep the sharp planes of her face, the lush curve of her breasts, and the fullness of her hips before it came to rest on the warm juncture of her thighs where gratification awaited.

Too soon? No, not for him.

Plunging abruptly within her, Morgan heard her protesting rasp, and a low grunt of pleasure escaped his throat. He raised himself, plunging deeper, the sound of her protests adding impetus to thrusts that grew stronger, more frenzied. Climaxing, Morgan collapsed upon her as he sought to catch his breath.

Morgan was about to withdraw when Conchita wrapped her arms around him and clutched him close. He heard the uncertainty in her voice as she whispered against his cheek, "Do you love me, *querido?*"

Withdrawing from her embrace, Morgan forced a smile. He was so tempted.

No, not yet.

Leaning closer, Morgan smiled and stroked the straight black strands splayed against the pillow. He whispered, "Of course I love you, Conchita. How can you doubt it?" The responsive catch of her breath as he twisted his fingers in the silky strands pleased him, encouraging him to continue more softly, "You always please me, Conchita. You know that, don't you?"

Conchita's heavy lids flickered as he leaned closer. Conchita's gaze darted to his lips.

His hand still locked in her hair, Will rolled to his back, drawing her with him so she lay prone upon him. He felt her heat and the wetness that lingered. He saw her uncertainty, and he inwardly smiled.

Morgan whispered, "Do you love me, Conchita?"

"*Si . . .*" Conchita's lips trembled and her eyes grew moist. "I love you, Morgan, more than I have ever loved."

"I'm glad." Morgan surveyed her face. He had been too quick. She was uneasy. Smiling his boyish smile, he reached up to caress her breasts. "You like me to touch you, don't you?"

Conchita's breathing grew heavier. "*Si . . .*"

He could see the hunger in her eyes as he brushed the dark crests of her breasts with his lips. "I like you to touch me, too."

Conchita bit at her bottom lip. He could feel the shuddering within her as he whispered, "You make me feel good, Conchita . . . better than any other woman ever made me feel."

Conchita's shuddering grew more pronounced. "That is want I want to do, Morgan. I want to make you happy."

"We only have a little more time until the boys come back in."

Conchita glanced at the door. Her eyes grew moist. "I love you, Morgan."

". . . only a little more time."

Morgan held his breath as Conchita lowered herself down upon him.

Thunder boomed. Chastity stiffened on the driver's seat beside him, and Reed turned toward her with a frown. She was unnaturally pale, her gaze fixed, her rigid figure outlined against the rapidly darkening sky. Her knuckles white, she clutched her locket, barely seeming to breathe, and Reed's agitation soared.

He must have been crazy to bring her with him! What in the world had ever made him think that this charade would work to his advantage?

Reed steeled himself against the obvious. Chastity was terrified. He had not expected the fear he'd seen in her eyes when he drove up with the wagon. He noted the courage it took for her to climb up onto the seat beside him, and he felt the shudder that racked her when the wagon snapped into motion. He purposefully dismissed her anxious glances as the day progressed, forcing them from his mind as he sought to reconcile the passing terrain with the course Jenkins had noted on his map.

Reed's jaw tightened. One day . . . maybe two, and he would be as close as he wanted to get to Morgan's door. The Indian mission was north of his hideout, but Reed's plan was simple. If he met up with Morgan or any of Morgan's men, he would pretend he had taken the wrong turn. His parson's collar and Chastity's obvious innocence would lend him the credibility he needed. He would linger only long enough to assess the situation and familiarize himself with the terrain and Morgan's camp. He would then proceed directly to the mission, where he would leave Chastity and his disguise behind.

Then Morgan—the thief and killer—would succumb to the hunter.

He owed Jenny that.

That thought a hard, cold knot within him, Reed studied Chastity's pale face a moment longer. Her hand was clenched around her locket. Why did that habit disturb him? Where had he seen it before?

Thunder rolled and lightning cracked overhead. The air grew so heavy that he knew it would only be minutes until the storm broke.

Chastity shuddered.

"What's the matter?" Reed asked. "Are you afraid of the storm?"

Chastity blinked. Her hand dropped from her locket. "No."

She was, damn it, and he had no time for childish fears! He offered gruffly, "You can sit in the back of the wagon if it starts to rain. You'll stay dry there."

She shook her head as the first drops of rain fell.

"Maybe you'd better. From the way things

look, there's going to be a downpour."

Chastity's eyes jerked stubbornly to his. "I'm not afraid of getting wet."

Reed studied her adamant expression. "It's senseless for you to sit here through the storm."

"You're going to keep driving, aren't you?"

Reed was puzzled by her resolution. "I have oilskins to keep me dry."

"I'll share them."

"You can't. Then we'll both get wet."

"I don't want to sit in back."

Thunder boomed again and the rain came down in earnest. Reaching for the oilskins behind the seat as the frigid drops pelted them, Reed ordered, "Get into the back of the wagon."

"No."

Rain pounded more roughly as he slipped on his protective garment. The drops darkened the fiery color of her hair and ran in glittering streams down her face. She was soaked within minutes but she did not move.

"Get in the back of the wagon, Chastity!"

Furious when she remained unmoving except for the tremors that shook her visibly, Reed pulled the team to a halt. Standing on the muddied ground beside her in a moment, he reached up and swept her from her seat despite her angry protests. He strode to the rear of the wagon and thrust her inside, pausing briefly to instruct her, with anger that was barely controlled, "I don't know what that was all about, but you're going to stay there—

where it's dry—until the rain ends, do you understand?"

Raindrops beaded on the clear skin of her cheeks as Chastity returned his adamant stare. They followed a steady path downward, past the firm set of her jaw, along the slender column of her neck, disappearing at last in the soft, female flesh at her neckline. Reed swallowed tightly, forcing his gaze up at the sky as thunder crashed more loudly and lightning briefly lit the blackening expanse. Looking back at her, he said more softly, "Do you understand?"

Chastity remained unmoving.

She did not reply.

Reed turned his back on her and returned to the driver's seat. Silently fuming, he whipped the team back into motion.

It was raining.

Conchita glanced out the window to see muddy pools rapidly forming in the corrals. Low male laughter turned her toward the men who were eating at the table a short distance away. She glanced at Morgan, where he sat at the head of the table, scooping up the last of the stew she had served. The men were conversing easily without looking in her direction.

Conchita straightened up slowly as she assessed the men one by one. Turner, the oldest of the gang, was dark, bearded, and barrel-bellied. He was a terrible man, unclean in mind and in body. She had known many men like him before reaching her present advanced age of seventeen years. He made constant attempts to touch her while Morgan's back was turned. She had kept a careful eye on him during Morgan's last trip to Sedalia. It was only the knife she carried concealed in a sheath on her thigh that had held him off on several occasions—*and* Turner's realization that she would not hesitate to use it.

Bartell was younger and only a little less foul. Short and balding, he was a braggart and a liar, who could not be trusted.

Simmons was not much better. Nor was Walker. They were as black-hearted as the others, but Morgan preferred them as traveling companions when the situation demanded. The reason was obvious. They were afraid of him and would follow his orders without question.

But Morgan was different from his men. Conchita's heart fluttered in her breast as a familiar agitation returned. He was young and handsome, his deep voice sweet music to her ears. She had loved him from the moment she saw him enter the cantina where she earned her living. Slenderly built, he was clean and well dressed, with shiny dark hair and a glowing, dark-eyed gaze. Dismissing all the other women who threw themselves at him when he entered, he had seen only her. And when he approached her, with a smile so beautiful and warm that it melted her heart, she was his.

Conchita closed her eyes briefly as the memory of the moment again thrilled her. She had known there would never be another man for her the moment he had first touched her flesh. She had silently made that vow, and when he had taken her north with him, she had not cared what some said about the life he led, or what they said he left behind him. And if she had come to know that there was a darker side of him, she told herself that nothing could be worse than losing him.

Conchita glanced again at Morgan as he laughed at one of the men's jokes. He was calmer since the time they had spent together that afternoon. It made her proud that she was able to give him ease when he was in need. There were times when she sensed a change in him and she became frightened that he might grow tired of her someday. But that fear left her each time they made love and she knew that he was again hers alone.

Conchita knew that the men considered her a fool because she lived to please Morgan. But she also knew that Morgan paid little attention to whatever those men said. And if Morgan did not always respond to her as she hoped he would, she did not allow herself to become disturbed. She did not wish to chance Morgan's displeasure.

For the truth was that she would suffer anything to remain with Morgan. He had singled her out and raised her above the life she had led—the only person who had ever held her above the others like her struggling to survive in a world where no one cared if they lived or died. She would do anything for him. Anything.

Morgan turned toward her and Conchita took an unsteady breath. Her heart began a slow pounding when he stood up and approached her. She remained still as Morgan curled his arm around her waist, ignoring the men at the table as he whispered into her ear, "You were just what I needed this afternoon, Conchita."

Morgan's words touched Conchita's heart. Sliding her arms around his neck, she whispered for his ears alone, "You are my joy, *querido.*"

She felt his body tighten when she pressed herself against him, and happiness stirred within her. She would bind Morgan to her with his need. She would do all she could to keep him hers.

Feeling safety in his ignorance of her native tongue, Conchita whispered against his lips, *"Seremos juntos siempre, mi amado."*

Yes, they would be together always. She would have it no other way.

Rain pelting the canvas cover over her head . . . the groaning creak of the wagon as it shuddered along the trail . . . the roar of thunder and streaks of lightning that lit the night sky . . .

The nightmare had returned!

Chastity stared at the canvas walls of the wagon where Reed had deposited her so unceremoniously an hour earlier. Rain hammered the trail unceasingly as the wagon plodded steadily forward. She told herself over and again that this wagon was not the family wagon in which she had traveled with her sisters so many years ago. She reminded herself that despite the growing power of the storm, the present situation bore little resemblance to that fateful day when she was a child.

But the sounds were so similar. The returning images were so clear. And the voices that trailed through her mind were increasingly vivid:

*"Can you hear me, sugar?"*

*"Papa?"*

*"No, don't talk. Just listen. Mama and I are going to take the wagon across the river soon. It's going to be a rocky ride."*

*"But Mama said—"*

*"Mama's going to drive the wagon while I lead the team. She won't be able to sit with you, but I don't want you to be afraid. Can I depend on you, sweetheart?"*

*"Yes Papa. I love you, Papa."*

*"I love you too, and I know my girls love each other just like I know they'll always look out for each other."*

Later, Honesty's rasping voice:

*"Papa's takin' us across the river now . . . to the doctor."*

*"Good, 'cause I'm sick."*

*"Me, too."*

*"Go to sleep."*

And Honesty's belated, final admonishment:

*"Don't be afraid, you hear? Papa will take care of us."*

The pain within Chastity sliced sharply at her heart. No, she didn't want to remember anymore! It was too late to change what had happened and remembering was too hard.

Thunder cracked, jolting Chastity to new rigidity. Lightning ripped across the sky, snapping her eyes wide as the tormenting memories threatened to return.

No, she wouldn't listen—not to the rain or the rush of the river! She wouldn't let the voices torment her either! She had had enough!

Clapping her hands over ears, Chastity lay down on the pallet beneath her. Her heart hammering, her jaw tight, she closed her eyes.

Jagged strips of lightning lit the night, followed by shattering sounds as the storm continued its relentless assault. Reed's expression was grim as he sat a short distance from where Chastity lay in the rear of the wagon. Surrendering to the darkness of the trail an hour earlier, he had drawn the wagon to a halt at last, grateful for the excuse to stop for the night. He had climbed into the rear of the wagon, ignoring the dull ache in his thigh as he stripped off his oilskins and shirt and put on dry clothes. His impatience with Chastity earlier in the day had gnawed at his conscience. He had known from the outset that Chastity had little experience with the wilderness. She was young, and he knew nothing could have prepared her for the awesome power being unleashed over their heads, or the feeling of helplessness it could evoke in such an isolated place.

Chastity did not raise her head or look in his direction. They had not exchanged a word since he had dumped her under the wagon's canvas roof hours earlier. He had been uncertain what his reception would be when he entered the wagon, but he had not expected to see her as she was now. Curled up tightly against the wooden side of the wagon, she made no move to turn toward him. Neither the coverlet drawn up over her shoulders nor the shadows of the darkened wagon concealed her shuddering or the hands she held clamped tightly over her ears.

Anger flared. She was behaving like a child!

Anger faded. No, it was more than that. Something was dreadfully wrong.

A shattering boom crashed suddenly overhead. The lightning flash that followed lit the interior of the wagon with the brightness of day, and Chastity gasped aloud. Unable to bear her distress a moment longer, Reed cursed softly, then slid down on the pallet beside her. He grasped her shoulders and turned her toward him, frowning at the realization that her dress was still damp from that afternoon's soaking.

The ashen pallor of her face tightened the knot inside him as Reed rasped, "I've had enough of this, Chastity. I know it isn't only the storm that's frightening you. It's something else. Tell me what it is. I need to know."

Chastity shook her head, her gaze frantic. "No."

"Tell me, Chastity."

Chastity shook her head, panic visibly rising. "I can't! I won't!" Suddenly struggling, Chastity shoved hard, attempting to break his hold. "Let me go! I want to get out of here!"

"Stop this, Chastity!" Regretting the force necessary to suppress her struggles, Reed rasped, "There's no place to run in this storm!"

"Let me go! I have to get out of here!"

"No, you don't. Chastity, *please* . . ."

Chastity's struggles abruptly ceased. Still shuddering, she looked up at him as he appealed softly, "I want to help you, Chastity. Please, tell me what's wrong."

Chastity's shaken gaze searched his. He felt the panic that lingered in her. He suffered her pain. He waited with anxious expectation as her lips moved soundlessly before a whisper emerged.

"I thought I wanted to remember what happened that day, but I don't. It's too hard remembering."

Chastity turned away from him, and Reed demanded softly, "Tell me, Chastity."

"No. It happened a long time ago."

"Tell me."

Pallid, Chastity turned back toward him abruptly. "My parents are dead! I was never more sure of that than I am now." She swallowed against welling tears. "We were traveling in a wagon just like this one, and it was storming, just like it is now. The thunder and lightning wouldn't stop. My sisters and I were sick, but Honesty wouldn't let us cry. My father wanted to get our wagon across the river so he could find a doctor. The river was flooded, but he told us not to be afraid. We were halfway across the river when we heard the sound. It was so loud! Honesty sat up. She screamed when she saw it coming—that monstrous wall of water rolling down the river toward us! My mother saw it, too. She scrambled into the back of the wagon. She was trying to reach us when the water struck!"

Chastity was sobbing freely, her face pressed against his chest as she rasped, "The water . . . it tumbled the wagon. The sounds of creaking and splintering wood . . . the roar when the wagon went under. I heard Honesty and Purity scream, but I couldn't make a sound! The water sucked me down. It filled my nose and my mouth. I couldn't see. I couldn't hear. I couldn't breathe!"

Clutching her close, Reed rocked Chastity gently. Uncertain of the words he spoke, he whispered consolingly against the bright hair under his cheek, breathing deeply of the scent of roses rising from it as her shuddering slowly lessened. He waited for her to regain control before he questioned, "No trace of your parents or sisters was ever found?"

"No."

Reed stroked back the fiery wisps from Chastity's face. Her skin was blotchy from tears, and her eyelids were red, but the intensity of her belief was not compromised by her emotion as she continued, "Everyone said the rest of my family drowned that day, but I know Honesty and Purity survived."

Taking his hand unexpectedly in hers, Chastity closed it around her locket. Her gaze holding his intently, she whispered, "I know my sisters are alive, and I know they're wearing the lockets my father gave them, just as I am, Reed. I know, because I can feel their hearts beating when I hold mine. You can feel it, too, can't you? The heartbeats are strong and steady, just as they've always been. They're waiting for me to find them somewhere out here. I'm sure of it."

Her eyes were so earnest and filled with hope.

"What does your banker in Caldwell say about this?"

"He's going to help me find them."

"Did he tell you that?"

"Not exactly . . ."

Reed's stomach clenched.

"I haven't asked him yet, but Emily said he'd help me whenever I decided I was ready to start searching."

"Emily..?"

"His wife. She died."

"Oh." He hesitated. "What if he won't . . . or *can't* help you?"

"Then I'll find them myself."

The knot within him constricted. "How?"

"I don't know how. I just know that I will."

Reed clenched the locket tighter. He wanted to tell Chastity that he felt her sisters' heart-beats—but he didn't. He wanted to believe just as strongly that Chastity's sisters were alive—but he couldn't. He wanted to tell her that she had not traveled all this way just to see her dreams crumble into dust—but he knew she had.

The only heartbeat he felt was Chastity's. It pounded against his chest, echoing the drumming of his own heart as he looked down into her sober gaze.

Blotchy skin that he longed to taste with his lips . . . reddened lids that he yearned to soothe with his touch . . . trembling lips that he hungered to still with his kiss . . . He wanted to console Chastity as he had never wanted anything before. He wanted to hold her tightly against him, her flesh against his. He wanted to breathe her in, to consume her, to make her a part of him and drive all the fears and insecurities from her mind. He wanted her so completely that he—

The locket's warm gold seemed suddenly to sear his skin, and Reed released it abruptly.

Forcibly striking all other thoughts from his mind, he whispered, "That nightmare's over and past, Chastity. The storm that's raining down on us now will end soon. There aren't any flooded rivers for us to cross, and you don't have to be afraid of tomorrow."

Chastity looked up at him in silence.

"The sun will shine tomorrow. Don't be afraid."

Chastity took in a shuddering breath. "I'm going to find my sisters." She held his gaze a moment longer, whispering as her eyes fluttered closed, "I'm not afraid anymore."

Reed drew her closer, the bittersweet pain of the moment acute. She wasn't afraid anymore.

Reed settled Chastity in his arms.

In some ways, he almost wished she was.

# Chapter Seven

The whirlpool of surging rapids and pounding debris dragged her relentlessly downward. She was sinking deeper.

"Mama!"

"Your mama's not here, little dear, but you needn't be frightened. You're not alone."

She heard the high-pitched voice, but she could not open her eyes.

"We found her lying by the river, doctor. We were so frightened. We thought she wasn't breathing! Poor child, she's so small and helpless . . . so alone. Do you suppose she can hear me?"

"How would the doctor know that, Penelope?"

"On the contrary, Miss Lawrence," A deep voice responded. "I believe the child can hear you."

"See, I told you, Harriet!"

*"You never miss an opportunity to say, 'I told you so.'"*

*"That isn't true!"*

*"Isn't it?"*

*"Ladies, please!"*

The high-pitched voices continued their indignant exchange and fear suddenly swelled within her. She called out weakly, *"Honesty . . . Purity . . ."*

A gasp.

*"Do something, doctor!"* The anger in the high-pitched tone changed to anxiety. *"The child is rambling! She's naming the virtues! Do you suppose she's dy—"*

*"Miss Lawrence, if you can't control yourself, I will ask you to leave!"*

Silence.

The tone of the deep voice grew coaxing. *"Will you open your eyes, dear? You have a fever, and you've had a terrible experience in the river, but I know you can do it if you try."*

She struggled to comply, seeing as she did a man with gray hair and a full mustache.

*"That's a good girl. Can you tell us your name . . . where you came from?"*

*"Chastity . . ."*

*"Oh, Lord . . . oh, Lord, she's rambling again!"*

*"Penelope, please!"*

*"Chastity?"* The gray-haired man spoke again. *"Is that your name?"*

Yes.

*"Can you answer me?"*

She nodded as two women moved into view

170

*and looked down at her. They were pale and
homely, their features similar. But their eyes were
filled with compassion as one whispered, "Don't
worry, little dear . . . little Chastity. You're not
alone. We'll take care of you until you find your
mama."*

*A scalding tear slid from her eye.*

*"Don't cry, little dear. Please don't cry. We
promise we won't abandon you. Harriet, tell her,
please!"*

*"We promise you. We give you our word, dear.
We won't abandon you."*

The images faded.

The rain continued.

Chastity sat silently inside the rocking wagon
as it moved forward along the muddied trail.
The night had been long as shadows of the past
deluged her dreams. She had awakened time
and again, the rain pounding at the canvas
cover overhead, reviving familiar fears. But her
fears had dissipated the moment she felt the
curve of Reed's arm around her and the steady
rise and fall of his chest against her cheek.

Strangely, she gave no thought to the impro-
priety of their intimate posture when she bur-
rowed closer to his warmth. The scent of him
had lent her comfort in the darkness, and the
hard, muscular wall of his body had been a haven toward which she was instinctively drawn.
The weight of his arm lying lax around her had
seemed so right, and when he drew her closer
in his sleep as the storm wailed overhead, she

realized that at that moment, there was nowhere else she would rather be.

The Reverend Reed Farrell was not the man she had anticipated he would be. In the time they had been together, she had felt the brunt of his anger, and she had responded in kind. She had endured his impatience with little patience of her own. She had witnessed the frightening menace of which he was capable when she was threatened and had been stunned at its scope. Those emotions had raised an awareness within her of the true power of the total man behind those startling blue eyes—but none had touched her heart as strongly as his unexpected gentleness.

Chastity recalled the breathless rush of emotion she'd experienced earlier, when she opened her eyes to find Reed lying so close. His body was curved around hers, his arm draped across her breast, and when his eyes opened unexpectedly, the light that surged to life there had set her heart to pounding. Mesmerized as his head dipped slowly toward hers, she had felt her lips parting. She had wanted as she had never wanted. She had needed as she had never known need. His mouth was only inches from hers when he drew back abruptly, and the sense of loss she felt when he stood up suddenly and donned his oilskins was so acute that she had almost called out in protest.

He left the wagon without a word. They shared a cold and uncomfortable breakfast later. Mentally berating herself, she told herself that she had responded foolishly to Reed's kindness. She told herself there was no anger in his silence, that he had merely dismissed those few moments between them as unwise and had moved ahead to contemplate the complications of the storm. And if he responded gruffly when she inquired if he thought the storm would end soon, she preferred to believe that his clipped response was due to annoyance at the delay the storm caused.

A deafening clap of thunder interrupted Chastity's thoughts, stirring the anxieties she thought she'd conquered. Reed had erred. The storm had not ended as he predicted. The persistent downpour had not yet abated.

A second thunderclap shook the earth beneath them, and Chastity gasped aloud. The wagon drew to a halt, and Chastity moved apprehensively to the front of it to peer out. The unrelenting downpour had shortened visibility to a scant few yards in front of the wagon. Reed was not in the driver's seat.

Leaning forward, Chastity saw that he had dismounted from the wagon and was walking slowly along the trail. He halted and remained motionless for long moments. He turned back briefly toward the wagon, his eyes narrowing as an endless sheet of rain cascaded from his protective oilskins.

Then she heard it.

The sound was hardly discernable over the steady pounding of the rain.

It turned her blood cold.

* * *

"You're crazy!" Turner's adamant statement twisted his bearded face into a tight snarl. Morgan's mood of the previous evening had changed abruptly with the storm that had hit overnight. He had awakened that morning on a rampage. Aware of the viciousness of which he was capable, Walker and Simmons remained silent as Turner concluded defiantly, "If you want somebody to go out brandin' in this rain, you can do it yourself!"

"I ain't doin' it, neither." Quick to join Turner in his revolt, Bartell slapped his hand down on the table, unmindful of the remains of breakfast that had not yet been cleared. "I ain't goin' to get soaked to the skin and get my bones chilled when there ain't no need! If I wanted to do that, I would've stayed a drover! Hell . . ." He spat on the floor beside him. "Them days are gone forever."

Morgan responded with equal heat, "You would've been done with the brandin' if you'd have done what you were supposed to while I was in Sedalia! If you think I'm goin' to let you lay around on your lazy hides, waiting for the weather to change, you're wrong!"

"I ain't lazy. . . ." His mood as dark as the weather, Turner challenged Morgan softly, his barrel-shaped belly tightening as his gaze slanted toward his gun lying nearby. ". . . and I ain't about to let nobody call me lazy."

"You think you can take me, Turner?" The sudden warmth of Morgan's smile was belied by the deadly gleam in his eye as he continued softly, "Go ahead, strap on your gun and I'll do the same. I haven't had much action lately. You just might be able to beat me to the draw." His smile tightened. "But I think it's only fair to remind you about Abilene . . . and Kansas City. You were there, weren't you?"

Turner's complexion paled.

Morgan demanded, "Weren't you?"

Turner's unshaven cheek twitched. "Yeah, I was there."

"Of course, that was over six months ago. Things can change in six months. You might be faster than that fella who said he was the fastest gun in the territory."

Turner shrugged.

"Then there was that fella who said there wasn't nobody who could make him turn tail and run." Morgan paused. "There wasn't too much difference between them, though. They both bled just as red."

Turner's hand fell limply to his side.

Morgan turned toward the others with snake-like quickness. "Anybody else here think their trigger finger's faster than mine?"

Morgan waited for the mumbled responses. "All right, I'm makin' things clear, once and for all. I've had enough of this place. I did my part. I made a good deal for this beef in Sedalia, and now it's time for you to do yours. And I'm tellin' you now, I'm not lettin' anybody or anything hold me back from the good time I got comin' to me. So that means we're goin' to brand those steers. We're goin' to start now, rain or not, and we're goin' to keep brandin' until I say quit, is that understood?"

A reluctant chorus of agreement turned Morgan toward the door. Shrugging on his oilskins, he paused with hat in hand. "I'm goin' out to start a fire in the shed firepit. Those brandin' irons will be hot right quick, and I expect every one of you to be right behind me. Those who aren't had better be ready to make some hard decisions."

Slamming the door behind him, Morgan stomped across the muddy ground toward the shed without looking back.

Staring after him, Turner growled, "Hell, he's crazy!"

"Yeah, maybe he is." Walker walked slowly toward the rack beside the door. He picked up his rain gear and slipped it on. "But there's no changin' his mind when he's set on somethin'. And there ain't a one of us who could take him, and you know it."

"What in hell's the matter with him, anyway?" Following Walker toward the door with obvious reluctance, Bartell ran a nervous hand over his balding head. "I ain't never seen his moods change so crazy as they've been doin' since he got back from Sedalia with you fellas."

Simmons gave a knowing grunt that turned Bartell toward him. "What's that supposed to mean? Did somethin' happen in Sedalia?"

"No, nothin' happened. We took care of what we had to do there, and then we left town." Simmons's small eyes narrowed into a squint. "The problem is that Morgan's been thinkin' about what *might've* happened if we had the time to stay."

"What are you talkin' about?"

Walker looked at Simmons and shook his head. "You're thinkin' the same thing I've been thinkin'. It's that red-haired woman, all right. I told him she'd be nothin' but trouble, but he don't listen to me."

"What red-haired woman?"

"You know Morgan when he's got a woman on his mind. He met this one the mornin' we left town. Hell, you should've seen him when she looked up at him with that smile like pure honey. He put on that act of his, charmin' her right out of her skin. He might've fooled her, but he didn't fool me. I knew what he was thinkin', and I knew it meant trouble. Them church types are all the same."

"Church types?" Turner laughed harshly. "Since when did Morgan start lookin' at that kind?"

"She was a good-lookin' woman, but I'm thinkin' it wasn't only her looks that heated Morgan up inside. Whatever it was, he waited outside that store where he met her, as itchy as a flea-bit cat. She came out lookin' for him, all right. And let me tell you, I knew then and there that he wasn't goin' to be satisfied with that bein' the end of it."

"I should've known a woman was at the bottom of it." Joining the others at the door, Turner grabbed his oilskins, his sweaty face grim. "Hell, if I had known what Morgan was thinkin' with instead of his brain, I wouldn't have said nothin'." He sneered. "He's worse than a dog in heat, that one. I've seen him in action before. We'd better get out outside or we'll be in for trouble, all right."

Another low chorus of agreement sounded as Turner jerked open the door and stepped out into the rain. The other men quickly followed.

Silent in their wake, Conchita stood rigidly beside the fireplace. As was their practice, the men had conversed as if she did not exist. They had not even bothered to glance in her direction to see her reaction to their exchange.

Conchita's face flamed. They considered her to be nothing—not worth a moment's thought! They did not believe her capable of any true feeling, nor did they believe Morgan had any true feeling for her!

*Puercos!* Pigs, every one of them!

Every one of them but Morgan.

A heated rage suffusing her face, Conchita strode to the window. Trembling, she saw the men disappear into the shed just as the first white puffs of smoke rose from the chimney.

Liars, that's what those men were! And cowards! Not a word of what Walker and Simmons said about what happened in Sedalia was true. They were so afraid of Morgan and what he would do if they tried to face him down that they would make up any story to stop him.

Conchita stood staring blindly as the relentless rain continued. Morgan loved her. He had told her so many times. She gave him more pleasure than any other woman—he had told her that, too.

The fury in Conchita's expression settled gradually into hard lines that drained the blush of youth from her cheeks. Her jaw tight, she slid her hand down her leg toward the sheath concealed on her thigh. The story that Walker had told about the red-haired woman was untrue. But even if it was not, it made little difference. Her blade had tasted blood before. If necessary, it would again. There was no woman who could take Morgan from her.


Reed stared at the trail ahead of him, incredulous at what he saw. What had obviously been a crossing that Jenkins had not even felt worthy of marking on the map was now a roaring river. He had seen things like this happen before—a trickle of water in a harmless gully that was dry the greater part of the year swelling into a rush of churning currents after a prolonged storm.

Reed glanced back at the wagon. His choices were few.

He could remain here, hoping the storm would dwindle and the currents would slow, but that could take days. He would lose valuable time and he could lose Morgan as well.

He could take the alternative route that Jenkins had mapped, but he would have to backtrack, and the result would be the same.

Or he could ford the crossing now.

Reed's strong jaw hardened. He had made a mistake in taking Chastity along with him. He had not thought the situation through. Watching Chastity as she slept, breathing in the scent of her skin, wanting her—she had compromised his concentration so efficiently that even now, when his choice should be clear, he could not oust her from his thoughts.

Damn it all, he had no time for this! Yet, Chastity's renewed shuddering with each flash of lightning and each roll of thunder through the long night remained with him. Her fear was real. The tormenting memories were scars that ran deep.

Reed glanced up at the leaden sky. He cursed as the steady torrent beat down on his face, then adjusted his oilskins against the rain. Looking ahead, he studied the flow of the flooded gully. He was certain it wasn't deep. The water would barely reach the body of the wagon at the highest point. His team was strong and would have no trouble overcoming the currents. He would not hesitate for a minute if he were alone.

But he was not alone.

The scent of roses rose strongly in Reed's mind, flushing him with heat, and his decision was made. He could not afford to prolong the journey, as much for Chastity's sake as his own.

Turning back toward the wagon, Reed was startled to see Chastity emerge from the rear and start toward him. Unprotected against the storm, she was soaked to the skin before she had taken more than a few steps.

Furious, he approached her with angry strides.

*No, not again!*

Chastity halted, hardly aware of the battering rain as she stared at the rushing river in front of her. She had heard the roar of the current and now saw the hungry whitecaps swirling against the bank. The sound was burned as deeply into her mind as the echoes of Honesty's and Purity's screams and the memory of her mother's hand reaching for her.

Reed turned toward her. He approached, shouting over the roar of the continuing torrent, "What are you doing out in the rain like that? Get back in the wagon! You're already drenched!"

She shouted back accusingly, "You said there was no river to cross!"

"I was wrong!"

Chastity jerked her arm free of Reed's grip as he attempted to lead her back to the wagon. "You said the rain would stop and everything would be all right!"

"This is no time to discuss the weather!"

Avoiding him as he attempted to grasp her arm again, Chastity fought to control the shivering that beset her. "Let me go! You lied! You said the sun would come out and the rain would stop. You said there was no river and—"

"All right! That's enough."

Taken by surprise when Reed scooped her suddenly from her feet, Chastity struggled to

free herself. She halted abruptly when he
clutched her tightly against his chest, the incredible blue of his eyes glaring as he ordered,
"Be still, damn it! I'm doing this for your own
good!"

Her strength suddenly depleted, Chastity
closed her eyes against the abuse of the ele-
ments, against the reality she could not bear,
against the furious pounding of Reed's heart
against her breast as he carried her toward the
wagon.

The pallet beneath her back, she opened her
eyes again to see Reed crouched over her. Stripping off his hat, he reached for the coverlet
nearby and wrapped it around her. She saw the
tight set of his jaw as he brushed a wet strand
back from her cheek, then grated, "Taking you
with me was a mistake. I can see that now. You
shouldn't be here. You have your objectives and
I have mine. They take us in different directions, even though I thought for a while that—"
He paused. "It doesn't matter what I thought. I
was wrong."

Her teeth chattering so hard she could barely
speak, Chastity managed, "I won't go across the
river."

Reed's light eyes did not blink. "You have no
choice."

"I do have a choice! You can go across if you
want, but I'm staying here!"

"Listen to me, Chastity!" Reed's expression
hardened. "This isn't a river! It's nothing more
than a flooded gully a few feet deep!"

Chastity did not respond.

"The horses can easily get the wagon across it."

"That's what my father thought."

"That was then. This is now."

"I won't go across."

"I'm not going to backtrack and lose two days. There's too much to lose."

"We can't make it across!"

"We can!"

"No, you're wrong! You were wrong when you said the rain would stop by morning! You were wrong when you said there was no river to cross, and you're wrong now. We can't get across the river! The water will stop us somehow, and it'll happen all over again!"

"No, it won't."

"Yes, yes, yes, it will!"

"Chastity, listen to me!" Chastity turned away and Reed gripped her arms, demanding, "Look at me, Chastity!"

The tremor in Reed's voice, a note of desperation she had never heard before, touched a chord deep inside her. Turning slowly back to face him, Chastity caught her breath at the flush of emotion coloring Reed's face. His chest heaving, his hands shaking as they cut into the flesh of her arms, he rasped, "Do you think I'd take you across that river if I thought there was any danger? Do you think I'd risk your life, for any reason, if I thought there was any chance at all that the wagon couldn't make it?"

The new trembling that beset her bore no relation to the cold as Reed continued hoarsely, "Trust me, Chastity. That's all I ask. We'll get across, I promise you that. You're right. I was wrong when I said the rain would end today. I was wrong when I said there was no water to cross. But I'm not wrong now." Reed cupped her cheek with his palm, his voice catching as he whispered, "Don't you know I'd never do anything to hurt you?"

Chastity swallowed. The mortifying words she had loathed to say emerged in a hoarse whisper. "I'm afraid."

"Chastity . . ." Reed's gaze dropped briefly to her lips. She felt its heat, then saw the determination with which he forced it back up to meet hers. "Stay here. Don't be afraid, and don't worry. We'll be safe on the other side in a few minutes and then it will all be over."

"Reed . . ."

"Just stay where you are, Chastity, please. Tell me you will."

Chastity swallowed against the sudden dryness in her throat. She tried to speak, but realized she could not as the brilliant blue of Reed's gaze pleaded with her as avidly as his words.

Controlling the sob that rose to her throat with sheer strength of will, Chastity nodded. She closed her eyes.

Reed released her. She heard him turn and leave the wagon. Her eyes were still closed when the wagon jerked into motion. She squeezed them tightly shut, holding her breath when she felt the wagon's gradual descent into the water.

The roaring grew louder.

The horses whinnied in protest when the first surge of water struck.

The wagon swayed.

The icy torrents of rain thickened. Reed strained to see as the flow of the swollen stream hit the wheels full force, rocking the wagon. His hand firm on the reins, he forced the balking team forward.

His jaw set, Reed scanned the surface of the angry water as the currents dragged at the wagon and it teetered precariously. He cursed as a log driven with punishing force pounded the wagon's side, causing it to shudder beneath them. He was intently conscious of Chastity's silence in the wagon behind him as he proceeded to mid-stream, where the current gripped the wagon more strongly.

The team whinnied loudly in protest, and Reed snapped a sharp command that drove them forward. Thunder boomed and lightning cracked across the sky as the leaden expanse above them opened up with sheets of rain that pounded his shoulders like hammers. The fierce assault continued, the storm howling as the team reached the opposite bank at last.

Halting the team the moment firm ground was underneath them, Reed jumped down from the driver's seat and started toward the rear of the wagon. He was stripping aside the rear flap when he saw it—the spare wheel that had been ripped loose from its position on the side of the wagon. It was caught on a rock a distance from the water's edge.

The current dragged at it, lifting it. He needed to reach it before it was swept away.

Striding forward, Reed waded into the water. He caught the wheel just as the current freed it. Almost pulled from his feet, he struggled to maintain his grip, turning too late to avoid a broken limb rushing toward him. It struck him with pounding force.

Knocked into the churning rapids, Reed felt consciousness waver.

Chastity screamed as Reed lurched forward into the water. The horror of the moment froze her into immobility as he disappeared from sight beneath the surface.

On the muddy bank in a moment, Chastity was running wildly toward the churning rapids when Reed surfaced, fighting to regain his feet. She called his name, the sound a panicked plea that resounded over and again in her mind as she plunged into the water.

She couldn't lose him! She couldn't lose Reed, too. Not now . . .

Disoriented, Reed floundered, momentarily helpless against the current. Water filled his throat and he gasped for breath, struggling to retain consciousness. He heard someone calling him. The sound drew him back, feeding him strength.

His mind clearing, he recognized Chastity's voice. He turned to see her beside him. His strength returning, he regained his feet, grasping her arm as they fought their way back toward the bank.

Chastity fell to her knees on the muddy soil, and Reed sagged to his knees beside her. Taking long moments to catch his breath, he then pulled himself to his feet and drew Chastity up with him. He slid his arm around her waist, looking down as she raised her face to his and leaned against his side, sobbing incoherently.

Helping her into the rear of the wagon moments later, he climbed in beside her. He sat, silent and still for long minutes as the maelstrom continued overhead, until Chastity regained her breath and her hysterical sobbing ceased.

He waited until she was as still as he, then reached out and took her into his arms.

A sob of pure joy escaped Chastity's lips as Reed's strong arms closed around her. His mouth caressed hers with his kiss, and Chastity welcomed him. His lips separated hers, and she gave her mouth to him willingly. His kiss surged deeper, more powerfully, more consuming. The sounds of the storm faded as Reed spoke soft, loving words unintelligible in the rush of heated emotions.

Returning kiss for kiss, caress for caress, Chastity tightened her arms around his neck, forcing away the horror of the moment when she saw Reed slip beneath the churning rapids. It had all become so clear to her in that terrifying moment—the instinct that had drawn her to him that first day, the intuition that made her remain despite the friction between them, the strange conflict within her that had grown stronger with each passing day. Those few moments in the river had forced a trust that went beyond the spoken word.

Reed's lips left hers as passion swelled. Stroking back the wet strands from her face, he drank the droplets of rain from her brow with his kiss, he stroked her fluttering lids with his lips, he left not a patch of her clear skin untouched by his loving caress. He returned to her mouth again and again with increasing ardor. Whispering heated words of love, he tasted the hollows of her ear, then worshipped the tender lobe, trailing the line of her jaw and the slender column of her neck. His mouth was warm against her chilled flesh as he slid her dress from her shoulders, baring the white mounds of her breasts beneath. Emotion swelled as he stroked her gently, then lowered his head, his strong body shuddering as he closed his mouth over a pink crest.

Stunned as a brilliant joy rose within her, Chastity gasped.

Halting abruptly, Reed drew back from her. She saw the restraint he expended as he searched her face, waiting for her to speak. But her throat was tight, her emotions so keenly drawn that she was somehow incapable of speech.

The silence between them grew taut.

Chastity was lying beneath him, and the anguish within Reed swelled to new depths. The fiery color of her hair darkened by their watery fray lay splayed against the pallet, glinting with subdued brilliance. Water beaded against the smooth skin of her face, and dampness clung to the thick brush of lashes surrounding eyes that glowed with radiant flecks of green. Her lips were parted and he viewed them hungrily, his gaze descending for short moments toward the warm, female flesh he had tasted so briefly moments earlier.

She was beautiful and giving. He saw the trust in her eyes. She had braved the swirling currents to save him minutes earlier, despite her fear. Her emotions were running high. It would be so easy to overwhelm her. He could not be sure if that was his original intent when he took her into his arms, so much did he want her, and so confused had his thoughts become where Chastity was concerned. The only thing he was sure of was that they were alone in a wilderness where the world was kept at bay, where nothing meant more to him than the wonder he knew they could feel in each other's arms.

Stroking back a wisp of hair from her cheek, Reed whispered the only words that bore the true import of the moment—words that originated from a spot within him that was chaste and untouched despite the furor of past moments and the bitterness of anguished years.

"I want to make love to you, Chastity. I've wanted to make love to you from the first moment I could clearly see you, but I never wanted it more than I do right now. I didn't think it was possible to want again the way I want you. I didn't think it was possible to feel again the way you make me feel."

Reed paused, the hypocrisy in his words cutting deep, despite his earnestness, "But I want to make sure you want this as much as I do. I have to be sure because . . . I don't want to hurt you. I don't ever want to hurt you."

Chastity's eyes searched his face. He saw the tears that threatened as she whispered, "You said you want to hold me close to you. Reed . . . I want that, too. I remember other things you said as well. You said that you have your objectives and I have mine, that they take us in different directions, that you thought for a while it could work out, but you had made a mistake."

Chastity paused to take a stabilizing breath. He saw the effort it took for her to continue, "All that may be true. I don't know." Chastity's lips trembled. "But there's one thing I'm sure of. I want you to make love to me, Reed. Nothing could be more right than that right now." She paused again, seeing a lingering hesitation in his eyes. "Are you as sure as I am, Reed?"

\* \* \*

Yes, he was.

Reed expressed those words with his lips, with his touch, and with the fervor of soaring passions.

Chastity breathed against the rapid beating of her heart. Their lovemaking grew more frantic, more impassioned. Her yearning became almost more than she could bear, and as Reed had stripped away the barrier of clothing between them, pressing his naked flesh to hers, she believed her heart would burst with elation.

The wonder of it . . . the power. Chastity wrapped her arms around Reed's neck, winding her fingers in the sun-burnished gold of his hair, savoring the bliss of the moment. Strangely, she knew with a profound certainty that she had been born for this moment in Reed's arms, that there was no fulfillment that could be greater than knowing she was giving herself to him as totally as he was giving himself to her.

But the ache within her was growing with each kiss. The need was becoming more demanding with each caress. Touching her soul with a tenderness so sweet and acute that she was almost undone, he raised her to a plane of sustained emotion where the joy seared as deeply as pain. There was no indulgence he withheld—save one.

She knew the time was coming. She felt it in the ferocious ardor with which he again took her lips. She sensed it in the shuddering of

Reed's strong frame, and she read it in his passionate gaze as he drew back to slide his hand between her thighs.

"It's time, darlin'." He caressed her intimately, making her gasp anew. "I want you to want me the way I want you. Tell me you want me, Chastity."

Her response trembled on her lips as emotions that were new and filled with raw heat shuddered through her in successive waves. She managed haltingly, "I want you, Reed."

His caress slipping deeper, Reed fondled the bud of her passion, the brilliant blue of his eyes glittering as he whispered, "I want you to need me the way I need you. Tell me you need me."

Chastity's reply was choked as the wonder soared to breathlessness. "I . . . I need you."

"Say it again, Chastity. I need to hear the words. Tell me you want me and need me, that you yearn as much as I do to have me inside you." Separating her thighs, smoothing the soft flesh there with quick, gentle strokes, Reed paused above her. The hard swell of his passion moved against her and she caught her breath.

"Tell me, Chastity."

The words rising from the font of loving hunger deep within her, Chastity rasped, "I want you inside me, Reed. Yes, I want that more than I ever wanted anything before."

Her words were swallowed by a gasp as Reed slid inside her. Chastity closed her eyes. The brief stab of pain was overwhelmed by Reed's grunt of pleasure as he settled hot and deep

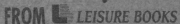

within her. She heard him groan softly as her body closed fully around him, and she clutched him close. She felt his anticipation growing, and her own swelled as well. He moved hesitantly, then with increasing passion until she had no thought but the moment, until there was no breath that did not speak Reed's name, until the colors assaulting her mind became a brilliant cataclysm that exploded brightly before her eyes as Reed carried her with him to ecstatic reward.

The rain hammered the battered canvas roof of the wagon, but the sound no longer caused fear as Chastity lay with Reed's moist flesh still intimately pressed to hers. Reed had transformed the sound to a drumming rhythm of love that would forever quell her fears.

Grateful for that gift, with the tender moments they'd shared still warm between them, Chastity opened her eyes slowly to see Reed studying her face.

Morgan's mood was foul. Conchita realized it the moment he walked back into the cabin, his oilskins dripping and the mud thick on his boots. The men followed close behind, but there was little conversation between them as they stripped off their outerwear and hung it on the hooks beside the door.

They had been branding in the rain most of the day, and it had not gone well. She had heard Morgan's voice echoing angrily from the corral as the rain continued and the mud lent endless

# Elaine Barbieri

complications to their work. She had not needed to count the stock successfully branded to know that Morgan would be furious when he returned, and she had done all she could to compensate. She had taken special pains with the meal and had spent time and care with her grooming, brushing her dark hair until it shone, going so far as to use the last few drops of scent in the bottle Morgan had bought her months earlier before donning a fresh blouse and skirt.

The men lingered at the door, waiting for Morgan to make the first move toward the table and the food that was waiting for them. She saw Morgan's eyes slant toward them with contempt. Her throat tightened at the thought that he might look at her in a similar way one day. She waited, her skin prickling, for the explosion to come. It did not take long.

"What are you waitin' for?" Morgan's dark eyes flashed with anger as he turned sharply on the others. "You're hungry, aren't you? So sit down. Just because you didn't earn your keep today doesn't mean you can't eat."

The men grumbled as they took their seats. It was Turner who spoke up, obviously unable to restrain a response.

"It wasn't our fault—you know that as well as we do. Brandin' in the rain ain't right, and it don't work out!"

"It's right when you had all the sunny days you needed to get the job done and you let them slip away." Morgan dug his fork into a slab of beef on the platter in front of him and slapped it down on his plate. He looked up, his dark eyes vicious. "And it's right when I already made the deal to sell a herd that isn't ready yet!"

"Yeah, you made the deal in Sedalia."

The subtle inference in Turner's tone didn't escape Morgan. "That's right. You got somethin' to say about it?"

"Yeah, I got somethin' to say, all right." Turner could hold it back no longer. "You should've stayed a little longer and gotten yourself a piece of that red-haired witch, so's you wouldn't be takin' it all out on us right now!"

Morgan went still.

Conchita took a sharp step backward that brought her up against the far wall. She swallowed, noting that the table had fallen silent and that Turner had paled. A slow shuddering began inside her as Turner shrugged, his gaze flicking around the table before he met Morgan's lethal stare. "I didn't mean nothin' by what I said. Simmons told us about that red-haired woman, is all."

Conchita realized with a start that Morgan was trembling, but she knew instinctively that there was not a shred of fear in him. Instead, she recognized his supreme effort at control as he hissed, "That was one nail in your coffin, Turner. I'm warnin' you now that the next one will come straight from the barrel of my gun. And I'm tellin' you somethin' else. I don't want to hear anythin' else about a red-haired woman—not now, not ever! If you all want to stay healthy, you'd better remember that. And while you're at it, there's somethin' else you'd better keep in mind. We're brandin' tomorrow, rain or shine. We're goin' to take up right where we left off, and there's only two ways any of you'll get away from it. Either you'll ride out, knowin' you won't be welcomed back . . . or you'll be carried out. Make your choice."

His chest heaving, Morgan picked up his knife and fork and cut into the meat on his plate. He chewed it briefly as the men maintained their silence, then spat it out in disgust.

Slapping the silverware back on the table, Morgan stood up abruptly. Conchita trembled visibly as he stared darkly in her direction, then walked into the rear room and slammed the door behind him.

Conchita managed a smile. Morgan was angry that the men had told stories about him—*untrue* stories. He was tense and cold, but she would change his mood and this darkness—this part of him that was *muy mal*—would fade.

Conchita started toward the door.

"You're makin' a mistake goin' in there."

Conchita turned back toward Walker. She spat out, "I do not listen to you! Your lies made Morgan angry."

"They wasn't lies." Walker's small eyes narrowed as he glanced at the door. His voice dropped a note lower. "Look, I don't care what you do, but if you was smart, you'd stay away from Morgan for a while. I've seen what he can do, and it ain't pretty."

"Morgan is not angry with *me*."

196

"He don't have to be."

Not bothering to respond, Conchita approached the door. She knocked lightly. "Morgan. It is Conchita." When he did not respond, Conchita repeated, "Morgan . . . it is Conchita."

"Leave me alone."

Conchita's hand stilled. Suddenly aware that she held her breath, she forced herself to breathe, then pressed, "I would like to come in, Morgan. I would like to speak to you."

"Get away from the door. Leave . . . me . . . alone."

Morgan's tone chilled Conchita's blood.

It stopped the beating of her heart as all came suddenly clear.

The *lies* were truths.

The *truths* were lies.

Conchita turned woodenly from the door, uncaring of the stares that followed her as she crossed the room, drew open the door, and stepped out into the storm.

Shrugging, Simmons darted a knowing glance around the table as the door clicked closed behind her. He gave a scoffing laugh. "Hell, that *puta* sure learned a hard lesson. Did you see the look on her face when Morgan told her to leave him alone?"

"Yeah . . ." Bartell flicked a piece of beef from his teeth. "She actually thought he was crazy about her. She so much as told me so when I tried feelin' her out while he was gone."

Turner's unshaved face tightened. "She didn't

pull no punches with me. Hell, before I knew it, she had a knife in her hand!"

"Yeah, but you keep forgettin'," Walker contributed with a sneer, "You ain't as pretty as Morgan is. You ain't got a baby face and that smooth way of talkin' that he has when he's after somethin'. Women fall all over themselves gettin' in line to be next—even them red-haired church types."

"What was so great about her, anyways?"

Walker stared thoughtfully at Bartell. "Can't rightly say. All that red hair and white skin . . . and she was taller than most. She had a way about her, kinda prim and proper." He gave a short laugh. "But Morgan said she knocked that storekeeper flat on his back when he tried to put a hand on her."

"She did! He liked that, did he?"

"Yeah, I think he did."

Bartell frowned, then slapped down his fork. "I'm tellin' you one thing. If Morgan brings that woman back here from Sedalia, I'm leavin' as soon as he sells off the herd. Between that hotheaded *puta* and the other one, I ain't about to wait around to catch a stray bullet."

"You think it could come to that?" Turner addressed Walker. "You know Morgan better than the rest of us. You think he'd bring that woman back with him while that *puta's* still here?"

Walker shrugged. "I wouldn't worry about it, even if he did."

"You're so sure he could handle them?"

"Handle them?" Walker continued without

hesitation, "He'd put a bullet through both their hearts if they got him mad enough, and you can bet on it."

The rain continued its hammering assault above them as Reed raised himself from Chastity's warm flesh, his expression sober.

The residue of sated passion glittered in her eyes. Her lips were swollen from his kiss. The creamy color of her skin was brushed a rosy hue by his ardent lovemaking. Her body accommodated his weight naturally, totally accepting, and he ached with the beauty of her.

She had confronted and conquered her worst fear to come to his aid in the flooded gully. She had given herself to him wholly, holding nothing back.

The only lies between them were his own.

Sliding his arms under and around her, Reed clutched Chastity close to him. The mental list of those deceits tormented him: the bogus collar he wore, the countless lies he had told to hide the real reason he traveled into Indian Territory, his selfish purpose in taking her with him. It occurred to him that Chastity did not really know him at all. But he dared not tell her the truth. If she balked, the risk of losing Morgan now, when he was so close, was too great.

And the risk of losing *her* was even greater.

Her silence concerning him, Reed raised his head to look down into Chastity's face. His lips only inches from hers, he asked, "Are you all right, Chastity?"

"Yes."

A smile touched her lips, and he lowered his mouth, consuming it. He pulled back reluctantly, drawing her with him as he rolled to his side. Satisfied only when the warm, naked length of her was stretched fully against him, he held her there, somehow unable to release her. Her gaze locked with his as he said, "It's still raining. The team had a hard time in the river. The horses should rest for a while. I think we should, too."

He kissed her again. Her lips separated, accepting the probing warmth of his tongue. His heart began a new pounding as he pressed his kiss deeper and Chastity's flesh molded itself instinctively to his. His hunger stirring anew, he drew back, cupping her cheek with his palm, wanting to etch each delicate detail of her face into his mind as he whispered, "I'll unhitch them . . . let them graze for a while."

Chastity nodded. The catch of her breath as he dipped his head to press his mouth lightly to her breast, then seized the nipple for a lingering kiss, sent new tremors of yearning down his spine. His heartbeat thundering, he separated her thighs to probe her moistness. He slipped inside her, closing his eyes briefly as her body shivered and ecstatic emotions rose again full bore.

*Chastity*

Reed moved within her and his heart began a new pounding. A world of loving hunger in his tone, he whispered huskily, "I guess the horses can wait."

201

# *Chapter Eight*

"I bet you're all glad the sun is shinin' this mornin'."

The men turned cautiously toward Morgan as he emerged from the bedroom and walked into the main room of the cabin. They did not respond.

Morgan looked at Conchita where she stood beside the fireplace. She did not turn in his direction. He knew the reason. He'd sent her away, and he had never done that before. He supposed that lent credence to the talk about the red-haired woman in her mind, but the truth was, he didn't really care. After a long day in the rain, he had not been of a mood to pander to the feelings of a sensitive whore.

Morgan pulled out a chair and sat down at

the table, watching as the men filled in the chairs around him. Conchita put the biscuits on the table. He did not question where or how she had spent the night. He knew that if Turner or any of the others put a hand on her, she'd cut it off.

A familiar annoyance surged inside him. Turner and Bartell thought he didn't know that they had both tried to bed Conchita while he was gone. If he hadn't known that it was just a waste of time on their parts, he would've faced off with them about it. Instead, it had merely irritated him. The truth was, he didn't really care who Conchita went to once he turned her loose. And he intended to do just that as soon as he got back from Sedalia.

There was something about the red-haired witch that set his blood to rushing hot even at the thought of her. He hadn't been able to get her out of his mind. He didn't expect to have much trouble finding her when he got back to Sedalia. How many women looked like her, with that bright red hair and skin like warm cream? He wanted a taste of that cream, and he intended to get it. Walker's comments aside, he knew that the red-haired witch was his for the taking. He had seen that look in a woman's eye too often not to recognize it.

But, with the return of sunshine and a better mood, he was beginning to feel he had made a mistake in turning Conchita away the previous night. It could be a week until he could start back for Sedalia. He could use her until then.

His thoughts interrupted by a crashing sound, Morgan turned toward the fireplace to see that Conchita had dropped the second tin of biscuits. He saw her flush as the men laughed at her clumsiness. He spoke up opportunely.

"What's the matter, Conchita?" He waited until she retrieved the biscuits and placed them on the table before he affixed an apologetic smile on his lips and said, "Come over here, darlin'." He saw her hesitate and repeated, "It's a new day and yesterday's in the past." He caught and held her gaze. "Come on."

He took her wrist gently as she approached. Her wariness lingered. He ignored it and the men who watched his every move as he spoke to her softly.

"I've been thinkin'. We're goin' to be finished brandin' here in a few days, and when that's done, I'll be headin' back to Sedalia for a while. I'm goin' to take you with me. There's a real nice hotel there where we can spend some time in comfort, without anybody else around. They've got a nice store there, too, and I'm goin' to take you shoppin'. I'm goin' to get you a new dress— somethin' nice and bright. And some new shoes—and some perfume." He waited for her reaction. "Would you like that, darlin'?"

Conchita nodded.

He pressed, "What color dress would you like?"

Conchita remained wary.

"Come on . . . tell me."

"Green. I would like a green dress."

"All right, green. Now let me see you smile."

Conchita looked intently into his eyes. She searched his gaze deeply. He felt the tears she restrained as she glanced down at his lips, then raised her chin with a wobbly smile.

Hell, she was no challenge at all. . . .

Morgan released her. "You'd better pour some more of that coffee so these boys can get started. The sooner we get done out there, the faster we're goin' to make it to Sedalia."

Conchita moved to his bidding. Her smile faded as she glanced back at him. It amused him to realize that although she had been unable to hold out against him, she was still suspicious . . . and jealous.

Herding the men out the door ahead of him when breakfast was done, Morgan saw Conchita's gaze linger on him. He gave her a parting smile that dropped from his lips the moment he pulled the door closed behind him.

He was striding toward the shed, Walker beside him, when Walker laughed, "You sure do know how to handle women! There was no way I would've thought last night that you'd bring that *puta* around so easy this mornin'. Are you really goin' to take her to Sedalia with you if you go back?"

"Not *if* I go back . . . *when* I go back."

Walker looked surprised. "I thought you was just leadin' her on!" He shook his head. "So, you're really takin' her with you."

"Not a chance."

"Wh-what?" Walker appeared confused.

"I've got me an appointment in Sedalia, and I'm sure as hell not takin' her with me when I keep it."

"That red-haired woman . . ."

"That's right."

"You're so sure it'll be worth the trip?"

"Damned right I am!"

"What if that woman's got other ideas?"

"She won't . . . for long."

"You don't mess around, do you?"

"Not when I want somethin' bad enough."

"And you want her."

"Almost as much as I'm goin' to make her want me."

"You're a cocky bastard."

Morgan smiled, his gaze darting toward the others as they threw their branding irons on the fire. "Cocky, maybe, but—"

His smile freezing, Morgan looked at the far corral. It was empty, and there wasn't a steer in sight.

"Damn it!" His agitation returned. "The storm must've panicked the beeves." He turned accusingly toward Turner. "I told you that fencing needed to be repaired. They could've run for miles in that storm last night!" His chest heaving, Morgan spat, "Get your horse saddled, Turner—you and Bartell—and find those steers! And don't come back until you've rounded up every last one of them!"

Waiting only until the two men moved resentfully to his bidding, Morgan turned back toward Walker, their former conversation forgotten as he grated, "If they don't find every one of those critters, I'll take it out of their hides!"

Livid, Morgan headed toward the shed.

The sun was shining. The violent storm had ceased during the night, the muddy trail was already beginning to dry under the sun's intense heat, and the horses were drawing the wagon forward with new enthusiasm.

Glancing at the driver's seat beside him, Reed saw Chastity staring at the passing landscape. He had been the first to awaken that morning, and he was glad. It had allowed him the opportunity for a few minutes of silent thought as Chastity lay pressed intimately close against him. But she had awakened too soon for him to get a clear perspective on the events of the day and night past, other than to know with unshaking certainty that he could not get enough of her.

Chastity had opened her mouth to speak, and he had swallowed her words with his kiss. She had turned toward him, and he had enveloped her in his embrace. She had given herself to him, and he had consumed her voraciously. And he had despised the moment when he had been forced to surrender her at last to reality, and had to don his parson's clothing again for the trail ahead.

Strangely, there had been little conversation between them as the morning hours passed. Knowing the need to steadily survey the passing landscape so he might follow Jenkins's directions with as little deviation as possible, he had forced aside all personal thoughts. He had noted belatedly as he turned toward Chastity a short time earlier that her gaze had grown increasingly contemplative.

A whispered word had turned her toward him then, and he had been momentarily breathless at the sight of her. Her hair, loosely confined, bobbed in fiery wisps against the graceful contours of her cheek. Pensive sparks of green glittered in her gaze, her creamy skin was touched with color by the morning sun, and her lips were parted in warm appeal. It occurred to him that he had never seen a woman more beautiful than she was at that moment. When he touched his mouth to hers, he had been hard pressed not to take her into his arms, then and there.

But Chastity's pensive posture had gradually become more rigid as the morning passed. Silent, she now clutched her locket tightly in her hand. Her eyes were narrowed, her lips compressed in a tight line as she scrutinized the passing landscape.

Closing his hand over the fist she clenched in her lap, Reed asked softly, "What's wrong, Chastity?"

Chastity turned toward him, uncertain. "I don't know. There's something about the land . . . it's familiar to me, but I know I've never been here before."

He questioned, "Are you sure?"

"My aunts found me in Texas. They brought

Chastity

me directly back to their home in the East. This is Indian Territory. I know they never would have brought me here. They couldn't wait to get back to civilization."

Reed frowned. "Maybe this land resembles a place you saw with your family."

"No . . . that's not it." Chastity's knuckles whitened around her locket. He saw the effort she made to draw her mind back as she asked, "How soon do you think we'll reach the mission, Reed?"

The question took him by surprise. "I'm not sure. Maybe a day . . . maybe two."

Lies.

"What will you do then?"

He could not manage another lie. "I'm not sure."

Chastity shook her head. "What do you mean?"

"I have to find out how things stand at the mission first."

"Oh." Hearing the hesitation in Chastity's voice, Reed asked, "Why?"

"Because . . ." Chastity took a breath, her gaze silently intense. ". . . Because my sisters are close. I can feel it."

"Close? Where?"

"I don't know."

Apprehension slowly coming to life within him, Reed pressed, "What are you trying to say?"

"I can't stay at the mission, Reed, not until you get everything settled. It'll take too long. I

209

need to start looking for my sisters now or I may never find them."

"But you said—"

"I know. I said I'd stay until another teacher could be sent to take over the mission, but I can't."

Reed did not respond. He wanted to tell her it would be no longer than a week, maybe two, before he finished his business with Morgan and his gang. He wanted to confess that the situation wasn't what she believed it to be, that there was too much danger in a change of plans that was not thought through. He wanted to tell her that he'd take her anywhere she wanted to go, then, but too many lies were in the way. They tied his tongue, allowing the only reply he could make.

"Are you sure that's what you want?"

"I don't want to leave you, Reed. You know that, don't you?" The torment in Chastity's eyes tore at his heart as she continued, "But I have this feeling . . . this sudden certainty deep down inside me that if I wait too long, my chance to find them will pass."

Reed could not respond.

"Reed, please try to understand. I made the commitment to find my sisters a long time ago. I made it to them as much as I made it to myself, and I can't abandon it. If I did, it would be like abandoning *them*. I couldn't do that, Reed. You do understand, don't you?"

Yes, he understood about commitments—only too well.

210

"Reed . . ."

Reed frowned, all joy seeming to drain from his heart as he replied, "I understand."

"It's a good thing I took the time to pack us somethin' to eat."

Bartell glanced up again at the afternoon sky, then turned toward Turner when he did not respond. Turner's jowled face was fixed in a scowl. He had had the same look since they saddled up and rode off with Morgan's warning ringing in their ears.

Bartell slanted another sideward look at Turner. It was Turner's fault that the steers had broken loose in the storm. He was supposed to have fixed the fencing and he didn't. But he wasn't about to remind Turner about it. It was bad enough that they had been in the saddle most of the morning without finding even half of the steers that were lost. They had herded the ones they'd located into a spot where the grazing was good enough to keep them for a while, with Turner's disposition growing worse by the minute. It wasn't just that Turner wasn't in the mood to work. He never was. This was different. Something was eating at him, and Bartell had a feeling that he wasn't going to have to wait long to find out what it was.

"I've had enough of him, you know! Who in hell does Morgan think he is, talkin' to us like he does?" Turner spat on the ground beside him, then jerked his mount's bridle with a viciousness that elicited a sharp whinny of protest. "He's gettin' worse all the time. I was willin' to go along with the things he did at first, because he's smarter than most of the lawmen around. I had to hand it to him when he got the idea of rustlin' Texas cattle and drivin' them over the line into Indian Territory where Texas law couldn't touch us. I figured it was real smart of him to realize that a Texas lawman would have a hard time tryin' to find a local sheriff who'd be willin' to put his life on the line for somethin' that didn't directly concern him. I figured we didn't have nothin' to worry about." Turner gave a low snort. "I never figured Morgan would get crazy like he is."

"He ain't crazy."

"He ain't?" Turner raised a hairy brow. "What do you think would've happened if we said we wasn't goin' to go after them steers like he said?"

Bartell shrugged. "I don't know. And I wasn't about to find out."

"I'll tell you what would've happened. He would've pulled his gun and put a bullet in both of us."

"He wouldn't go that far."

"Would you bet your life on it?"

Bartell did not respond.

"That's what I thought."

"So, what're you goin' to do about it?"

"Me?" Turner shrugged. "I ain't doin' nothin' about it—not until Morgan sells that herd and I have my share in my hand. And then I'm goin' to hightail it out of here so fast—"

"You're makin' a mistake." Raising his hat,

Bartell wiped the sweat from his balding head. "We both know what's got Morgan all hot and bothered, and it ain't no steers that run off durin' the night."

"I'm sick and tired of hearin' about that red-haired woman!"

"A little bit of her and he'll be fine again. Didn't you never have the hots for a woman?"

"No, not like him. Hell, one woman's as good as another to me!"

"He'll settle down."

"If everythin' goes his way."

"I never did see a woman who could turn him down."

"Maybe not, and just maybe this one will be the first. Whatever, I ain't goin' back to the cabin tonight."

"What are you sayin'?"

"And neither are you."

"Speak for yourself!"

"Wait a minute. Hear me out!" Turner sneered. "Morgan told us not to come back until we find them steers, right?"

"Yeah."

"Well, we'll just take our time findin' them. We'll go back tomorrow—late—drivin' those steers in just like he told us. The boys should have almost all the brandin' done by then. It would serve Morgan right if he ended up doin' my part of the brandin', and yours, too."

Bartell did not reply.

"What can Morgan say? He told us not to come back without every one of them steers."

Elaine Barbieri

"We have to find them first, which might not be as easy as you're thinkin'."

"We'll have them all rounded up in another hour."

"What makes you so sure?"

"Look over there." Turner pointed toward a grassy knoll in the distance. "How much to do you want to bet we find them steers waitin' for us there?"

"And when we do?"

"We just lay ourselves down in a nice, shady spot for a while."

Bartell paused. He was as sick of Morgan's ways as Turner was. And he would enjoy putting one over on Morgan just as much as Turner, too. What could Morgan do about it if they showed up with all the cattle, just like he'd told them to? Bartell shrugged. "Sounds like a good idea to me."

"I'm bettin' them fellas back at the cabin are sweatin' over them brandin' irons right now."

"And cursin' up a storm . . ."

That thought tickling him, Turner laughed aloud, then kicked his mount into a gallop.

Daylight was fading. Reed had drawn the wagon to a halt for the night. He was tending to the horses while Chastity walked off along the narrow stream where they had camped.

Chastity stared at the glistening trickle of water, at the sun's setting rays reflected there. A myriad of feelings overwhelmed her, things she could not truly put into words. By accompanying Reed on his journey to the mission, she had put parts of her past to rest in ways she had never thought she could. She had faced her nightmare in the rushing water of the gully, and she had conquered it. She knew she would never be a slave to it again.

But with each passing hour, new sensations grew stronger. The sun on her shoulders, the scent of the passing landscape, the vastness that surrounded her in all directions, the light-hearted freedom it all evoked that warmed her heart and raised her spirits—all were familiar to her in ways she could not explain, except to know with ever-increasing certainty that she was, indeed, coming home.

Suddenly aware that she was trembling, Chastity raised a hand to eyes that were moist. She turned abruptly at the sound of a step behind her.

Reed stood beside her, the startling blue of his eyes so intense that they seemed to touch her soul. "Why are you crying?"

She avoided his gaze. "I'm not crying."

Reed wiped the moistness from her cheek with his palm.

How could she explain to him how she felt? How could she say that she had discovered a truth she had not expected during the dark hours of the storm—that his arms were a haven she had sought all her life, without knowing it? How could she say that when she lay with her flesh pressed close to his, there was no past or future, only the present and the shattering emotions he made her feel? How could she say that right here and now, when he looked at her as if there was nothing in the world more important than the two of them, and there was nowhere else she wanted to be?

How could she say all that, and in the next breath tell him she was willing to say good-bye?

"Chastity, don't torment yourself, please, darling."

"Oh, Reed, I wish . . ."

Conflicting emotions warred in Reed's gaze as Chastity's words trailed away. She saw the resolution slowly overwhelming him as he whispered, "There are things you must do, and there are things I must do. We're both bound to follow paths in separate directions." Grasping her arms, Reed continued more intently, "But we don't have to think of that here and now. This place is ours. And today is ours. Tomorrow is hours away. The world can't intrude here. It's just the two of us now, Chastity."

Taking her into his arms, Reed held her close. She felt his strong body shuddering, and she raised her face to his. She saw the torment in his gaze, and the pain of it squeezed tightly inside her. His need was her need. She lifted her mouth to his. She slid her hands into his hair and drew his mouth to hers. She parted her lips to taste his kiss more freely, offering herself to him with all the love in her heart.

"What do you suppose they're doin' now?"

Turner gave a harsh laugh. The sun was setting; they had made a campfire and laid out their bedrolls in a spot where the brisk breeze and the steady heat of the afternoon sun had removed all trace of dampness from the ground. And it looked as if it was going to be a balmy night. Hell, nothing could be better!

Biting off another piece of jerky, Turner chewed it with a satisfied smile, continuing, "I'm bettin' that just about now, Morgan's fit to be tied. I'm thinkin' he had Walker and Simmons jumpin' this way and that all day long while he was watchin' over his shoulder for us to come back."

"Yeah, but I don't know what you're smilin' about." Bartell frowned. "I'm not so sure what we're goin' to be in for when we get back if Morgan's that mad."

"Losin' your nerve, Bartell?" Turner's familiar sneer returned.

"You talk real big out here." Bartell turned angrily toward him. "I don't know how I let you talk me into this!" He glanced at the cattle grazing close by. Second thoughts about the prudence of their actions had loomed ever greater as the day passed. The cattle had been waiting on the other side of the knoll, just as Turner said. They had rounded them up, driven them to join the others, and had settled down for a leisurely afternoon. Turner had dozed most of the time, but he hadn't been that lucky. He had lain awake and started thinking.

"Do you know what the matter with you is, Turner?" Bartell was growing more angry by the second. "You think you're smarter than Morgan, but you ain't."

"I ain't listenin'."

"Well, you'd better! I had a lot of time to think while you was sawin' wood all afternoon! I must've been crazy to let you talk me into this. Hell, if it wasn't gettin' dark, I'd get these beeves movin' right now!"

"Yeah, but it is gettin' dark, and it wouldn't do you no good, and you know it."

Bartell glared.

"Relax! Morgan ain't goin' to do nothin'! He's so hot to get back to Sedalia that he can't take a chance of doin' nothin' that might complicate things." Turner smiled. "He needs us. And when he don't need us anymore, I'm goin' to be long gone."

Bartell reached for his canteen and took a long drink. The water was warm and it tasted foul. He spat it out. He looked up to see Turner still staring at him.

"What are you lookin' at, Turner?"

"You don't have to look so worried. We're goin' back tomorrow."

"At sun-up."

"Hell, no!"

"At sun-up, I said, damn it!" Bartell's face flamed. "And if you give me any trouble, I'll make sure you regret it."

Turner stiffened. "Is that a threat?"

"We're startin' back at sun-up, and that's the end of it." Standing up abruptly, Bartell walked into the bushes and out of sight.

\* \* \*

The cabin was silent. The supper meal had been eaten in silence. The table had been cleared in silence. The silence was so heavy that neither Walker nor Simmons dared look at Morgan's face for fear of what they would see.

The day had stretched on, with Morgan driving Simmons and Walker relentlessly, but neither had dared to complain because Morgan had worked right alongside them, pushing himself as hard as he was pushing them. The tension had started growing at midday. Walker did not care to remember how many times he had raised his head to see Morgan scanning the horizon. All he knew was that each time, the knot in his stomach had twisted tighter.

Walker silently cursed. He had the feeling that Morgan knew as well as he did that he had made a mistake sending Turner and Bartell after those cattle. And he had the feeling that Morgan suspected just as he did what was happening. There was no way those cattle ran so far that they couldn't be driven back before sundown. Those boys thought they were teachin' Morgan a lesson and gettin' out of some heavy branding at the same time.

Walker glanced at Morgan, who sat tight-lipped. He looked at the Mexican whore to see that she was as tense as he was. He didn't trust the look in her eyes, either, and he wondered if Morgan realized that she was smarter than he gave her credit for.

Walker shifted uncomfortably and pulled at

# Elaine Barbieri

his wiry mustache. Unable to stand it any longer, he addressed Morgan.

"What do you suppose happened to them?"

Morgan snapped back toward him. The expression on his youthful face was so vicious that it forced Walker back an involuntary step as Morgan hissed, "Those bastards—you know as well as I do what's keepin' them."

Walker darted a look at Simmons. Realizing there would be no help there, he managed a casual shrug. "Maybe they ran into some kind of trouble that held them up. This is Injun territory, you know."

"The Indians aren't the problem, and you know it."

"Yeah, well . . ."

Morgan's face twitched. "They'll drive those cattle in here tomorrow like nothin' happened, thinkin' they put one over on me, but they've got a surprise comin'."

A chill crawled up Walker's spine. "What do you mean?"

Morgan's dark eyes met his with a gaze so cold that Walker almost shivered. "Turner's got to be taught a lesson."

Walker swallowed. "Turner's all right. He's just been cooped up here too long. He'll be all right when he gets back to civilization for a while and gets a chance to blow off some steam."

Morgan did not reply. Instead, he stood up abruptly and walked with a slow, measured tread toward the bedroom door. Walker saw the

Mexican whore follow him with her gaze. She was still staring when he slammed the door behind him.

Walker looked at Simmons, then back at the woman. The look in her eye compelled him to offer, "I wouldn't worry about Morgan. He's a little upset, is all. He'll be all right in the mornin'."

Conchita turned toward him, her expression frigid. "Do not waste your pity on me. Pity Turner! He is the one who will need it!"

Dismissing him with a scornful glance, Conchita walked to the bedroom door. She paused only briefly before knocking. He saw her raise her chin as Morgan replied with a admonition to enter.

"Women!"

Walker turned toward Simmons's low-voiced comment, responding, "I don't give a damn about that whore. All I know is that Turner's in for it, and it looks to me like Bartell just might get caught in the crossfire. When them two get back tomorrow, I'm goin' to make sure I give them all plenty of room."

"Morgan's gettin' crazier every day."

Walker glanced at the door, then hissed, "What's the matter with you? What if Morgan heard you? He'd kill both of us!"

Simmons held his gaze. "Yeah . . . I know."

Simmons was a man of few words, but his message came through loud and clear.

The message lingered as Walker drew himself

to his feet. He was going to have to make some hard decisions soon.

Tomorrow would tell the tale.

The sun was up. The day was clear.

Reed glanced cautiously around him as he affixed the parson's collar that chafed more at his conscience with every passing day. But he was never more aware that he was bound to the course of action he had set for himself, just as he was bound to the parson's collar that would be Chastity's greatest protection in the days to come.

Reed reviewed Jenkins's map again in his mind. If all went well, he would be in the vicinity of Morgan's hideout sometime that day. He had already decided to keep his surveillance as brief as possible.

Involved with harnessing the horses, Reed looked up as Chastity returned from the stream. His heart jumped in his chest at the sight of her. Freshly bathed, her skin was almost luminous. Her hair was knotted loosely at her neck, the color seeming to glow in the light of early morning. She was lost in thought, her expression sober. As he watched, she touched her locket, then gripped it in her palm . . .

. . . *and he remembered.*

Reed swallowed, the import of his recollection setting his heart to pounding. It had been a year earlier. He had been in Texas, on the trail of a rustler who was raiding ranches in the south. He remembered passing the camp of some drovers. He had asked for the boss of the outfit and the foreman said the boss had ridden ahead. He made his inquiries and was about to leave when the boss rode up. The boss was a woman. He didn't speak more than a few words to her. Dressed in drover's gear with her hat pulled down low on her forehead, she was tall and slim. At first glance, her gender was betrayed only by the long, blond braid that trailed down her back . . . *and the gold, heart-shaped locket visible in the open neck of her shirt*. Her face was in the shadows. He did not get a good look at her, but looking back, he saw her seated on her mount, supervising as the men cut an injured calf out of the herd. She was frowning, and while he watched, she reached up to grasp her locket in her palm. She was still clutching it when he turned away and rode off.

Reed swallowed. Chastity was right. She had said her sister was close by.

But so was Morgan.

Reed stared at Chastity. Should he tell her? So much depended on the next few days.

Reed abruptly realized the full absurdity of that thought. One more omission . . . a few more lies.

Chastity turned toward him and her frown became a smile. The dwindling hours before the full scope of his deceit was revealed to her were suddenly priceless. He could not sacrifice them.

The image of Jenny's lifeless countenance suddenly bright before his mind, Reed felt his throat close. Images haunted Chastity. She needed to put them to rest.

But he had haunting images of his own.

Breaking contact with Chastity's gaze, Reed buckled the harness tight, then checked it, allowing long moments to regain control of the tumult inside him. He turned back to Chastity at last and forced a smile.

"Are you ready to go?"

He approached her, unable to resist sliding his arm around her when he reached her side. She leaned against him, and the knot within him tightened to pain.

Chastity's locket glinted in the rays of the morning sun, mocking his smile as he brushed her lips with his, then lifted her up onto the seat.

The scent of slaughter abounded.

Mounted, quaking with rage, Bartell surveyed the carnage before him. Five steers—no six—lay butchered and bloody. Nearby, several others stood wobbling on their feet, slashed and bleeding profusely. Such had been the scene when he had awakened and ridden out to check on the steers they had assembled for the short drive back to the cabin.

He had ridden back to their camp and awakened Turner. He had pulled him to his feet, furious when he resisted. He had dragged him back to see the result of the nighttime predators' attack, with Turner getting more surly by the moment.

Perspiration trailed from beneath the brim of Bartell's hat despite the brisk, early-morning breeze. He turned toward Turner where he sat his horse beside him. His unshaven face twitching, Bartell shouted, "This is your fault! I wanted to bring them steers back yesterday! Now look what happened!"

"Pull yourself together. It ain't the end of the world! So we lost a few steers! What's Morgan goin' to do about it?"

"It ain't only the steers we lost . . ." Bartell looked back at the bloodied scene, disbelieving he could have slept through the sounds of the savage attack. He took a shaken breath. "We can't be sure how long it's goin' to take us to round up the rest of them steers again. Morgan will be foamin'."

"You make me sick, you know that, Bartell!"

"Yeah . . ." Bartell was seething. Turner was a big talker, but he knew what would happen to all that big talk when he faced Morgan again. He was tired of covering for Turner, and he had been a fool to let himself be talked into a situation that was getting worse by the minute. He stated flatly, "Well, I'm tellin' you somethin' here and now. We're goin' to round up them cows quick, and we're goin' to drive them back to Morgan just as quick, or I'm ridin' back by myself. And if I do, there's no way you'll live to collect your share when Morgan sells off that herd."

"Remember somethin', Bartell! You agreed to

this little game we're playin'. I didn't twist your arm!"

"Get movin', Turner, or I swear—"

"All right!" Turner jerked his reins tight. "Let's go, but don't say another word, damn it! I'm warnin' you, I've had all I can take!"

Turner rode off at a gallop, leaving Bartell in his dust. He sneered at the sound of Bartell riding up behind him. The yellow-bellied coward! All Morgan had to do was blink, and he wet his pants. Well, he'd show him what he was made of. When he got back to the cabin he'd tell Morgan off and set him straight. Then he'd—

Drawing back on his mount's reins at the sight of a dust trail rising from the road, Turner saw a wagon moving steadily toward them. He looked back as Bartell drew up beside him.

"What are you stoppin' for, Turner? Anybody can see them steers ran north."

Turner squinted back at him. "That's a wagon on the trail. What a wagon like that doin' in Injun Territory?"

"I don't know, and I don't care."

"Well, you should! Ain't no settlers allowed in here."

"Who says they're settlers? And if they are, maybe they're passin' through."

"Yeah, we can tell Morgan that. And when he asks us who was in the wagon, we can tell them that maybe they were settlers . . . or maybe they wasn't."

Bartell looked more closely at the wagon as it approached. "What else could they be?"

"If we go down, we'll find out."

"We ain't got time!"

"Maybe you ain't, but I'm goin'."

Turner spurred his horse forward. Taking a page from Morgan's book, he affixed a smile on his lips. It didn't escape his mind that there was no law to speak of in Indian Territory, and that there might be something of value in that wagon. A little extra cash never did nobody no harm. . . .

Turner's smile widened as he neared the wagon.


"There's somebody on the trail ahead."

Chastity attempted to identify the approaching riders. One horse . . . no, two. She looked at Reed, her expression freezing when Reed reached down underneath the seat and withdrew a gun. He slid it out of sight nearby, his explanation terse.

"Just a precaution."

Reed drew the wagon to a halt as the men rode up. Chastity watched as he greeted them cautiously with a forced smile.

"Good morning, gentlemen. We weren't expecting to meet anybody on the trail today."

She saw the heavier of the two men blink when he saw her. Her flesh crawled as he studied her for a long moment, his smile stretching his thick lips to the limit when he responded, "We wasn't expectin' to see nobody, either." He paused, looking back at Reed with open scrutiny. "What are you all doin' out here in Injun Territory?"

Reed's smile grew strained. "We're on our way to the mission to replace Reverend Stiles. They've been waiting a long time for his replacement."

"The Injun mission?" The smaller of the two men responded, his gaze shifting between them. "Yeah, I heard about that." He paused. "Even the Injuns figured the new parson would never come. I guess they was wrong."

The bigger man prodded, "Where are you from? Kansas City?"

"No."

"Came by way of St. Louis, did you?"

Reed paused. "That's right."

"Came along the rail line . . . Sedalia, and then Baxter Springs . . ."

"Seems like you know the route well enough."

"Sedalia's a nice town. Did you stop there long?"

"A few days."

Chastity inched instinctively closer to Reed as the bigger man's perusal of her intensified. She felt Reed's responsive stiffening as he offered, "My name's Reed Farrell." She noted that he avoided introducing her as he said, "I'm pleased to meet you, Mr—?"

"The name's Turner." The bigger man motioned with his chin at the man beside him. His name's Bartell." He added, "You missed the turnoff, you know. The mission's north of here."

"I did?" Reed frowned. "I had no idea." Somehow Reed's words did not ring true as he continued, "I don't suppose you could point us toward the quickest route back."

"It ain't hard. Just keep followin' the trail like you are and turn north when you get to the next fork. Another day or so and you'll be there."

Reed nodded, adding as if in afterthought, "Will you be traveling along with us?"

"No," the man called Bartell responded. "We got some cattle to round up."

Reed appeared surprised. "The Indians don't object to herding on their land?"

The man called Turner replied, "They're real nice neighbors if you know how to handle them. And our boss does."

"Your boss?"

"Yeah." Turner's response was clipped as he turned his mount abruptly. "You just keep right on in the direction you're goin' and you'll ride right onto that fork I told you about."

"Thank you, gentlemen."

"Nice meetin' you, parson . . . ma'am."

The haste with which the two men rode off turned Chastity toward Reed with a frown. She saw the set of Reed's jaw, and a chill coursed down her spine as she said uncertainly, "Those men . . ."

"Don't worry about them. You're safe with me." Reed slapped the reins against the team's back. "We'll be at the mission soon."

The determination in Reed's voice turned Chastity's attention forward.

\* \* \*

Turner drew his horse to an abrupt halt out of sight of the wagon. He grinned when Bartell reined up beside him. "Yeah, nice meetin' you ma'am . . ." He laughed aloud.

Bartell's expression was incredulous. "Do you think it was *her*?"

"Who else could it be?" Turner's grin faded. "How many women do you suppose look like her with all that red hair and that white skin that Walker was talkin' about? And how many of them was church types who came through Sedalia a few days ago?"

"Walker didn't make no mention of her husband."

"Maybe he didn't know. Besides, a husband never made no difference to Morgan when he was after a woman."

"Yeah, but how many of them husbands looked like that Farrell fella?"

"Farrell's a parson! It don't make no difference how big he is! He ain't never goin' to be no match for Morgan."

"I don't know . . . there was somethin' about him. Did you see his eyes? Hell, I ain't never seen a parson with eyes as cold as that fella's."

Turner gave a mocking laugh. "You can tell Morgan all about them eyes of his when we get back, if they bother you that much, 'cause that's where I'm headin' right now."

"What about the cattle?"

"The hell with them sorry steers. Morgan's goin' to be so excited about who's happenin' to pass by that he's goin' to forget all about them.

230

And he'll be real grateful that we didn't let him miss her. You can go after them steers if you want, but I know a good thing when I see it. I'm headin' back."

Digging his heels into his mount's sides, Turner spurred him into a jump forward that left Bartell cursing in his wake.

Something was wrong.

Reed scanned the passing terrain with growing caution. The two riders had ridden out of sight, but not out of mind. He hadn't liked the looks of them. The descriptions of the men in Morgan's gang were so vague that they fit any number of men, those two included. Morgan was the only one he could positively identify from wanted posters, but the hackles on his spine had never failed him.

Bothering him even more was the way they had looked at Chastity. They had asked too many questions and had been too evasive when he questioned them in return.

Reed glanced at Chastity to see that her expression was stiff. Even with her inexperience, she had sensed danger.

Reed silently cursed. He remembered the excuses he had formulated for taking Chastity with him on this chase. A parson and his wife were expected at the mission—so a parson and his wife were what they were going to get. Chastity would provide him the cover to get necessary work done. He had actually talked himself into believing that nonsense, when the truth was that however hard he had fought it, he had been unwilling to let her go.

Reed's stomach clenched. He had lost one woman he loved to Morgan, or a man just like him. He would not lose another. He needed to get Chastity to the mission as soon as possible. She would be safe there.

Reed strained his mind to recall the extended map Jenkins had given him. If he remembered correctly, the fork in the road was no more than a few hours away.

Gripping the reins tighter, Reed slapped them hard against the team's back. His jaw locked tighter as the wagon jumped forward at an increased pace.

"Here they come."

Morgan looked up at Walker's solemn pronouncement. He straightened up slowly, his hand tightening around the branding iron he had just pulled from the fire. He cursed under his breath as he raised his arm to wipe the sweat from his forehead, never taking his eyes from the two horsemen steadily approaching.

"What do you supposed happened? Where's the cattle?"

"I don't know, and I don't care," Morgan replied through gritted teeth. "I told them not to come back without those beeves. I warned them."

Throwing the iron back into the fire, Morgan walked the few steps to the fence and picked up his gunbelt. He strapped it on.

"Somethin' must've gone wrong, Morgan. Hell, they ain't fool enough to come back without them beeves otherwise!"

"Walker's right," Simmons joined in reluctantly. "Turner's a bastard, but he ain't stupid. He knew you meant every word you said when he left."

The two horsemen drew closer, and Morgan adjusted his gun in the holster. He didn't care what excuse they had for coming back empty-handed.

Morgan squared his stance as Turner and Bartell reined up a few yards away. He watched them as they dismounted, the thought crossing his mind that they were too stupid to realize what was coming. Walker and Simmons stepped back warily as he spoke.

"I told you two not to come back without those steers."

"We had some trouble." Bartell was sweating profusely despite the cool breeze. "We got them all rounded up and it was too late to start back. Then, the next mornin' when we went to get them, somethin' had gotten into the herd durin' the night, and them that wasn't driven off was lyin' dead and wounded."

"Good work." Morgan sneered his sarcastic response, taking a slow step backward. "And good work demands good payment."

"Wait a minute, Morgan." Turner interrupted, his gaze darting toward Morgan's hand as it dropped toward his hip. "Don't go jumpin' to conclusions. We wouldn't have come back here without them that was left if we didn't have somethin' to tell you that we knew you'd want to hear right away." His eye on Morgan's twitching hand, he stammered, "Y-you got company passin' by. We rode ahead to tell you, 'cause we knew you'd want to know right away."

Morgan's dark eyes were as cold as death. "Spit it out! What are tryin' to tell me?"

"There's a wagon headin' this way. It's a preacher and his wife. They took the wrong cut-off for the mission."

"I don't give a damn about a preacher and his—"

"His wife's young and real good-lookin'. She got red hair and skin as smooth as milk. They said they spent some time in Sedalia on the way. . . ."

Morgan went still, his heart suddenly pounding so loudly that it echoed in his ears. He stared at Turner. "What did she look like? Was she tall and were her eyes kind of green?"

"We couldn't see how tall she was 'cause she was sittin' down, but I'd say she wasn't the petite type." He frowned. "I don't remember nothin' about her eyes."

"It was her husband's eyes I was lookin' at." Bartell interrupted anxiously, "He was wearin' a parson's collar, and he said all the right things, but I ain't never seen a parson who looked like him, not with them eyes that looked right through you. And I ain't never seen a parson that big, and with all that hard, workin' man's muscle."

Morgan hardly heard him. "Did she say what her name was?"

"She didn't say nothin'. Her husband did all the talkin'."

"What else did he tell you?"

"He said they was comin' to the Injun mission to replace that Reverend Stiles who died a while back. I told them they took the wrong turn-off and to stay on the trail as far as the fork, and then turn north. Then we headed right back here. I knew you'd want to know."

Morgan took an unsteady breath. It had to be her. He stared at Turner for a long time, noting that Turner was sweating. He did well to sweat.

"You just bought your life back. You know that, don't you, Turner?"

Turner did not respond.

"You did the right thing comin' back here like you did, but I want you to listen real close to what I'm tellin' you now, because it's the last time I'm goin' to say it. I'm the boss here. I give the orders. You take them. If you don't, you either get out, or you get carried out. Do you understand?"

Turner gave a jerky nod. Morgan turned toward Bartell.

"You got a choice, too, Bartell. My advice is to think twice the next time you let Turner talk you into tryin' to put somethin' over on me . . . or you might end up regrettin' it."

The taut silence that followed was broken when Morgan added as he turned back toward the cabin, "I'm goin' to get cleaned up and then we'll be ridin' out. Get yourselves ready."

Conchita appeared in the doorway as Morgan approached the cabin. He frowned, realizing he had forgotten she existed.

"Something is wrong, Morgan?"

Morgan reached for the bucket and poured water into the wash basin beside the door. He stripped off his shirt and tossed it aside.

"Get me a clean shirt."

He took off his hat and tossed it on the bench nearby as Conchita turned to his bidding. He lathered his face and upper body liberally, then rinsed away the soap and wiped himself dry. He combed his dark hair carefully, then grabbed the shirt Conchita offered him.

"Where are you going, Morgan?"

Morgan continued buttoning his shirt, his gaze frigid. "What makes you think you've got the right to ask me questions?"

Conchita's lips tightened.

"You haven't got the right . . . just in case you're wonderin'. As a matter of fact, you haven't got any rights at all here."

Conchita raised her chin.

"Make sure you've got somethin' good cookin' when I get back."

Conchita did not reply.

"You heard me, didn't you, Conchita?"

"I heard you, Morgan."

Patting his hair carefully into place, Morgan took a last look in the mottled mirror before reaching for his hat and walking away without another word.

A slowly expanding ache within her, Conchita followed close behind Morgan as he headed back toward the barn and disappeared inside. She waited a distance from the men, listening as they grumbled.

"I'll tell you one thing . . ." Walker addressed Turner softly. ". . . You'd better be right. That had better be the woman he's expectin' it to be, or you're goin' to regret it."

"Morgan don't scare me!" Turner sneered. "Maybe it'll be better if it ain't her. Then everythin' will come to a head once and for all."

"Yeah, and you'll be lyin' on the ground lookin' up at the sky with eyes that don't see nothin' at all!"

"I ain't so sure of that!"

"If it ain't her, it ain't our fault, anyways!" Bartell addressed Walker defensively. "We was only goin' by what you and Simmons said—a real good-lookin' woman with red hair. Maybe it wasn't her in that wagon. If it isn't, Morgan just might like this one better!"

"I wouldn't bet on it. He—"

"Quiet! Here he comes."

Conchita looked at the barn as Morgan emerged, leading his horse. Not bothering to speak, he mounted quickly and headed out. The men fell in behind him.

Conchita watched them until they disappeared from sight. She walked back to the cabin, a solemn litany drumming in her mind.

A dream that was dead.

Tears to be shed.

Blood soon to be flowing.

# *Chapter Nine*

Chastity stretched, then took a few stiff steps toward the wagon where Reed was tending to the horses. Reed had pulled the wagon to a halt a few minutes earlier—their first stop since meeting the two men on the trail that morning. Grateful to be on her feet for a little while, she glanced up at the sky. She realized with a moment's wry amusement that she had assumed Reed's habit of checking the position of the sun to determine the time of day. She had become completely comfortable with a custom that would have seemed somehow backward to her only a few weeks earlier when doubts still prevailed about the wisdom of leaving the "civilized" East behind her.

But she was a different person now, both in-

Elaine Barbieri

side and out. The pale, drably dressed, severely coiffed, bespectacled young woman who had boarded the train for Caldwell, Kansas, those weeks ago no longer existed. The sharp edges of discipline and propriety had softened, allowing a new side of her to emerge.

Chastity considered that thought. No, the side of her that had emerged was not new. It had been lying beneath the surface, smothered by years of latent memories from which the fear had finally been dismissed. Only hope remained. Reed had done that for her. The strength of his presence beside her and the emotions he had raised within her had opened her heart and mind.

Her thoughts sober, Chastity looked up again at the sky. It was nearing noon. Reed had pushed the wagon to a faster pace after their meeting with the two men on the trail earlier that morning. She was uncomfortable with the tension she sensed in him. She knew he didn't trust those men to be what they claimed. Somehow, neither did she. There was something about the way they looked at her that had sent chills down her spine. She had the feeling that Reed would be making as few stops as possible until they reached the mission. The thought stirred conflicting emotions.

Turning instinctively at a sound behind her, Chastity gasped at the sight of an Indian partially concealed in the bushes a short distance away. Startled into speechlessness, she was unable to move under the intense scrutiny of his

dark eyes. Her heart thundering, she swallowed
past the lump of fear in her throat, then turned
toward the wagon.

"Reed!"

Reed looked up. At her side in a moment, he
slipped his arm around her.

"What's wrong, Chastity?"

"That Indian—"

Chastity looked back at the bushes where the
Indian had stood. Her eyes widened. "He's
gone!"

"You saw an Indian here?"

"Yes." Chastity realized belatedly that she was
trembling. "There in the bushes. He didn't say
anything. He just stared at me."

Chastity stood rigidly immobile as Reed
searched the bushes. He returned to her side,
frowning. "He's gone. There's no use trying to
follow him. Don't worry about it. There hasn't
been any trouble with the tribes here for a
while."

Chastity nodded, struggling to subdue her
trembling. "Of course."

"I think we'd better get moving, anyway. The
sooner we get to the mission, the better." Pausing, Reed looked wordlessly down at her. She
saw regret, concern, and an emotion she could
not quite identify in his eyes as he whispered,
"I'm sorry, Chastity. I never should have
brought you here."

"Don't say that, please, Reed."

"Chastity, if I could—"

Reed bit off his words abruptly, his expression hardening as he stepped back from her. "We'd better get going."

Responding to the sense of urgency in his tone, Chastity glanced apprehensively around her, then complied without a word.

*Chastity, if I could—*
The unfinished sentence dangled in Reed's mind.

*If I could go back to the beginning so we could start all over. If I could erase the image of Jenny's face from my mind. If I could be sure I wouldn't lose you. . . .*

They were back on the trail, the horses maintaining a steady pace. Chastity was seated close beside him, the warmth of her leg against his compensating for the dull ache of the wound in his thigh that had not yet completely healed. Even that had been a lie. He had not made the mistake of attempting to stop a gunfight. He had *instigated* that gunfight with three simple words: "I'm taking you in."

But he had been careless. He had entered Mc-Coy's cabin believing McCoy's partner had gone to town. That mistake had almost cost him his life.

He survived, but McCoy did not. He managed to get McCoy's partner to jail before collapsing, and when he was able, he collected the reward, ignoring the marshall's obvious contempt as he counted out the sum.

Would he see that same contempt in Chastity's eyes when she learned the truth about him? He would find out soon enough. The events of the morning had made it clear that he needed to get her to the safety of the mission as soon as possible. The hackles that had crept up his spine when Bartell and Turner approached was an instinct he had learned not to ignore. The Indian who had appeared and disappeared so quickly was another complication.

Reed looked at Chastity. She turned toward him, her brow knit in a frown. He slid his arm around her and touched his lips lightly to hers.

He loved her. He had avoided acknowledging that truth to himself for countless reasons that now seemed unimportant. He needed to say the words. He needed to let Chastity know that he—

Reed's head jerked up abruptly as riders appeared over the rise in the distance.

Indians?

No. Reed stiffened. His arm dropped from Chastity's shoulders. He almost wished they were.

Reaching underneath his seat, Reed adjusted the position of the revolver hidden there. He felt the smooth stock of the rifle he had secreted beside it. He hoped he wouldn't need to use them.

His attention acute, he watched the riders approach. There were five of them. The number was right. He strained to make out the features of the lead rider. He was of slight to medium build. That was right, too. He recognized the two riding beside him as the men he had spoken to earlier. He drew the wagon to a halt and waited for them to rein up.

One good look at the leader was all he needed. Morgan, the murdering bastard . . .

"Mr. Jefferson! How nice to see you again!"

Reed's head jerked toward Chastity at her unexpected greeting. Stunned, he saw true warmth in her eyes as she smiled at Morgan.

Morgan returned her smile and tipped his hat. "Nice to see you, too, Chastity. You're the last person I expected to see out here, but it sure is a fine surprise. Bartell mentioned that he had run into your wagon this mornin' and I had to ride by to see if there could possibly be *two* beautiful red-haired women in these parts."

Reed stiffened at Chastity's flush of pleasure. He didn't like the way Morgan looked at Chastity. And he didn't like the shifting glances of his men. He had the feeling that they were as uncertain as he was what Morgan was going to do next.

"This is Mr. Will Jefferson, Reed." Chastity turned toward Reed. "The incident in the store with Mr. Dobbs while you were ill . . ." She hesitated, obviously embarrassed as she continued, "Mr. Jefferson was there when it happened. He was very helpful."

Reed forced a smile. "I'm glad to be able to thank you for helping Chastity, Mr. Jefferson. My name is Reed Farrell. Chastity and I are on our way to the mission. Your men told me that I missed the turn."

"You sure did. But it looks like your loss is

my gain. I probably would've missed the pleasure of seein' your beautiful wife again if you
hadn't."

His wife. Chastity glanced at him. He knew
what she was thinking. Deception went against
her grain, and she was about to correct Morgan's mistaken impression. He averted her reply, responding, "I didn't realize that the
government had opened this land to grazing."

"They didn't . . . officially. The Indians and I
have an understanding."

Reed nodded, maintaining a pleasant facade
with pure strength of will. "Your place is near
here?"

"It is. It isn't much, but it works out real fine."

Yeah, he bet it did.

Morgan's earnest smile was a true master-
piece as he added, "It would be my pleasure if
you'd stop off and spend the night. My cook isn't
much, but she puts a satisfyin' meal on the table, and there's always more than enough."

"That's kind of you." The words stuck in
Reed's throat. "But Chastity and I are anxious
to get to the mission."

"That's real disappointin'." Morgan turned to
Chastity. The blood boiled in Reed's veins as
Morgan appealed to her directly. "I'd appreciate
it if you'd use your influence to get your husband to change his mind, Chastity. It isn't often
the fellas and I get a chance for enjoyable company out here."

Chastity turned hesitantly toward Reed.

"I'm sorry," Reed said, adding firmly, "I can't

in good conscience delay reaching the mission another day. I hope you understand."

Morgan's smile faltered, and Reed reached down to rub his calf, his hand hovering near the gun. His hatred was so intense that he almost wished Morgan would draw.

"All right. I guess there's no changin' your mind," Morgan continued with another of his ingratiating smiles, "I'm hopin' you won't object to my visitin' the mission after you get yourself settled."

"Of course not." Reed slowly straightened up. "Everyone is welcome at the mission. No one is turned away."

"I appreciate that, Reverend."

Nauseated by the mutual hypocrisy expressed, Reed knew he could not take much more. "Sorry to cut this visit short, but we have to be on our way."

"I'm sorry, too, Mr. Jefferson." Chastity's voice held a true note of regret. "I hope we have a chance to meet again."

"You can count on it, ma'am."

Morgan tipped his hat, and Reed slapped the reins sharply against the team's back, startling the horses into a jump forward.

Chastity's rigid posture was revealing as they rode away. Reed knew the silence between them would not last long.

His smile dismissed, Morgan watched the wagon continue down the road. His men exchanged glances as Morgan maintained a tense silence.

Walker ventured, "That was a waste of time."

Turning sharply toward him, Morgan spat, "You think so? I think it worked out real fine."

Walker's wiry mustache twitched. "Maybe you saw somethin' that I didn't, but I think that parson made it pretty clear he didn't like the way you was lookin' at his woman."

"I wasn't payin' much attention to him. I was lookin' at his wife . . . and she was lookin' at me. She made it pretty plain that she was glad to see me."

Walker shrugged. "I'd say that's right."

"She's better lookin' than I remembered. There's somethin' about her." Morgan's chest began a slow heaving. "I'm thinkin' all the fire in that woman ain't just in the color of her hair. She wanted to get to know me better . . . and I'm goin' to give her the chance."

"Not if that parson has any say about it, you ain't."

"He won't."

The wary silence that followed Morgan's response was broken by Walker's cautious question. "You ain't thinkin' what I think you're thinkin' . . ."

"This is wild country—Injun country." Morgan raised his dark brows. "Accidents happen."

Walker looked at the men beside him. They were watching Morgan incredulously, their thoughts obviously running in the same vein as his as Walker responded, "You can't be serious!

We got a good thing goin' here. Killin' off that parson will start all kinds of trouble. There'll be marshals ridin' all over Injun Territory!"

Morgan shook his head. "I don't think so."

Walker's shoulder twitched. "What about Conchita? She ain't goin' to take this lightly."

"She doesn't have anythin' to say about it."

"That one's smarter than you give her credit for. You're goin' to have to watch out for her!"

Morgan's expression grew suddenly vicious. "There isn't any problem that I can't handle, and that includes gettin rid of a Mexican whore who can find a new home at the nearest *cantina!*"

"You really are a cold bastard."

"Maybe . . ." His gaze drifting back toward the trail where the wagon had disappeared from sight, Morgan repeated, "Maybe, but I got a feelin' that Chastity can warm me up."

"I got a bad feelin' about all this," Simmons said, speaking up at last. "I don't want no part of it."

Morgan's expression grew rabid. "Who asked you?"

"I'm goin' back to the cabin."

"No, you're not. We're goin' to find those steers first and take care of business." He turned toward Turner. "And Turner's goin' to lead the way."

Turner's jowled jaw drew tight. "Them steers run off durin' the night, like I told you. They could be scattered all over creation."

"You know where they are!" Morgan's gaze grew deadly. "You were just too lazy to round them up again and drive them back. Well, you aren't gettin' out of it this time, 'cause we're gettin' those steers now, and we're not goin' back without them. So, lead the way!"

Cursing under his breath, Turner wheeled his horse sharply, then kicked it into a burst forward.

Following behind, Morgan stared at Turner's back. His thoughts returned to the woman presently traveling in the opposite direction, and he grunted low under his breath. She had slipped away from him again, but only temporarily.

Morgan consoled himself. It would only be a little longer.

Chastity's question emerged through stiff lips. "You didn't like him, did you?"

The wagon moved along the trail at a clipped pace. It had been hours since they left Morgan behind them. The conversation between them had been stilted.

Reed did not immediately respond. How could he explain to her the true danger of the situation—a danger intensified by a complication of which she appeared unaware. Morgan *wanted* Chastity. He had seen the desire concealed behind that courteous facade. It had wrenched at his gut, flushing him with a rage he had barely controlled. That rage had not yet faded.

"Reed?"

Daylight was fading. The extravagant colors of sunset lit the delicate contours of Chastity's face as Reed turned toward her. He knew he would never see a sight more beautiful than the one he was presently beholding.

"Reed . . ."

Reed struggled to conceal his emotions. "Didn't like who?"

"You know very well who I mean."

Reed chose to remain silent.

"You were rude to him."

"Was I?"

"You know you were."

"We didn't have time for a detour that might add another day to our trip."

"You were rude."

"If you say so."

"Why? He helped me, Reed! He made sure that Mr. Dobbs knew he would stand behind me. I don't really know what would've happened if he hadn't been there."

"You're too gullible, Chastity."

"What's that supposed to mean?"

Suddenly unable to conceal his anger any longer, Reed snapped, "It means you don't see the obvious when it's hidden behind a smile."

Chastity stiffened. "Are you saying that Mr. Jefferson isn't sincere?"

Clutching the reins in a tight fist, Reed turned to face Chastity squarely, "Yes, that's part of it."

"What are you trying to tell me?"

"He *wants* you, Chastity!"

Chastity gasped. Her face flamed. "You're wrong! He was never anything but courteous and polite. You spoke to him! He's a gentle-men."

Reed bit back the response that rose to his lips.

Chastity's expression softened unexpectedly. "I suppose I should be flattered that you think I'm so desirable." Chastity's warm color darkened. "You're prejudiced, Reed, because of everything that's happened between us, but you see me in a different light than most men. Mr. Jefferson was just being friendly."

Frustrated, Reed replied, "You're going to have to trust my judgment about this, Chastity. I've seen this kind of thing a thousand times. I *know* what I saw in his eyes."

"You're wrong."

"No, I'm not."

"I don't want to argue with you, Reed. But neither do I want you to be rude to Mr. Jefferson because of me. Promise me you won't act that way again."

"I won't promise."

"Why are you so stubborn?"

Reed's jaw locked tight.

"You're not going to answer me, are you?"

Chastity took an angry breath when he did not respond. "When are we going to stop for the night?"

"We're not."

Chastity looked at him. Her lips parted with confusion. "What do you mean?"

"I'm telling you that we're going to drive on through the night."

Elaine Barbieri

"It's getting dark. We won't be able to see!"

"It's a clear night and there's a full moon. If necessary, I'll walk ahead with the lantern and you can drive the team."

"This is insane!"

"It's necessary."

"Necessary . . . because of Mr. Jefferson? Is that what you're trying to say?"

"It's necessary because the situation has changed. It isn't safe here any longer."

"Because of Mr. Jefferson . . . or because of that Indian?" Chastity's flushed cheeks suddenly paled. "Is that it . . . you're afraid the Indians will attack?"

"No."

"Then what is it?"

Reed did not respond.

"It *is* because of Mr. Jefferson!" Chastity shook her head. "What's the matter with you, Reed? He's just a cowman like any other. He's trying to make a living raising cattle, just like any other cowman."

"No, he isn't."

"What do you mean, he isn't?" Chastity grasped Reed's arm, forcing him to draw back on the reins as she shook it roughly. "Tell me!"

"All right!" Angry frustration pounding through his veins, Reed rasped, "You have to find out sooner or later. His name isn't Jefferson. It's Morgan—Will Morgan. He isn't a cowman trying to make a living raising cattle. He's a rustler—a criminal—a man who makes his

252

living *stealing* cattle, not raising them, Chastity."

"How do you know all this?" Chastity struggled to catch her breath. "He doesn't know you."

"I've seen the wanted posters."

"Wanted posters."

"He's wanted in Texas for cattle rustling . . . and murder."

"Murder!" Chastity closed her eyes. She snapped them open again a moment later, shuddering visibly. "No, I don't believe it. You made a mistake. You're as new to this territory as I am. This Morgan person you're referring to is someone else who just happens to look like Mr. Jefferson."

"Listen to me, Chastity!" Reed gripped her shoulders, forcing her to meet his eyes. "It's not a mistake. He's Morgan, all right. I know because I've been on his trail for over a year."

"On his trail?" Chastity's eyes widened, her bewilderment apparent. A new light gradually dawning in her gaze, she replied slowly, "Mr. Jefferson's name isn't Jefferson. It's Morgan." She raised her chin, her voice rising as well. "Does that mean your name isn't Reed Farrell, either? Who are you, Reed?"

"Chastity, please . . ."

"You aren't a minister are you, Reed?"

Reed stared intently at her. "No, I'm not."

"Who are you? *What* are you?"

Reed felt the hysteria rapidly building within Chastity. He whispered, "Don't be afraid of me,

Elaine Barbieri

Chastity, please. My name is Reed Farrell, just as I told you."

"Are you a lawman? Is that it?"

"No."

"What are you, then?"

Reed gripped her shoulders tighter. "I'm a bounty hunter."

Reed felt the shock that rippled through her. He attempted to draw her close, but she fought against him, her voice rising as she ordered, "Take your hands off me! Let me go!"

Reed released her, then whispered, "We don't have time for this, Chastity. Whatever you think of me, we have to go on. We have to get out of here. It isn't safe!"

Chastity drew back, her stiff shoulders quaking. "I should have known. The bullet wound in your leg . . . you didn't get it trying to stop a gunfight, did you?"

"No."

"You were shot. Did the other man survive?"

"No."

"Oh, God . . ."

Reed reached for her.

"No!" She paused her breathing heavy. "That man—Mr. Jenkins—he wasn't a Federal Indian Agent, was he?"

"No. He brought me a map to Morgan's hideout. It's only a short distance away."

"That's why you came here."

"Yes."

"Everything you told me about yourself is a lie. You aren't expected at the mission. You

254

aren't a preacher. You don't care about the Indian children or the teacher they need so badly." Chastity gave a short, hysterical laugh. "You made it all up!"

Reed did not respond.

"Didn't you!"

"Yes."

"Why?"

"A preacher and his wife were expected at the mission."

Chastity blinked. "So you decided to give them what they expected. I was convenient and I was gullible. I believed everything you said." Chastity raised a trembling hand to her forehead.

Reed glanced around them. Night was rapidly falling.

"We don't have time for this now, Chastity. We have to get out of here. We have to get to the mission as soon as possible. You'll be safe there."

"You didn't care if I was safe before."

"I did, but the situation has changed. I didn't know you had met Morgan. I didn't expect him to come looking for you. I didn't know he—"

"He *wanted* me?" Chastity took a shuddering breath. "Who are you, Reed? Are you telling me the truth now? I don't know what's true or what's false anymore. Were you acting when you took me into your arms?"

"No."

"Were you laughing at me all the while?"

"No!"

255

Reed reached for her, but Chastity drew back. "Don't touch me!"

Unable to bear the pain in her eyes, Reed reached for her again. He was unprepared when she drew back and swung her fist with all her might.

Momentarily dazed, Reed saw the look of true horror that crossed Chastity's face the second before she turned and jumped to the ground. A long moment passed before he jumped to the ground behind her and saw her disappear into the shadows.

"Chastity! Don't run away from me, please!"

Reed's voice sounded in the darkness behind her. She heard the sound of his heavy footsteps pounding increasingly closer as she dashed through the shadows, stumbling her way through the densely foliated section of trail.

It was getting darker. Darkness wasn't her enemy, but she couldn't be sure what was. There was no truth. All were lies. Reed had told her he needed her, and that was a lie. Every whispered word, every endearment, every look, every touch . . . lies, all of them!

Chastity ran faster. Her breath came in short, hard rasps. She heard a sob and was startled to realize that it was her own. No, she would not cry! She was a fool . . . she was gullible, but she wasn't weak! She didn't need Reed! She didn't need anyone! She'd get back to civilization by herself and then she'd go on as she had originally intended. She would forget that this whole nightmare ever happened!

The heavy footsteps behind her were drawing closer! Chastity turned to look behind her.

She didn't see the sudden downward slope of ground in front of her until it was too late, and she fell, tumbling head over heels into the darkness below.

Reed paused in pursuit, his chest heaving, the wound in his thigh throbbing. He listened. Chastity's thrashing footsteps ahead of him had ceased. He strained to penetrate the shadows with his gaze, but he could not. Anxiety burgeoning within, him he called out, "Chastity, where are you?"

Silence.

"Answer me, Chastity. Don't be afraid . . . please."

The silence prevailed.

Something was wrong. She wasn't hiding. She wouldn't do that. Something had happened.

Abruptly aware that he had left the wagon without his gun, Reed cursed softly under his breath, then continued slowly forward.

"Answer me, Chastity!"

The ground sloped downward unexpectedly. Realization pounded through him as he called out, "Chastity, are you all right?"

He started down the slope. Stumbling and sliding, his throat tight, he called out again when he reached the bottom.

He heard a whimper and froze. He heard it again, and then he saw Chastity lying a few yards away. She struggled to sit up when he reached her.

Her face was shadowed. He couldn't see her clearly.

"Are you all right, Chastity?" His hand trembling, he stroked back a strand of hair from her face.

"Is it you, Reed?" He heard the crack in her voice as she repeated hoarsely, "Is it *really* you?"

She was in his arms, then. He was kissing her wildly, lovingly. He was telling her in all the ways that words could not express that he loved her . . . that he would always be there when she needed him . . . that he had discovered that nothing in the world meant more to him than holding her in his arms and that he would never let her go.

But Chastity was not responding. He drew back. "Are you all right, Chastity?"

"My head hurts."

Fear struck, roughening his voice. "Can you stand up?"

He helped her to her feet. She wavered, and he scooped her up into his arms.

"You can't carry me, Reed."

"Yes, I can."

Chastity's head was bobbing against his chest when he reached the wagon at last. He carried her to the back and put her inside. He climbed in behind her and lit the lamp there. He picked up the canteen and dampened a cloth, then

258

sponged the dirt from her face. Her cheek was bruised and her forehead was scratched, but she had never looked more beautiful to him than she did at that moment.

Cupping her cheek with his hand, he whispered, "I love you, Chastity."

Chastity's moist eyes held his. Her voice was ragged. "Truth . . . or lies?"

Ripping the parson's collar from his neck, Reed tossed it aside. "You can believe me now, Chastity. And you can believe that I never lied to you when I held you in my arms."

Chastity did not reply. Instead, she struggled to sit up.

"What are you doing?"

"You said we have to keep going. You said it wasn't safe here."

"I know." Reed attempted a smile. "But not yet. I want to hold you just a little longer."

Chastity relaxed slowly against him, and Reed held her close as her shuddering gradually lessened.

The lamplight flickered as he whispered again, "I love you, Chastity." The words fell from his lips as naturally as rain. "I love you."

Dawn stretched lacy fingers across the night sky as Morgan awakened. He glanced around the bedroom, disoriented. He frowned at the chaos of discarded clothing, miscellaneous saddle gear, and Conchita's spare belongings, all crammed into the limited space. The thought struck him that he needed to make sure that

Conchita cleaned up the place and removed all trace of her presence there. Chastity was a lady. She would not suffer the thought that a tramp like Conchita had preceded her.

Morgan sat up slowly. Things had gone poorly after they left the wagon. Turner led them to the scene of the steers' slaughter. They trailed the remaining steers, found them a short distance away, and drove them back to the cabin. The men protested when he demanded that they start the branding immediately. They worked until dark.

Conchita was unnaturally silent when they returned to the cabin. She had made no attempt to follow him into his room when he retired for the night, and he realized then that part of what Walker had said was true. Conchita *was* smarter than he thought she was. She saw it was over between them, and she realized the futility of protest. In their way, both Walker and he had been right about her. She was smart, and she was a whore. She knew her place, and she knew when to move on. As for her cooking . . . Morgan paused at that thought, recalling Chastity's smooth, white hands. He doubted he'd get much work out of her, but there was much to be said for smooth hands and the wonders they could work.

Morgan stood up abruptly. The outer room was silent. It was early. Conchita was not yet working at the fireplace. The men wouldn't like to start work without breakfast, but they'd do it. They'd do it because they knew better than to buck him, most especially when he had *plans*.

Morgan smiled his boyish smile. And his plans were something very special. He would get those steers branded and sold as soon as possible, he would pay off the men, and then he would take Chastity with him for the time of their lives. They'd go wherever she wanted. He suspected that her parson husband hadn't given her much of a taste of the good life, but he would. He would spoil her and he would please her until she could resist him no longer.

She was a lady, all right. It might take him some time to bring her around, but he knew instinctively she would be worth the trouble. He could almost taste those warm lips now. He could almost feel that smooth skin pressed against his. He could almost hear her voice gasp his name as he plunged deep inside her.

Oh, yes, she'd be worth the trouble . . . but he'd be damned if he'd wait a minute longer than necessary to have her.

Morgan snatched up his clothes and dressed quickly, the heat of his thoughts propelling him. He stepped into the outer room, where the men lay asleep in their bedrolls. He announced loudly, "It's time to get up! We're startin' out early this mornin'. That buyer in Sedalia isn't goin' to wait forever, and there's a lot of work to be done."

The men grumbled awake as Morgan walked to the fireplace to find a pot of coffee waiting. He looked at Conchita, pleased as she drew biscuits from the fire. The whore knew her place,

Elaine Barbieri

all right. He might miss her, after all.

Morgan drank his coffee as the men stirred to life behind him.

Reed stirred. His arm tightened spontaneously around the woman lying curled against him. He breathed in the scent of her hair. He caressed her softness.

He awakened with a start!

Reed stared at the sunlight peeking through the flaps of the wagon, incredulous that he had actually allowed himself to sleep through the night. He looked down at Chastity lying beside him, then cursed softly under his breath. The bruise on her cheek had darkened, and a lump was visible on her forehead. Her blouse and skirt were stained by her fall, and particles of leaves still clung to her fiery curls. He remembered his fear when she disappeared in the darkness, and the relief that had surged through him when he found her again. He had taken her into his arms when they returned to the wagon, waiting for her trembling to cease. He had been loath to release her.

Chastity's eyelids fluttered, and Reed held his breath. Her eyes opened. They were clear, free of confusion. She attempted to move, then groaned, her hand snapping up to her forehead.

"What's the matter, Chastity?"

"My head hurts."

Reed frowned. It was his fault that she was hurt. He had been angry and jealous of Chastity's defense of Morgan. He had blurted out the

262

truth and frightened her into running away from him.

"I'm sorry, Chastity." He attempted a smile. "You have a lump on your head. You'll probably have that headache for a while."

Chastity looked at the sunlight seeping through the wagon flaps. "It's morning."

"Yes."

"You said you wanted to travel through the night."

"I know."

She took a shaky breath. "We'd better get started."

"No, not yet. There's something I have to say first."

Reed paused, suddenly uncertain. He had said it all the previous night, but shadows of doubt remained in her eyes. He needed to erase that doubt.

The pounding of his heart and the emotion that choked his throat made words difficult as he began.

"I didn't start out to deceive you, Chastity. But I did, and now you aren't sure you can trust me. I suppose I deserve that. But I give you my word that I won't lie to you again—no matter how hard the truth may be. Part of that truth is that we still have to get to the mission as soon as possible."

"Is it much farther?"

"No. I don't think so. We should be there by nightfall."

"What are you going to do then?"

263

"I'm going to make sure you're safe, and then I'm going back for Morgan."

"You can't!" Chastity winced as she raised her head. "There are too many of them!"

"Chastity, listen to me." The words he was about to speak were harder than any he had ever uttered. "I can't change the past, and I can't change the reason I came here," Reed whispered. "If I could, I would. The only thing I wouldn't change is loving you."

"Reed . . ."

Reed drew himself up to crouch beside her. He pulled up the coverlet and adjusted it across her breast. "It's early and your head hurts. Rest a little longer." The words came simply, from the heart. "I love you, Chastity."

Brilliant shards of green glistened with sudden moisture as Chastity's gaze held his. Her voice was tremulous. "I don't want anything to happen to you, Reed."

"Go back to sleep, Chastity. You'll feel better when you wake up. I'll be here."

Reed pressed his mouth lightly to hers. Her lips were soft and warm, but he forced himself to draw back. Standing outside the wagon moments later, Reed looked up at the clear morning sky. Chastity had not said she loved him. She had said she didn't want anything to happen to him. He wished he had been able to give her that reassurance. He wished he was able to tell her that everything would turn out all right when he went after Morgan.

But he had promised her the truth.

And the truth was hard.

Damn, it was hot!

Morgan looked up at the clear blue of the sky, cursing. He looked down at the branding irons in the fire, then at the steers yet to be branded in the far corral. They had been at work since dawn. The men were grumbling, and he knew that if he hadn't been driving them every step of the way, they would have stopped working hours earlier.

Morgan's stomach grumbled loudly. It was almost noon, and he was hungry. The smell of Conchita's cooking had been teasing the men for the past hour, but food was far from his thoughts despite the sounds his stomach was making.

He was tired of this! Things were going too slowly. He wasn't accustomed to waiting. The schedule he had set for himself had soured more in his mind with every passing hour.

Morgan's hand squeezed tightly around the branding iron as the memory of Chastity's smile returned. The heat of it had lit a fire in his belly that was consuming him. Why had he felt the need to wait until they reached the mission before making his move? An incident on the trail was easy enough to arrange if he was cautious. He would appear unexpectedly to help her after the light-eyed bastard breathed his last. He knew all the right things to say. Chastity would lean on him then. He could bring her back to the cabin to recuperate from her grief, and her dependence on him would deepen.

And he would console her. Morgan's body tightened in response to thoughts of that consolation.

His mind suddenly set, he threw the iron back into the fire. Responding to the men's inquiring looks, he said, "That's it for the day. Just make sure you put the rest of those steers back in the corral before you eat."

Ignoring the men's surprised looks, Morgan turned back toward the house. He was pouring water into the washbasin when Conchita appeared in the doorway.

"You come in to eat now, Morgan?"

"No, I'm not hungry." He did not bother to look up.

Conchita watched as he tossed his hat and shirt aside, then soaped his torso, face, and arms fastidiously.

"You are going somewhere?"

"That's none of your damned business!"

He saw her lips tighten, and he scowled as he dried himself and slipped back into his shirt.

"I'll be back in a couple of hours. I want my room cleaned up before I do. And I want your things out of it. Do you understand?"

Conchita remained silent.

"*Comprendes, puta?*"

Conchita's expression turned to stone. "*Sí. Comprendo . . . comprendo muy bien.*"

Snatching up his hat, Morgan headed for the

barn. Mounted a few minutes later, he galloped past the men without a word.

Simmons turned to follow Morgan's hasty departure with a surprised glance. "What do you suppose got into him?"

Bartell gave a short bark of laughter.

Slamming the corral gate behind the last of the steers, Turner joined the others as they started back toward the cabin. He growled, "You ain't that stupid, are you, Simmons?"

"No, I ain't stupid. And Morgan ain't, neither, if you're saying he's headin' back down the trail. There's no way he'd make a move on that preacher's wife now—especially in broad daylight!"

"What's to stop him?"

"Common sense, that's what!" Simmons shook his head. "I've seen Morgan hot for a woman before, but he ain't never lost his head."

"It's time you wised up, Simmons." Turner would not back down. "Morgan's not thinkin' with his head no more. He ain't goin' to be satisfied until he's got that woman underneath him, and I got the feelin' it ain't goin' to be long before he does."

Turner pushed open the cabin door. Ignoring Conchita as she placed food on the table, he pulled out a chair and sat down hard. He waited only long enough for the others to be seated before he continued, "Morgan ain't thinkin' straight anymore. It's time we start doin' some thinkin' for ourselves if we want to get out of this territory alive."

"You're all gurgle and no guts, Turner!" Walker interjected heatedly. "When Morgan gets back, you'll back down just like you always do."

"Not this time! Not if I know I've got you all behind me."

"Why should we get behind you?" Walker sneered. "You ain't never done nothin' to make us think you got half the brain Morgan does."

"I ain't half as crazy as he is, neither."

"He ain't crazy."

"He ain't? Are you waitin' to see him bring the whole territory down around us before you admit it? Killin' a parson and takin' his wife when we're supposed to be hidin' out here and keepin' ourselves clear of the law—if that ain't the talk of a crazy man, nothin' is!"

"He ain't crazy. And I ain't goin' against him."

"That's 'cause you're yellow, Walker." Turner turned toward the others. "Are you goin' to listen to a yellow-belly like Walker so's you all end up catchin' a marshal's bullet?"

"Morgan will be all right once he settles down again. He's smart. He ain't goin' to get himself killed over a woman. Besides, we'll be done brandin' them beeves in a few days and then we'll be out of here."

"That's if we live to drive them out of the territory. He's crazy, I'm tellin' you! He—"

Turner halted in mid-sentence when he spied the pile of clothing folded neatly in the corner.

He addressed the woman standing silently nearby.

"What happened, Conchita? Did Morgan tell you to get your things out of his room? Maybe he told you to clean it up, too, because he was bringin' company back with him?"

Conchita's smooth face went rigid, and Turner laughed aloud. "He did, didn't he! I don't believe it! I hit the nail right on the head!"

Conchita snatched up her belongings and walked stiffly toward the door. Turner laughed again when she slammed it shut behind her. His laughter fading, he shot a victorious look around the table. "So, anybody else want to tell me that I'm not makin' sense?"

"Morgan was sick of the whore, that's all. He wanted her out. That don't mean he's plannin' on bringin' that parson's wife back with him."

"Want to bet your share of the take that he ain't?"

Walker did not reply.

"That's what I thought." Turner reached for a tortilla and filled it liberally from the plate in front of him. "I'm done talkin' for now. Morgan will do the rest of my talkin' for me—when he brings that parson's wife back with him to-night."

"You're crazy!"

"All right, I'll make you a deal." Turner leaned forward, his heavy jowls sagging as he stared directly into Walker's eyes. "If I'm wrong, I'll shut up and stay shut up. But if I'm right and Morgan brings that woman back with him, I

want you all to agree that we'll start makin'
some plans of our own."

"And who's supposed to be the one to give the
orders? You?"

"What are you afraid of, Walker?"

"I ain't afraid of nothin'!"

"You're sayin' Morgan ain't stupid enough to
kill that parson and bring the whole territory
down on us—ain't that right?"

"Right!"

"If you're so sure of that, you ain't got nothin'
to lose. If he brings that woman here, we start
makin' plans of our own. If he don't, you ain't
goin' to hear nothin' more about it from me."

Walker did not reply. Turner scanned the
faces of the men around him. "What do you say,
boys? Are you goin' to wait for Morgan to get
us all killed?"

Simmons spoke up hesitantly. "Everythin'
goes on as usual if Morgan don't bring her
home?"

"Right."

"And we don't do nothin' unless we all agree."

"Right."

The silence stretched taut as Turner looked at
each man in turn. Satisfied when each nodded
his agreement, Turner smiled.

"Let's eat."

Turner folded the tortilla and shoved it into
his mouth. He chewed enthusiastically, ignoring the silence around him as he reached for
another before swallowing his last bite.

"Damn, that was good! I just might keep that

Conchita on here. She's a good cook."

"Don't go countin' your chickens, Turner."

Turner smiled. "I'd watch what I say, if I was you, Walker. You're goin' to be takin' orders from me soon."

Grumbles sounding all around were Turner's only response as Conchita walked back into the cabin. Invisible in their eyes as she always was, she picked up the coffee pot and refilled the cups as the meal continued.

The wagon rocked steadily underneath her as Chastity came slowly awake. She stared at the bright sunlight slanting through the rear flaps of the wagon. Momentarily disoriented, she heard the fevered moans of her sisters as they lay beside her. She heard her father speaking, his voice deep with concern. Her heart jumping to a wild pounding, she raised a hand to her forehead in confusion. The voices faded when she touched the lump there.

Chastity's mind cleared. That danger was in the past. She was in Indian Territory now. Reed was not really Reed. He was a bounty hunter. Mr. Jefferson was not really Mr. Jefferson. He was a rustler and a killer. They were not going to the mission to help the Indian children. They were headed toward disaster.

Chastity raised herself slowly to a seated position. The dizziness with which she had awakened earlier had disappeared, and the pounding in her head had faded to a dull ache. But her cheek was sore and her clothes were dirty.

Holding herself stiffly erect, she remembered something else, too. Reed had carried her back to the wagon after her fall. He had bathed her face and tended to her, his light eyes filled with concern. He had held her protectively close through the night.

And he had said he loved her.

The sound of Reed's throbbing voice returned, and Chastity closed her eyes against the pain the words evoked. Did she believe him? Were the words enough? She remembered that the incredible blue of his eyes had stared directly into hers as he declared in the next breath that he was going to leave her at the mission to go back after Morgan.

The thought suddenly more than she could bear, Chastity struck it from her mind. The present offered pressing dangers. She needed to ready herself so Reed would not face them alone.

Stripping off her stained clothing, Chastity reached for her case nearby. She withdrew her blue dress, gasping when she saw her image reflected in the mirror in the case. The right side of her cheek was bruised and swollen. The lump on her forehead was an ugly protrusion that was beginning to darken as well. Her eyes were darkly shadowed and her hair was filled with the residue of her fall. Her thoughts of the previous day returned. Truly, she was no longer the same woman who had boarded the train west several weeks earlier.

The true irony of the situation was never

clearer. Reed was not really Reed. Chastity was not really Chastity. They had met, and the metamorphosis had been complete. There was no going back to what they once were—for either of them.

Chastity picked up her dress and slipped it over her head. Biting back emotion, she brushed the debris from her hair, then worked her way determinedly toward the front of the wagon.

Pausing, Chastity took a stabilizing breath, then parted the flaps. Reed turned toward her. His brown brows drawn over his light eyes, he searched her face.

"How do you feel, Chastity? Are you sure you should be up?"

Her throat tight, Chastity could not respond. She saw a spark slowly come to life in Reed's eyes. She watched it gradually soar to flame. A sob of jubilation sounded deep within her when he wrapped his arm around her and swept her onto the seat beside him. His hand curled in her hair, holding her still as he covered her mouth with his.

Reed's kiss lingered. It spoke words of silent promise, confirmed by the ardor in his gaze when he drew back from her reluctantly. When she spoke at last, the words came softly, with gentle earnest.

"I love you, Reed."

Reed's throat worked with obvious emotion. Wordless, he tightened his arm around her, a happiness mixed with pain clearly reflected in his expression as he brushed her lips with another brief kiss. She felt the restraint that shuddered through him when he turned back to the trail ahead and snapped the reins for another burst forward.

Morgan rode cautiously along the trail, his mind racing. The cabin and the work he had set to be accomplished that day left far behind him, he realized that his thoughts of the red-haired woman had become an obsession. By riding out of camp that morning, he had signaled a dangerous surrender to that dangerous emotion. But the thought excited him. The red-haired beauty presented a challenge he had never faced before. It lent so keen an anticipation to the victory he knew would be his that he shuddered at the thought of what awaited him.

But the need for caution did not escape him. For that reason, he had proceeded carefully after his first rush from camp. He knew that the wagon could not possibly reach the mission before nightfall on a trail as rough as the one they traveled. He had time.

Drawing his mount to a halt, Morgan surveyed the trail from a rise above it. Going still when he saw dust rising in the distance, Morgan waited. He was rewarded moments later by the sight of the bulky wagon lumbering into view.

Spurring his horse forward without conscious volition, Morgan rode slowly toward it. At the first flash of the blazing color of Chastity's hair, his heartbeat turned to thunder in his chest—and his decision was made.

Reed stiffened as a rider appeared on the trail ahead. He felt Chastity stiffen as well as he dropped his arm from around her shoulder.

"It's him, isn't it?" Chastity turned toward him.

"It looks like it is. Get back into the wagon."

"No, he'll think something's wrong if I'm not sitting beside you."

"Get in back, Chastity!"

"No."

Reed reached down under the seat to check the location of his revolver, whispering as he did, "I want you out of range if anything happens."

"No."

"Stubborn . . ."

The horseman drew closer. It was Morgan, all right. Reed straightened up slowly. He didn't like this. He hadn't expected to see Morgan again so soon. The bastard was planning something. If things were different, he would have snatched at the opportunity to take Morgan now, when he was alone.

Reed glanced at Chastity. Her attention was focused on Morgan as he approached. No, he couldn't risk it before he could get her to a point of safety.

Forced to rein up when Morgan continued his direct approach, Reed managed a neutral expression. He waited for Morgan to make the first move.

Farrell was watching him intently as he approached the wagon head-on. He wasn't wearing his parson's collar. It occurred to Morgan as he drew closer that Bartell was right. He had never seen a parson with eyes that cold.

Assuming a properly concerned expression as he drew his mount to a halt beside the wagon, Morgan began, "I'm real glad I ran into you out here on the trail. I was plannin' to find you anyways, but this makes it easier."

Chastity turned toward him fully for the first time. Her face was bruised black and blue, and Morgan was possessed of a sudden rage at the distortion of her beauty. He glanced back at Farrell, whose expression was unrevealing— *but he knew what had happened*. Barely suppressing his fury, he inquired softly, "What happened to you, Chastity?"

He noticed that the warmth was missing from Chastity's manner, and that she glanced hesitantly at Farrell before responding, "I fell. It was dark and I didn't realize there was a slope. It really is embarrassing to be so clumsy."

He didn't believe a word of it! He was well acquainted with the type who enjoyed causing pain in the name of religion. Her bastard husband had done that to her because he was jealous. He'd make sure Farrell paid for that.

His raging thoughts carefully hidden, Morgan continued, "Well, I'm glad to hear that it didn't have anythin' to do with the Indian trouble nearby."

Chastity stiffened. "Indian trouble?" She looked again at Farrell. "That Indian I saw near our camp the other night . . . you don't suppose . . ."

"I told you not to worry about him, Chastity. If he was going to cause us trouble, it would've happened already." Farrell looked back at Morgan. "There wasn't any talk of Indian trouble out here when we left Baxter Springs."

"That's because nobody knew about it yet."

"What kind of trouble are you talking about, Mr. Jefferson?"

"The usual kind, Indians gettin' liquored up and goin' out shootin' up things. We lost some cattle last night."

"This *is* Indian land."

"Right." Morgan refused to be ruffled. "But like I said, we have an understandin'." He continued with no sign of the agitation that had his trigger finger twitching. "What I was really thinkin' was that maybe it might be a good idea if you came to spend the night at the cabin—to give things a chance to cool off before you go on to the mission. You'd be safe there. You could start out in the mornin', and I could send a few of my men along with you if you liked."

"That won't be necessary."

"If those braves are still swillin' the red-eye, they aren't goin' to wait to see if you're a parson or not." He looked directly at Chastity. "I'm worried for your safety, ma'am."

"I don't think we're in danger."

Morgan scrutinized Farrell's expression. The bastard didn't want him anywhere near his wife. He replied, "Well, I suppose you trust in the Lord to get you through, but I'm thinkin' it just might be wiser to take some additional precautions."

"We'll be fine."

Morgan glanced up at the position of the sun in the cloudless sky. "I need to be gettin' back to my men. If you change your mind, you just drive that wagon up to my front door and you'll be welcome."

Farrell's smile was hardly worth the effort as he replied, "We'll remember that."

Tipping his hat, Morgan smiled at Chastity. "You still are the prettiest woman my eyes have ever seen."

"Thank you, Mr. Jefferson."

"Yes, thank you, Mr. Jefferson." Farrell's voice dripped ice. "We'll be saying good-bye, then."

After another look at Chastity's bruised face, Morgan turned his horse. He rode off without looking back.

Reining up out of sight a short distance away, Morgan sat his mount silently. An Indian had been skulking around their camp the previous night. That couldn't be better. It lent credence to the ground work he had laid.

Morgan looked up again at the sky. It would be dark in a couple of hours. He had just enough time.

\* \* \*

"Here he comes."

The shuffle of footsteps sounded against the board floor of the cabin as Bartell and Simmons joined Walker at the window, with Turner following behind. A victorious smile stretched underneath Walker's wiry mustache as Turner reached the window and looked out.

"He's *alone*. I told he would be." Walker laughed out loud. "You were so sure you knew Morgan better than the rest of us, but you were wrong. Maybe now you'll keep your mouth shut so's we can all have a little peace around here!"

But Turner was hardly listening. Instead, he was watching Morgan's advance. "He's ridin' like a crazy man."

"I'm sick and tired of you tryin' to say Morgan's crazy!" Walker took an aggressive step. "I've got half a mind to let him know what you were tryin' to pull off while he was gone. He'd set you straight!"

"Keep your mouth shut, Walker," Simmons grated. "I ain't lookin' forward to seein' Morgan get on one of his shootin' sprees."

"Don't worry, I ain't goin' to say nothin'." Walker sneered at Turner as he walked back to the table. "You're safe."

"Yeah, I'm safe . . . just as safe as any of us are."

All eyes turned back to the yard as Morgan drew his mount to a sliding stop. There was no sound within as Morgan covered the remaining distance to the cabin in a few long steps. He

## Elaine Barbieri

pushed the door open and halted abruptly when he saw them waiting.

"What's goin' on in here?"

"Nothin'." Walker responded with a shrug. "We was wonderin' what brought you back in such a hurry, is all."

"You're goin' to find out soon enough. Get mounted up. We got things to do."

"Like what?" Turner faced Morgan boldly. "You said we didn't have to do nothin' else to-day."

"I changed my mind. We're goin' out to play a little game."

"What're you talkin' about?" Turner's daring expanded. "I ain't no kid and I ain't playin' no games."

"What kind of game, Morgan?" Walker interrupted the exchange, his small eyes narrowing into a nervous squint. "The boys were expectin' to play a little cards tonight."

Morgan's face flushed with anticipation as he responded, "We're goin' out to do some fancy ridin' in the dark. We're goin' to do some hootin' and hollerin' and noisy shootin', actin' like some wild Indians."

"You was out by that parson and his wife again, wasn't you?" Turner shot a knowing glance at the men around him. "What's the plan? You goin' to fool that woman into thinkin' they're bein' attacked by Indians so you can shoot her husband dead without her knowin'?"

Morgan faced Turner, the flush fading from

280

his face. "And there I always thought you were stupid."

"No, I ain't stupid! I especially ain't stupid enough to do your dirty work for you!"

"You'll do what I tell you to do, Turner." Morgan eyed each man individually. "You'll all do what I tell you to."

"I . . . I don't want no part in no killin' a preacher, Morgan."

Simmons took a backward step when Morgan faced him. "You don't have to do any killin'. All you have to do is make a little noise. I'll do the rest."

"She ain't worth the trouble, Morgan." Bartell ran a hand over his balding pate. "There's too many women in the world to make a fuss over any one of them."

"She'll be worth the trouble."

"Not to me, she won't. And I ain't goin'." Turner looked at the men around him. "What do you say, boys? Are you goin' to follow this crazy man so you can go chasin' around in the dark after a red-haired whore?"

"I'm warnin' you, Turner."

"I've had enough of your warnin's too!" Turner's sweaty face glowed with triumph. "You ain't makin' me do nothin' I don't want to do."

Walker's small eyes twitched. "Shut up, Turner."

"No, let him talk." Morgan smiled. "I want to hear what he has to say."

"I'm sayin' that me and the rest of the fellas

have had enough, and we're not goin' to follow you into the grave just because you got the hots for some woman."

"Is that right?"

"Yeah. I'm takin' over. From now on, I'm givin' the orders. We're going to be doin' what I say to do, and we're goin' to sell them steers when I say they're ready—and you ain't got a thing to say about it."

"Draw, Turner."

Silence.

The men fell back.

"I said, draw!"

"I ain't goin' to draw!" Sweat beaded on Turner's jowled face. "And you ain't goin' to make me!" He turned toward the men around him. "You goin' to let him get away with this? He's crazy, just like I told you!"

"I'm tellin' you one last time . . ."

Silence his only response, Turner jerked back toward Morgan. His hand snaked toward his gun.

Gunshots shattered the silence.

A heavy thud resounded as Turner hit the floor. When the smoke cleared, the sight of his blood-soaked shirt and his lifeless eyes staring upward left no doubt that the bullets had done the job intended.

"Damn it—you killed him!" Walker stared at Morgan. "You killed him!"

"He had it comin'. I warned him, but he wouldn't listen." Morgan frowned. "Get him out of here. Put him in the barn. We can bury him tomorrow."

"We can bury him now!"

"We haven't got time. We got things to do."

Walker shook his head. "You ain't never goin' to let it go until you get that woman, are you? You're goin' to do whatever it takes."

"That's right. You got any complaints?"

Walker did not reply.

Morgan addressed the others. "You got any complaints?"

Their silence speaking wordless assent, Morgan ordered, "Then get him out of here."

Morgan sneered as Turner's heavy bulk was carried out the door. Turner never could keep his mouth shut. It had only been a matter of time.

The bloody puddle that remained on the floor turned Morgan's sneer to a frown. He looked around him, his gaze settling on Conchita, who stood silently in the corner of the room. Motionless, she looked back at him, her gaze inscrutable as he growled, "Get this mess cleaned up, and do it right."

Conchita's dark eyes held his boldly for long seconds before she nodded.

*The arrogant whore* . . . "Did you get your things out of the other room?" Morgan snapped.

Conchita did not flinch. "Yes, Morgan."

"That room had better be clean, or you're in trouble."

"It is clean."

Morgan turned back toward the door at the sound of footsteps returning. He met the men in the yard with a sharp command.

"Mount up. We're runnin' out of time."

He did not bother to look back as their horses thundered into the distance.

The shadows of the trail were closing in. Pressing the team steadily forward, Reed scrutinized the surrounding foliage. Seated beside him, Chastity leaned against him, the tension within her growing. She looked up as his arm tightened around her.

"You're worried, aren't you?"

Reed hesitated in response. She suspected he was regretting his promise to tell her the truth as he replied, "Yes."

"Mr. Jefferson—Morgan—" She shook her head uncertainly. "Whatever his name is, he seemed concerned about the Indian trouble, but he didn't seem suspicious about the real reason you're here. He seemed satisfied to let you handle things your way."

Reed's gaze bore into hers. "There is no Indian trouble, Chastity."

"How can you be sure?"

"Because I know him. Because I've been chasing him for years—him, and men like him. Listen to me, Chastity." Reed's voice deepened. "He's a killer. He's set on a course that allows for no thought but what he wants. He doesn't care about anybody or anything that doesn't relate to his own personal needs."

"What are you saying?"

"I'm saying that he wouldn't have gone out of his way to warn us about Indian trouble unless he had a purpose in mind."

"Maybe you made a mistake, Reed." Hope filled Chastity's voice. "Maybe you're chasing the wrong man. He seems so sincere."

"He's so sincere that he killed a man in Texas six months ago just to prove that he was faster with his gun. He's so sincere that he drove the last herd he rustled right over the top of one of the cowpokes who was guarding it. He's so sincere that there isn't a lawman in Texas who doesn't have him at the top of his wanted list."

The horror of Reed's statements was momentarily overwhelming. Studying Reed's adamant expression for a long moment, Chastity finally managed, "You're sure he's the right man?"

"I'm sure, all right."

"Morgan's wanted by the law for those terrible crimes . . ." She paused again to muster her courage before pressing, "But that doesn't tell me why *you're* chasing him. Why, Reed?" Her heart in the question she could no longer suppress, she whispered, "You said you're a bounty hunter. That means you hunt men for the money—like animals. I don't believe that's true. I can't make myself believe you could do that."

Reed's expression hardened. "Don't try to make me out to be something I'm not, Chastity. I've been that man for more years than I choose to remember."

"Why?" Chastity hesitated, braving the question she had not dared ask before. "Is—is it because of Jenny?"

Pain flickered briefly in Reed's eyes as Chastity held her breath. She saw the uncertainty in his gaze as he searched her face, then responded slowly, "I'd like to tell you what you want to hear. I'd like to make you believe that my motives are noble, that I wanted to right a wrong that really couldn't be righted. Maybe that was my reasoning at first. I loved her, Chastity." Reed's voice grew hoarse. "I knew Jenny all my life. So big a part of my life was gone when she was killed so senselessly by rustlers that I couldn't accept it. I couldn't give her up, and I suppose that while I tried to find the men responsible for her death, I felt I could keep her with me."

Reed paused. "But so many years passed . . . and I gradually began to realize that no matter how many outlaws I brought in, or how much money I was paid for doing it, nothing changed. Jenny was still gone. I started tracking those men for *myself* then, Chastity. I wanted to get even. There was nothing noble about my feelings when I looked at those men over the barrel of my gun, hoping they'd give me the excuse to fire. Some of them did—and I never hesitated or looked back."

Reed's gaze implored her understanding as he whispered, "It was only in the past few weeks that things started to change for me. I couldn't understand the change at first. I resented it. I was determined not to acknowledge it . . . just as determined as I was not to admit the real reason I couldn't let you take that train out of Sedalia and out of my life. I don't suppose I'll ever forgive myself for coming to the realization so late, but the truth is, I couldn't let you go."

Her throat so tight that she could barely speak, Chastity felt the intensity of Reed's light-eyed gaze bite into hers as he rasped, "Whatever you think, however many doubts still remain, there's one thing I never want you to doubt. I love you, Chastity. I curse the day I brought you into this danger. If I could undo it, I would, but—"

"No, don't say that." Chastity shook her head, Reed's words cutting deep. "If we had parted in Sedalia, if you hadn't been driven to keep me with you, for whatever reason prevailed at the time . . ." Her words trailing away, Chastity whispered, "What I'm trying to say is, if I were given a choice between being perfectly safe on my way west to Caldwell right now, or being here with you, no matter how much danger we're facing, I'd choose being with you."

"Chastity, I—" Reed halted abruptly, his gaze snapping back to the foliage alongside the trail.

"What's wrong, Reed?"

"Quiet . . ."

Apprehension crawled up Chastity's spine as Reed's eyes went cold, as he scrutinized the rapidly encroaching darkness surrounding them.

"Tell me what's wrong, Reed."

"Get in the back of the wagon, Chastity."

Reed urged the team to a more rapid pace as

Chastity looked around them, her heart pounding. "I don't see anything. What's wrong?"

"Get in the back!" The shadows making Reed's expression unreadable, Chastity was unprepared as he swept her from the seat and dropped her in the wagon behind him. Thrown off balance as Reed whipped the horses into a pounding surge forward, Chastity tumbled helplessly, terror striking as a wild yell signaled a barrage of gunfire from the surrounding darkness.

Savage war whoops rent the darkness as the wagon thundered along the darkened trail. The gunfire drew closer, the feral yells louder. Finally regaining her feet, Chastity fought her way forward, emerging at last behind Reed as he whipped the team to a frenzied pace.

"Get in the back, Chastity!" Reed turned briefly toward her. He pushed a gun into her hand. "Take this and get into the back of the wagon, damn it!"

The handle of the gun was cold against her palm as she shouted, "No, I won't! The Indians—"

"They're not Ind—"

Reed lurched sideward as the bullet struck him. Blood streamed from his temple, and Chastity screamed aloud, grasping his arm as he teetered over the edge of the seat. The gunfire continued as she strained to draw him toward her, sobbing as he began slipping from her grasp. She was clutching him with terrified desperation when a hot, piercing pain pounded into her, thrusting her backward.

Fighting to hold herself upright as the wagon raced onward, Chastity stared at the empty driver's seat in front of her. Consciousness wavered at the realization that Reed was gone.

*Gone . . .*

A loud buzzing sounded in her ears as Chastity touched her chest to find it wet with blood.

She struggled for breath.

She gasped Reed's name.

# Chapter Ten

"Which one of you shot her, damn it?"

The savage war whoops and gunfire had ceased. The runaway wagon had been drawn to a halt. Morgan had noted the blood on the driver's seat with satisfaction as he climbed into the back of the wagon to console the frightened widow.

And then he had found her.

Morgan leaned over Chastity's still form, his chest heaving with agitation. A desperation unlike any he had ever known beset him. She was unconscious, and the bodice of her dress was covered with blood.

Ripping open the bloody garment, he saw the bullet hole just below her shoulder. He grabbed a nearby cloth and pressed it tightly against the wound, grating to the silent men around him, "I told you to keep your shots high, damn it! I told you *I'd* take care of the preacher! I told you I didn't want anybody shootin' anywhere near the wagon!"

"She's bleedin' pretty bad, Morgan," Walker interrupted Morgan's tirade. "I'd say there's no time for talkin'."

Morgan was shuddering with fury. He hadn't expected this. Nor had he expected to feel such a frenzy of loss as Chastity lay motionless in front of him, her blood flowing against his hand. But Walker was right. He had no time for accusations.

He barked in brief command, "Simmons, get this wagon goin' toward the cabin. Bartell, you get my horse. Walker, you go back over the trail and find Farrell's body. Take Simmons's horse with you so you can bring him back."

"It's too dark! I'll never find him tonight."

"You heard me! This woman is goin' to be askin' about her husband when she wakes up, and I want to be able to show her his body if she wants to see it."

"She won't be askin' about nothin' tonight." Walker was adamant. "It's a waste of time. I can come back in the mornin' and bring him back."

"Listen to me, Walker . . ." Morgan stared levelly into his eyes. He shuddered with the emphasis of his words, "I want to make sure he's *dead.*"

"He's dead. There ain't no doubt about that! You saw the way he went off the side of that wagon. Either he died from a bullet or a broken neck, but he's dead, all right."

"Go back along the trail. See if you can find him."

"But—"

"You heard me!"

Walker left the wagon without another word and Morgan snapped, "Let's get goin'! We don't have any time to waste."

He leaned over Chastity, staring at her still face as the wagon jerked into motion.

She heard it coming long before she could see it in the darkness. It was a wagon, large and lumbering.

Conchita ran to the window of the cabin, a gun in her hand. She drew back the hammer as the wagon drew to a halt a short distance away. Her eyes narrowed when she recognized the man at the reins.

Rushing to the corner of the room, Conchita hid the gun in the woodpile there. She returned to the window in time to see Morgan jump down from the rear of the wagon. She frowned as a woman was lowered into his arms and he started toward the door. She stepped back as Morgan kicked the door open, calling over his shoulder as he proceeded toward the rear room, "It's a good thing you're up. I'm goin' to need you."

Conchita looked at the woman lying limply in Morgan's arms. Her hair was a bright red color . . . and her dress was soaked with blood.

Conchita raised her chin and smiled.

Morgan disappeared into the rear room, Simmons behind him. She waited.

"Conchita, get in here!"

She walked slowly into the room. She stepped back spontaneously at the sight of Morgan's savage wrath. "You come quick when I call you, you hear?"

Waiting only for her nod of acknowledgement, Morgan turned back toward the unconscious woman. Jealousy tightened into a hard knot within Conchita when Morgan touched the woman with trembling hands. The knot tightened to pain at the expression on his face the moment before he uncovered her wound. A single bullet hole just below her shoulder was still bleeding. Conchita watched as he turned the woman gently to her side to peer at her back, then looked up at her.

"The bullet didn't go clean through. You're goin' to have to take it out."

Conchita did not reply.

"I know what you're thinkin'." Morgan's face twisted into a savage mask. "You aren't deaf. You heard everythin' that's been said around here, and you know who this woman is. Well, she doesn't know it yet, but she's *my* woman now. I took care of her husband the same way I took care of Turner, and I'll take care of you the same way . . . if I need to."

Conchita winced as Morgan gripped her chin with a bloody hand. "Take the bullet out, Conchita. I know about you, and I know it isn't the

293

first time you fished a bullet out of somebody. But I'm tellin' you now—just so's you understand—take care how you do it, because if she dies, you die."

Morgan allowed enough time for his words to register, then rasped, "But I'm promisin' you somethin' else, too. If she lives, you'll be leavin' this cabin with enough money in your pocket to get you home, or anywhere else you want to go, in style. *Comprendes?*"

"*Sí.*" His words cutting deep, Conchita replied, "*Comprendo.*"

Conchita drew back, her mouth twisting when she felt the dampness of blood on her face. She walked back into the main room, leaving Morgan standing beside the unconscious woman. She poured water into a basin and washed away the blood, then threw the water into the bucket nearby. She carried the empty basin back into the room, snatching a bottle of red-eye and a cloth from the corner as she passed.

Back in the room, aware that Morgan watched her every move, she poured the liquor into the basin, then lifted the hem of her skirt to draw her knife from the sheath on her thigh.

Morgan snapped, "You're not goin' to use that filthy thing to get the bullet out, are you?"

"My blade is sharp. It cuts clean and deep." Conchita dropped it into the basin, waiting in silent challenge for him to reply.

"Go ahead then! You waited long enough!"

Conchita picked up the knife. The woman

was young. Her skin was white and smooth, her features delicate. The bright hair Morgan so much admired curled into ringlets around her still face. Morgan did not call her *puta*. Nor would he leave her side. He was consumed with desire for her.

Conchita dipped the cloth into the amber liquid, then rubbed the blood from the surface of the wound. The woman groaned softly. *Bueno*. She would not fully escape the pain.

Conchita applied her blade sharply.

It was like looking for a needle in a haystack.

Walker rode along the trail, scowling. Morgan and the wagon had disappeared from sight in the darkness. He was left behind to do Morgan's dirty work again. He supposed he should be accustomed to it by now, but he still didn't like it. He also supposed he should have walked out on Morgan a long time ago. But Morgan was smart—smarter than anybody he had ever ridden with. It had never made any difference to him that Morgan was also more deadly—as long as Walker wasn't on the receiving end of his anger.

A familiar agitation tugged at Walker's thoughts. He hadn't wanted to admit it, but he knew Turner was right. The parson's wife was making Morgan crazy. He had known he had to do something about her before Morgan got them all killed, just like Turner said. There was no way to trace a stray bullet . . . so he took a chance. But his bullet was a little too high. His only consolation was that judging from the amount of blood the woman had lost, Morgan was only putting off the inevitable by taking her back to the cabin. But he'd learned a long time ago not to argue with Morgan when he was determined to do something. It was too bad that Turner didn't.

Pulling the reins of Simmons's horse sharply as the animal lagged behind his own mount, Walker looked up at the night sky. Clouds moved over the moon, plunging the trail into darkness. Simmons hadn't liked the idea of his mount being used to carry Farrell's body back. He considered it bad luck. But he hadn't protested. He knew better.

Walker scanned the edge of the trail. The search was senseless. He had already been back and forth over that section several times without finding Farrell. The wagon had been traveling so fast, there was no way he could pinpoint exactly where Farrell fell. He could be anywhere in that heavy foliage. It would take most of the night to locate him in the dark.

A gust of wind stirred the shadows into a sudden burst of movement. Walker's mount shied, rearing so unexpectedly that he was almost thrown. Bringing him under control at last, Walker realized that Simmons's horse had spooked as well and had disappeared into the darkness.

All right! He had had enough. He didn't care what Morgan said, he was going back to the cabin!

Walker turned his mount resolutely. He'd handle Morgan. He knew how. That red-haired witch might be dead by the time he reached the cabin anyway, and finding Farrell's body wouldn't really matter if she was.

Walker considered that thought. Morgan might even thank him one day for saving him from that woman—if he ever found out.

Walker's wiry mustache twitched. But he wasn't fool enough to tell him. He valued his life.

That thought lingering, Walker dug his heels into his mount's sides and headed back.

Sharp whinnies and trampling hooves near-by . . . muttered curses . . . hoofbeats disappearing into the distance . . .

Reed groaned. Pain struck sharply in his temple as he attempted to move. He groaned again, his head spinning. He opened his eyes slowly.

Darkness.

He felt the ground underneath him, the foliage waving in the brisk breeze around him.

Where was he?

His body ached. The pounding in his head worsened as he attempted to clear his mind. He touched a hand to his temple and felt the stickiness of blood there.

*Chastity . . . the wagon . . .*

Reed struggled to a seated position. He looked around him. The trail was only a short distance away, and the wagon was gone.

Recall swept his mind in a sudden rush that

set his heart pounding. The gunfire and wild yelling behind them—a farce intended to make them think Indians were attacking them.

Reed swayed uncertainly, Morgan's plan suddenly clear. Morgan had warned them about an Indian problem, then orchestrated an attack to get rid of Chastity's "husband" so that she would turn to him for protection.

But where had everyone gone? Chastity would never leave with Morgan without trying to find him.

Something had gone wrong.

Dizziness again assaulting him, Reed fought to clear his mind. He had been driving the wagon at a frantic pace. Chastity had come to the front of the wagon. Chastity was directly behind him when everything went blank.

*Oh, God, no!*

Reed struggled to stand. He had to find her! He had to make sure she was all right.

On his feet, Reed took a staggering step, then another. But the darkness whirled around him. The ground swayed beneath his feet. He realized he was no longer standing the second before his head hit the ground with a stunning crack.

"She's opening her eyes. She's conscious."

"No, she ain't. She's driftin' off again."

"Conchita, get some water for her to drink!"

"She can't drink nothin'! She ain't conscious yet!"

"Mind your business! She isn't your concern!"

The angry voices swirled in Chastity's mind, punctuated by a stabbing pain in her shoulder that would not relent. She struggled to open her eyes, but her lids were so heavy.

"Chastity . . . how are you feelin'?"

*That voice . . .*

"Can you open your eyes? Look at me, Chastity."

Chastity recognized it. She forced her eyes open. She groaned as the pain seared more hotly.

"Those damn Injuns . . ." Morgan's face hovered over her. "We heard the shootin'. We got there just in time to run those drunken renegades off." Morgan's face moved closer. She could feel the warmth of his breath against her cheek when he whispered, "Can you hear me, Chastity?"

"Yes . . ." She felt so sick. It took all her strength to hold her eyes open as she rasped, "Reed . . . where is he?"

Morgan's expression softened to compassion. "He was shot."

"Where is he?"

Morgan's hand closed around hers. "I'm so sorry. We got there too late. He's dead."

"No!" Chastity's instinctive protest was a hoarse, grating sound that made Morgan snap, "Get her some water!"

Chastity averted her head from the cup that was held to her lips. "Drink, Chastity." Morgan whispered gently, "I know you feel bad, but you need to drink somethin' or you'll get the fever."

Chastity allowed a drop of moisture past her lips, grateful that her voice was stronger as she rasped, "Where is he? I want to see him."

"The boys carried him into the barn. You're too weak to go to see him now. You're lucky you're alive. An inch or so lower and . . ." He squeezed her hand tightly. "But don't worry. You're goin' to be all right. I'm goin' to see to that."

"Morgan . . ." A male voice called out, "Walker's here. He wants to talk to you."

"Morgan . . ." Chastity closed her eyes, not realizing the name had passed her lips. Reed was right. There had been no Indians . . . only Morgan. And Reed was dead.

Reed was dead.

Reed was dead.

Chastity's eyes drooped closed.


Grabbing Simmons's arm, Morgan jerked him roughly into the outer room. He hissed, "You damned fool! Now you did it! I told her my name was Jefferson, remember?"

Releasing Simmons's arm with a shove, Morgan looked at Walker where he stood frowning nearby. "Did you find him?"

Walker shrugged. "No."

"What?"

"I couldn't find him. I rode up and down that trail, but I couldn't see nothin'. It's too dark. I'll ride out first thing in the mornin' and bring him back."

"I told you to bring him back tonight."

"It's a waste of time! I couldn't see a thing. Take a look out there. It's black as pitch!"

Morgan glanced at the window, his lips tight. "All right, tomorrow. But I want you out of here as soon as it gets light. I don't want anybody else findin' that bastard but us. I already told Chastity that we put him in the barn."

"Next to Turner, huh?"

Morgan's youthful face twitched. "Get rid of Turner. I don't care what you do with him, but I want him out of the way."

Walker protested cautiously, "I don't mind draggin' Farrell back here, but I don't like dealin' with Turner. Hell, I rode with him for a year!"

"That bothers you, huh?" Morgan smiled unexpectedly. "But my guess is that you won't have an objection to splittin' his share of the take when the time comes."

Walker did not reply.

"That's what I thought. Just get rid of him, and make sure you do it before you bring Farrell back."

Turning, Morgan saw Conchita watching him intently. "What are you lookin' at?" he grated.

"Nothing, Morgan."

Morgan attempted to arrange his raging thoughts. He didn't like it when things didn't go as he planned . . . and he didn't like the look in the Mexican whore's eyes. He snapped, "Make somethin' for Chastity to eat. She has to get her strength back."

301

"She will not eat tonight. She is not well enough yet."

Morgan looked at Conchita in silence. He wondered what he had ever seen in the sullen witch.

He ordered, "Make sure you have somethin' ready for her when she wants it." He paused, adding with a note of chill warning, "And watch what you say to her. You know what's goin' on here. If you mess it up, you're done for."

Morgan walked back into the rear room and closed the door behind him.

Reed awakened slowly to the pale light of morning. His head was pounding, his vision blurred. He blinked, waiting long moments before he could see clearly and was able to draw himself to his feet.

The events of the previous night returned in a rush as he took a tentative step forward. The wagon was gone, and Chastity was gone with it. He needed to find out where she was, and if she was all right. If Morgan had hurt her . . .

A rustling sound in the bushes turned Reed slowly. He reached down into his boot toward the derringer concealed there, his hand halting when he saw a chestnut gelding moving through the foliage nearby. The animal stopped still when he spotted him. The animal was saddled, his reins hanging.

Reed approached him slowly.

"Easy, boy." Cursing his unsteady step, Reed continued his advance. He spoke softly past the throbbing ache in his head that would not relent. "They left you here, too, did they? I bet they'll be coming back for you. But they're not going to find either one of us."

Reed was almost at his side when the animal took a startled jump backward.

"That's all right, boy." Reed reached out a shaky hand, releasing a tense breath when his hand closed around the sagging reins. Throwing the reins over the nervous animal's head, Reed mounted, then looked unsteadily around him. Darkness was hovering at the edges of his mind. He needed to get away, quickly, before it was too late.

Reed dug his heels into the horse's sides, squinting against the pain as the animal started forward. Slumped low over his back, he allowed the animal full rein as consciousness dimmed.

Conchita walked into the rear room of the cabin, a cup of broth in her hands. It was morning and Morgan had gone outside to help with Turner. The red-haired woman was sleeping.

A mirthless smile curved Conchita's lips. Turner was having his last revenge. His body had stiffened overnight and his large bulk had become leaden. Morgan's help was needed to dispose of it. Morgan had not liked being called to such a task. He used his gun easily, but he was not accustomed to dealing with what followed.

Conchita raised her chin, recalling the pool of blood she had washed from the floor at Morgan's command. Morgan had shed that blood without flinching. She knew he had shed blood before, but it had meant little to her when she was in his arms.

A shiver of remembered rapture moved down Conchita's spine. She remembered so little when she lay in Morgan's embrace, when his clean, warm body was pressed against hers and his voice, as deep and smooth as velvet, whispered in her ear. She remembered only that he made her feel as no man had ever made her feel, and the simple sound of his voice was enough when he spoke promises of the loving times to come.

But the promises were broken. Morgan had turned cold. He had turned loving eyes to the red-haired woman instead of to her, and she knew that the pool of blood that had stained the cabin floor could just as easily have been her own.

The red-haired woman . . .

Conchita stood over the bed as the woman turned with a muffled word in her sleep. The wound was not severe. She had removed the bullet and had seen little damage to the surrounding flesh. The woman suffered pain and weakness, but that would soon end. And then Morgan would make her his own.

Conchita bore the thought with stinging pain. She had loved Morgan. She had given to him all she had to give, and she had made herself believe that he loved her.

Conchita raised her chin. He *did* love her. She

was sure of it. But his love had been stolen from her by lust for white flesh he longed to touch . . . by red hair that dazzled his eyes . . . by hunger for a long, slender body unlike her own meager height and rounded curves. If not for the woman lying in front of her, Morgan would *still* love her.

If not for the woman in front of her, Morgan would love her *again*.

The woman stirred and Conchita's hand trembled. It would be so easy. The woman was so weak.

The woman opened her eyes and looked up at her. Her lips moved soundlessly for long seconds before words emerged.

"W-who are you?"

Conchita wanted to tell her. She wanted to say she was the woman Morgan had loved. Instead, she leaned over her and held the cup to her lips.

"You must drink if you wish to be well."

The woman refused, questioning again, "Who are you?"

Conchita considered the question. Countless responses flickered across her mind. They were all discarded, and when she responded, the bitter irony of her words silently resounded.

"I am no one."

The sun of mid-morning shone hotly on Walker's shoulders as he scrutinized the foliage along the trail. Turning toward Simmons, who was riding alongside, he spat out, "Where in hell is he? The way he pitched off that wagon, I figured he must've landed somewhere in the bushes along this stretch, but there ain't no sign of him!"

Simmons stared at him. "There ain't no sign of my horse, neither."

"Don't talk to me about that horse of yours! He bolted like a jackrabbit in tall grass when my horse reared. I never did see such a skittish animal. He's probably still runnin'!"

"He's a damned good horse. I ain't never had no trouble with him. I don't like this."

"What are you tryin' to say?"

"That damned preacher's too big to miss. The reason we can't find him is because he ain't here! I'll tell you what happened. That big fella got up, found my horse, and he's headin' for that Injun mission right now. He'll be back here with help to follow our trail."

Walker laughed. "You mean that big fella rose from the dead and mounted that horse, just so's he could ride to the Injun mission to tell the Injuns there that Injuns attacked his wagon? Well, I wish him luck!"

"He ain't dead—and that ain't good!"

"He's dead, all right. We'll find him. Even if he isn't, he couldn't have wandered far. I saw the way he pitched off that wagon. He wasn't in no shape to catch a horse as skittish as yours, even if he did see it. He was hit and hit bad. I ain't worried about it."

"You ought to be. It ain't that preacher that's worryin' me. It's Morgan. What do you think he'll do when if we tell him we can't find that preacher's body?"

Walker's smile vanished. The memory of the grave they had dug that morning was too fresh to forget. "We're wastin' time talkin'. Like I said, even if he did get up and wander off, he couldn't get far. We're goin' to have to start scoutin' deeper. We'll find him."

"You'd better be right."

"I *am* right."

His frown belying the confidence of his words, Walker turned his mount into the foliage.

"What do you mean, you can't find him?"

Walker went silent. Morgan was livid. Walker had known he would be.

"I asked you a question."

"Like I said, we couldn't find him."

Walker took an unconscious step backward as Morgan advanced across the cabin, his step heavy with anger. "He's dead. A dead man doesn't get up and walk away."

"He ain't dead, and we couldn't find no trace of him. The ground was too hard to leave a trail."

"Go back and get him. He couldn't have gotten far on foot."

Simmons glanced at Walker. Morgan did not miss the look. "He isn't on foot, is he? He's got Simmons's horse."

"We don't know that he has, but we ain't been able to find either one of them."

"Stupid bastards . . ."

"It wasn't our fault. There's no way any of us could've known he was still alive. What's the difference, anyway? For all he knows, Injuns attacked his wagon. If he makes it as far as here, you can finish the job you started. If he goes to the Injun mission, they'll go lookin' for renegades. If they see the wagon here, we can just tell him that you brought the woman back here to care for, and that you thought the Injuns had taken Farrell off. He won't know the difference. Hell, he was shot, and after a fall like he had, he ain't likely to remember much of anythin' at all!"

"You forgot somethin'. I told Chastity he was dead."

"So? You could tell her you thought he was dead."

"I told her that we put his body in the barn."

"She probably won't remember any of it. And if she does, you can tell her that she was dreamin'. She trusts you. She thinks you're the next best thing to buttered toast. She'll believe anythin' you tell her."

"You got it all figured out, don't you?" Morgan smiled. "I'm thinkin' you puzzled it all out on the way back here for a reason—'cause you realize this whole thing is your damned fault!"

"My fault?" Walker shook his head. "It ain't *my* fault!"

"If you would've looked for that preacher last night like I said, you could've finished him off, then and there, and we wouldn't be havin' this trouble!"

"It ain't my fault . . ."

"I'm not goin' to argue with you!" Turning unexpectedly toward the hook on the wall, Morgan snatched up his hat and started toward the door. "Let's go."

Walker and Simmons followed behind him. Getting up his courage as they reached the door, Walker asked, "Where are we goin'?"

"We're goin' out to finish brandin' those steers. Bartell's already out there. We should be done by the end of the day, and then we're goin' to pack up and drive that herd out of here as fast as we can."

"What about the woman?"

"We're takin' her with us . . . in the wagon."

"That ain't smart."

Morgan stopped dead, a hot flush rising. "What did you say?"

Walker took a short breath. "I . . . I said, that ain't smart. When that woman's well enough, she's goin' to start talkin'."

"Right. She'll tell everybody how the Injuns attacked the wagon and took her husband. Then the law'll go out and find him dead somewhere. Because we're goin' to make sure that if we find him on the way, we fix it that he is."

Walker nodded jerkily. "All right. That's good."

"You're damned right, it's good. And that's the way it's goin' to be."

Dropping behind as Morgan strode ahead toward the branding corral, Simmons whispered under his breath, "Morgan's plum lost his head over that woman. I don't know about you, but I'm headin' out as soon as that money's in my hand, and I ain't lookin' back."

"Hurry up, you two!"

Walker's head snapped up when Morgan looked back at them. "We're comin'."

Reed opened his eyes slowly. Blue sky above him . . . the ground beneath his back . . . the sound of gurgling water . . .

He heard a rustling nearby and sat up abruptly. His head pounding, he saw the chestnut gelding drinking leisurely at the edge of a nearby stream. He stood up slowly and looked around him. Wilderness . . . no sign of habitation in sight.

The horse turned toward him as he approached, allowing him to take the reins. Securing the animal nearby, he lowered himself to his stomach on the stream's bank. He splashed his face and head liberally with the cold water, then washed the blood from his temple, his probing fingers ascertaining that the gash there might just as easily have taken his life.

Refreshed, his senses clearing, Reed walked back to the horse and withdrew the rifle from the leather sheath on its side. Checking the saddlebags, he found limited ammunition. He tore a piece from the beef jerky in the bottom of the bag and chewed gingerly. Still unsteady, he cursed his wavering steps as he walked to the top of a wooded rise.

Reed caught his breath. Stretched out below him were a cabin, a barn, and a few branding corrals . . . and standing a short distance from the cabin door, its bulky outline unmistakable, stood the covered wagon.

Reed's heart jumped to a sudden pounding. A crippling knife of pain stabbed simultaneously in his temple, driving him to his knees as he gripped his head, waiting for the pain to cease.

Reed took deep, fortifying breaths as the situation became clear. Semiconscious and hardly able to maintain his seat in the saddle after mounting that morning, he had allowed the gelding full rein. The animal's instinct had prevailed, and it had simply returned home. But fate had intervened, allowing him to slip from the saddle before they moved over the last rise. Trained as he was, the horse had remained close by. Ironically, he had been delivered, with no effort of his own, to a spot within walking distance from the man he had been trailing for more time than he cared to recall—but he was powerless to make his move.

Reed stared at the cabin below. There was no sign of Chastity. He drew back at a stirring of movement in the corral. Two men walked into view, a third following. And there was no mistaking Morgan or the men with him.

But where was Chastity?

The cabin door opened and a woman stepped out. She called, and Morgan started swiftly toward her. He spoke to her sharply, then entered the house in a rush.

His gaze fastened intently on the door, Reed held his breath. And he waited.

Seated at the side of the bed, Chastity took deep, strengthening breaths. She was determined to stand. The young woman who was looking after her had attempted to stop her, but she had warned her off. There was something about the way that woman looked at her. Her touch was gentle . . . but her black eyes were as cold as onyx. Her gaze sliced at her with a silent viciousness that she sensed could easily draw blood.

But she had no time for musings. She needed to regain her strength. She needed to be up so she might leave this place . . . so she might reach the mission somehow and find someone who would see to it that Morgan paid for what he had done.

Reed was dead . . .

Reed was dead . . .

Reed was dead . . .

The soul-wrenching litany drummed over and again in her mind. She had tried so hard to hold on to Reed when the bullet struck him, but she could not.

Despising the weakness that allowed a tear to fall, Chastity forced it back. She was still trying to stand when Morgan appeared in the doorway of the room.

She hated him! She despised him with every

ounce of strength in her body! She would see him pay for what he had done!

Morgan walked toward her, frowning.

Hatred forcing a new determination, Chastity reached toward him with a smile.

"You shouldn't be tryin' to get up yet."

Morgan approached Chastity. He took the hand she held out to him. She attempted to smile, but her lips trembled with weakness. Her glorious mane of hair was tousled, her light skin so pale, it was almost transparent. Shadows ringed her eyes, emphasizing the verdant color of orbs that glistened with moisture. The picture was one of a beauty as fragile and delicate as glass. Morgan longed to possess it. He hungered to make it his.

He whispered hoarsely, "You should be restin'. You lost a lot of blood."

"I want to get up."

Morgan slid his arm around her, supporting her as she wavered. "You'll start your shoulder bleedin' again."

"I have to get up. I want to see Reed."

Morgan tensed. He curled his arm more tightly around her. "He's not here, Chastity."

Morgan felt the shock that rocked her.

"But you said he was."

"No, you're mistaken." Jealousy swelled at the emotion Chastity struggled to withhold. He continued softly, "He was shot. He fell from the wagon. When the renegades rode off, we saw them dragging his body behind them."

Elaine Barbieri

Chastity gasped.

"I'm sorry, Chastity." Morgan tightened his arm around her. He drew her against his chest. He breathed in the scent of her hair, a sudden lust rising so sharply that he was hard put not to take her then and there.

No, he wanted more. He wanted this woman to *give* herself to him. He wanted to own her, body and soul. He would have it no other way.

Chastity was trembling.

"You have to lie down, Chastity. You have to rest." Morgan managed a tender smile. "We're goin' to be leavin' here in another day or so."

"We need to tell someone." He saw the difficulty with which she continued, ". . . about the Indians."

"We will. We'll tell them what the Indians did."

"Yes."

Morgan lay Chastity back on the bed. He lifted the coverlet and drew it up over her, frowning at the bloodstained dress she still wore. He wound his fingers in the fiery curls stretched across the pillow, then leaned over her to touch his mouth to her cheek.

He felt the shock that again rippled through her. It sent his blood surging. Drawing back, barely controlling himself, he whispered, "Go to sleep now."

Turning away from the bed, Morgan saw Conchita in the doorway. Taking her arm as he drew the door closed behind him, he spat out, "Get that dress off her when she wakes up and

314

put her in something *clean,* do you understand? I won't have her lying there that way."

"Yes, Morgan."

Releasing Conchita, Morgan dismissed her from his mind as well. He had a schedule to keep. They would be finished branding soon, and when the herd was sold, he'd leave this place and everyone in it behind him.

Then he would have time only for Chastity.

Reed watched Morgan emerge from the cabin and walk back to the branding corrals with a purposeful stride.

Reed withdrew from the edge of the rise. Was Chastity inside the cabin? He needed to know.

His head aching, Reed struggled to clear his mind. She had to be there. He had seen the look in Morgan's eyes. Morgan wouldn't have let her get away from him.

But he had to be sure.

His head was throbbing.

Conchita shook with rage.

*Put her in something clean, do you understand? I won't have her lying there that way.*

Morgan's words reverberated in her mind. His touch had once sought her female flesh hungrily. It was now cruel and hard. His words had formerly been gentle and loving. They were now cold and without heart. She had been a fool to believe he loved her.

Fury consuming her, Conchita approached the clothing folded neatly in the corner of the room. She withdrew a cotton nightgown, her smile rigid. She would dress the red-haired woman in this gown. Morgan would recognize it. She had worn that gown often when she lay beside him—those times when Morgan and she had made love with a passion so intense that her heart had almost stopped.

Yes, he would remember, and he would think of her. He would feel the heat of those moments again. He would not be able to look at the red-haired woman without thinking of the way they had loved.

Her hand twisting tightly in the soft white cotton, Conchita walked into the rear room and paused beside the red-haired woman's bed. She was sleeping. Her face was still, her breast heaving slowly beneath the bandage visible there. The gold locket she wore lay in the hollow of her throat. It mocked her, and Conchita reached out to tear it from its rest.

The red-haired woman's eyes snapped open the moment she touched it. Thrusting her hand away, the woman clenched the locket tightly in her palm, shielding it from her touch.

Conchita smiled, speaking with true pleasure. "I do not want your locket! I have seen one like it before. Another young woman wore it just as you do. She displayed it just as proudly against her white throat, holding it just as you do now, but she was more beautiful than you. Her hair was as black as pitch and her eyes as blue as the sky above. She worked in a saloon, this woman with a locket like yours. She was a *puta*. She cheated at cards, and she cheated at love, and everyone knew her for what she was. So, you may keep your locket . . . for it reminds all who see it that you are a woman who is no different than *me*."

The red-haired woman blinked. She rasped, "This woman you speak of . . . tell me her name."

Conchita laughed.

"Tell me her name!"

Conchita shrugged. "That woman had no name. Like me, she was no one."

Her smile never more true, Conchita threw the gown on the bed and walked away.

# *Chapter Eleven*

Twilight darkened the sky, muting the glory of vermillion clouds that floated in the brilliant pink and gold of the setting sun. But Reed had little thought for the beauty of the waning day. Instead, he lay on the summit of the rise where he had waited most of the day, watching the cabin.

It galled him when he awakened on several occasions that his concentration had lapsed and sleep had overwhelmed him. But the value of those moments became apparent as his strength rapidly returned. Thinking more clearly, he determined that he needed to ascertain whether Chastity was indeed inside that cabin before he could make his move.

Reed chewed the last, stringy strips of jerky

with determination. Morgan and his men had
been hard at work through the day. They were
only now leaving the branding fire. They made
no attempt to herd new animals into the enclo-
sure. He suspected they would soon be ready to
move the herd.

Morgan and his men approached the cabin.
Smoke had been rising from the chimney
throughout the day, an indication that the
woman he had seen earlier was hard at work
there. The woman had been young. Somehow,
he could not make himself believe that she
could belong to anyone other than Morgan if
his reputation with women was to be believed.

If so, where was Chastity? What had they
done with her? He could not believe they would
have gone through the trouble of driving the
wagon back to the cabin if Chastity had not
been in it.

Darkness was falling. Time was growing
short. Where was she? *How* was she?

"How do you feel, Chastity?"

Hatred rose inside Chastity, so sharp and
strong that it almost slipped from her lips as
Morgan approached her. She had dozed most
of the day, and she was grateful, for the waking
moments had been almost more than she could
bear. The memory of Reed's deep voice in her
ear as they had lain intimately close, his breath
on her cheek, the warmth of him pressed tightly
against her, had assailed her with aching grief.

Reed was dead.

Elaine Barbieri

The thought had drummed over and again in her mind. But with her returning strength came a strengthening of her resolve. She would not waste time on tears. Instead, she would see Morgan pay for what he had done. She had made that promise to Reed during the long night past. With all the anguished love in her heart, she had promised. Morgan thought she was a fool whom he could manipulate with his charm. She had been such a person once, but she would never be that kind of fool again. Her short acquaintance with Morgan had taught her that treachery often wore a smile. She intended to use that lesson well.

Chastity looked at Morgan. He was waiting for her reply. She managed a weak smile. "I feel better. I want to get up."

"No, you're too weak."

"I want to walk." Chastity was determined. "I . . . I've been too much trouble. I need to get back on my feet so I can take care of myself."

"Too much trouble . . ?" Morgan's boyish features twitched. "Did Conchita complain? Did she mistreat you?"

"No." A chill moved down Chastity's spine at the flash of viciousness in his words. That same viciousness had taken Reed's life. "No, I . . . I need to see that Reed's death is reported so someone will go after those renegade Indians. I need to know they will pay." Chastity took a breath as her composure briefly failed.

Morgan leaned closer. Chastity's flesh crawled as he whispered, "I know. Don't worry

320

about that now. I'll take care of that for you when we get to the nearest town. You shouldn't be thinkin' about anythin' but gettin' well. You aren't well enough to walk yet."

"I am."

"No."

*"Yes, I am."*

Chastity felt Morgan stiffen. He didn't like being challenged. She saw the conflict that raged behind his pleasant mask before he responded, "All right. Just a few steps."

Chastity stood up slowly, the desire to strike away Morgan's supportive arm almost more than she could withstand. Her legs wobbling, she took one step, then another. Willing herself stronger, she straightened her back, her step growing more steady. She looked up to see Conchita standing in the doorway, her expression cold.

The truth was suddenly clear. Morgan had thrust Conchita into the past when he marked her for his future.

Chastity took another determined breath. "I can walk alone."

Morgan's grip tightened. "No."

"I want to."

"No."

Lifting her suddenly from her feet, Morgan carried her back to the bed and laid her there. He pulled up the coverlet as she began, "Mr. Jefferson, I—"

His head snapped back toward her. "Call me Morgan." He frowned. "Everyone does. It's my middle name. I'd feel more comfortable if you did."

"Morgan . . ." The irony in his admission hardened Chastity's determination. She would see him admit to other things as well, if it was the last thing she ever did. "I know you think you know what's best for me, but—"

"I do know what's best for you, especially now." Morgan's dark eyes grew earnest. "You're alone, Chastity. You don't know this country. I do. You can rely on me to take care of you." He paused, his voice deepening, "I want you to trust me."

Trust him. Chastity's stomach revolted.

"Are you all right? You look pale."

"I'm fine."

"You need something to eat." Morgan looked back at Conchita, who still stood by the door. "Get Chastity something to eat." She did not move, and Morgan grated, "Get it—now."

He waited a long moment until Conchita turned away, then looked back at Chastity, his color high as he strove for control. "She's a moody witch, even if she is a good cook. I'll be glad to be rid of her."

"She talked to me a little this morning. She mentioned she saw another woman wearing a locket like mine. She didn't remember her name."

"I doubt there ever was such a person. What else did she say?"

"Nothing. She doesn't seem to like to talk."

"She's moody, just as I said. But you won't

have to worry about her much longer. We're goin' to start the herd movin' tomorrow."

"Tomorrow?" Chastity caught her breath.

Morgan smiled, his charm resurfacing. "You'll be ridin' in the wagon. Conchita can drive. When we reach town, I'm goin' to get you to the nearest doctor." His voice dropped a husky note softer." I want to make sure you're healin' right. You're special to me, you know."

*Hypocrite.*

"Then I'm goin' to the sheriff to make sure he gets the whole story on what happened."

*Liar.*

"I'm goin' to take good care of you—so good that you'll never have to worry about anythin' again."

*Murderer.*

"You're real pale." Morgan turned to address Conchita when she appeared in the doorway, a plate in hand. "Chastity isn't feelin' well. She might need some help."

"I don't need help."

Morgan looked at her, then back at Conchita. "Put the plate by the bed." He waited until the plate was within Chastity's reach and Conchita had left the room before he said, "I'll be back in a little while."

He leaned down unexpectedly and kissed her cheek again, this time grazing the corner of her mouth. Feeling defiled, Chastity watched as he left the room.

\*   \*   \*

"All right, what did you say to her?"

Morgan gripped Conchita's arm roughly when the bedroom door was securely closed behind him. He hissed, "I saw the way she looked at you."

"I said nothing! She lies if she told you I did!"

"Watch what you say about her, Conchita." The flush that colored Morgan's face sent fear coursing down her spine. "She isn't like you. She's a decent woman. She was raised right. She has morals."

Conchita spoke past the pain his words evoked. "Like you do, Morgan?"

She did not see the blow coming. Knocked backward as his fist struck her cheek, Conchita fell against Bartell, seated at the table. She heard his protest. She felt his arm support her as she struggled to regain her senses.

"Another thing—I told you I wanted the bloody clothes off her—something *clean* for her to wear, not that rag of yours! Take care of that tomorrow, or you'll be damned sorry you didn't."

In the blur that followed as Morgan pulled her free of Bartell's grip and thrust her staggering into the corner, only one thought became clear in Conchita's mind. Whatever the outcome of Morgan's exchange with this woman for whom he now lusted, there would be no going back. Morgan was done with her.

Facing her, rage seething in eyes as black as death, Morgan rasped, "If you tell her anythin' about this, I'll cut your heart out."

Drawing herself slowly erect, Conchita ignored the painful throbbing of her cheek as she held Morgan's gaze.

Cut her heart out?

Fool that Morgan was, he did not realize that his threat was meaningless.

That deed was already done.

The hours until Reed watched the cabin go dark and still for the night had stretched uncomfortably long. His strength had returned and his mind was now totally clear. The rifle strapped loosely to his back, he worked his way through the shadows. His plan was simple. He would ascertain if Chastity was in the cabin. If she was, he would get her out, any way he could.

Anxiety unlike any he had ever known choked Reed's throat as he peered in the first window. Four bedrolls were stretched out on the hard floor, one of them empty. With the fifth member of the gang absent throughout the day, there was only one unaccounted for.

Reed's heartbeat raced faster. Working his way around the cabin, he slipped up to the window in the rear and peered in. His heart went cold. The flame of a single candle lit the room. It illuminated Chastity's face where she lay sleeping on a cot. The bandage that was exposed in the neckline of the white garment she wore was stained with blood.

Reed swallowed thickly past the lump in his throat as Chastity moved, groaning in her sleep.

He glanced cautiously around him again. He was about to lift himself to slide through the open window when a rustle of movement in the corner of the room caused him to jump back. A shadowed figure moved in the chair in the corner. The man stood up and advanced toward the bed, allowing Reed positive identification.

Morgan.

Hatred swelled in a blinding rush that almost propelled Reed through the window. But common sense prevailed. Shuddering with the intense emotion he suppressed, Reed watched as Morgan leaned over Chastity's bed. He heard Morgan whisper to her, and he heard her mumbled reply. He saw Chastity turn her head away, appearing to sleep again, and he saw Morgan stand over her for long moments.

Reed strained to control the hard knot of rage tightening within him. He evaluated the situation with his last remaining reserves of composure. Morgan's gun was in plain view. He would never make it into the room before Morgan was able to use it. Nor could he risk Chastity's being hurt in the melee that would ensue if he fired a shot through the window to bring Morgan down.

Reed drew back. He must ascertain how badly Chastity was hurt first. He would form a plan from there. He had to be patient, to wait for a more opportune time when he could be certain he would not be putting Chastity's life in jeopardy when he rescued her.

But if Morgan made a move toward Chastity . . .

Morgan stood looking down at Chastity's pale face, his thoughts disquieted. The look in Conchita's eyes after he struck her had left him uneasy. The sensation that had prickled up his spine as he tried to sleep had contributed to the unrest that had forced him from his bedroll in the outer room an hour earlier. One look at Chastity's vulnerable beauty, and he had been unable to leave.

She was sleeping, her breast rising and falling in deep, steady breaths. His hunger for her was greater than any he had felt before. Chastity was the challenge he had been waiting for. He had sensed it the moment he saw her. He had felt her inner strength, and it had drawn him like a magnet. He had known he must possess her.

Seated in the corner of the room as he dozed fitfully, he had toyed with what the future would hold. He would court Chastity. He would make her believe in him. He would make her think the world was not complete without his loving—as he had done with so many women before her.

But would she surrender the tenets of her virtuous upbringing for him? He was unsure. He was positive of only one thing. He had killed to get her and he would kill to keep her—even if the life eventually sacrificed was her own.

All, or nothing at all. It was his way.

\*　　\*　　\*

Reed remained motionless as Morgan stared at Chastity, then walked back to the chair in the corner. He waited, shuddering with consuming enmity.

Despising himself, detesting his weakness, he waited until Morgan was sleeping, then forced himself to turn away from the window to slip back into the darkness.

"Get those horses hitched! Damn it, Bartell, you're useless!"

The morning sun beat warmly down on his shoulders as Morgan strode across the yard and ripped the harnesses from Bartell's hands. Fastening them, he tested the reins of the wagon, then snapped, "Get back to the herd and give the others a hand. I want them ready to move at my signal!"

Back in the cabin, Morgan glanced around the outer room. Satisfied that nothing but a few unimportant foodstuffs remained, he walked into the rear room to see Chastity seated on the edge of the bed and Conchita standing a short distance away.

Chastity looked up at him, and Morgan stopped still. She was dressed in a simple blouse and skirt, her hair loosely confined at the back of her neck. Moist tendrils clung stubbornly to her hairline even as she attempted to brush them back with her hand. The gleaming color made a sharp contrast with her pale skin and shadowed eyes that held a haunted quality.

She had never looked more beautiful to him.

She stood up as he approached. She started walking shakily.

Annoyed at her attempt at independence, he reproached her, "You're too weak. I'll carry you."

"I can walk."

"I said, I'll carry you."

He attempted to pick her up, but she pushed him away. "I said, I'll walk."

Morgan stiffened, anger flaring as Chastity looked into his eyes, confronting him directly. He saw Conchita's body instinctively twitch. He realized with surprise that if Chastity were any other woman, he would not hesitate to prove who the master was, then and there. But Chastity was not any other woman.

Instead, he nodded. "All right."

He saw the effort she expended in taking her halting steps. He frowned, following her as she continued out into the main room of the cabin without a word. He saw her waver halfway across, and he sensed that her strength was failing badly when she stepped out into the yard. She halted for breath. He waited for her to collapse from the weakness that had raised a fine veil of perspiration on her brow, but she did not. Instead, she continued toward the wagon, pausing when she reached the rear.

Determined to make her ask for his help, he watched as she negotiated the step there, then, with supreme effort, boosted herself inside. Furious, Morgan turned away to see Conchita watching him silently. He approached her and instructed in a carefully controlled voice, "I want you to drive out ahead of the herd. You know how to handle a wagon. Keep a fast enough pace so you won't be overrun. Somebody will ride alongside at all times to make sure you don't get lost." He moved a step closer. "Drive carefully, Conchita. You know what'll happen to you if anything happens to her."

Conchita's dark eyes held his. "*Sí*, I know."

He glanced at Bartell, who sat mounted nearby. "Make sure she keeps the pace."

The wagon lurched forward, and Morgan mounted and dug his heels sharply into his horse's sides.

Chastity closed her eyes as the wagon jerked forward. She swayed, barely able to hold herself erect. It had taken every last ounce of energy she possessed to make it to the wagon. She had truly believed she would not be able to lift herself up onto the bed, but the thought of depriving Morgan of another chance to practice his smiling hypocrisy had infused her with the last-minute strength she needed.

The torment within her almost more than she could bear, Chastity smoothed the pallet on which she sat with her palm. The memory of Reed lying beside her was so acutely vivid at that moment that it stole her breath. Never to see him again, never to hear his voice or feel his touch . . . she brushed away a tear.

A second sense turning her toward the

driver's seat, Chastity looked up to see Conchita looking back at her, reins in hand.

Raising her voice over the rattle of the wagon, she sneered, "So, you cry for the man you lost."

"No," Chastity responded with firm determination. "I don't waste time crying."

A hard smile touched Conchita's lips. "*Bueno*. Neither do I."

Standing just beyond the rise, Reed mounted the chestnut gelding. His mind had raced, preventing sleep during the long night that had followed his furtive visit to the cabin. Morgan's attitude toward Chastity and the deference with which he treated her made him certain that Chastity had not revealed his true identity or the real reason he had come to Indian Territory.

He wondered what Chastity thought had happened to him. Did Morgan tell her he had been killed in the Indian raid Morgan manufactured? The thought tormented him.

Was she even now mourning him? The thought sliced deep.

Chastity was still weak. He had seen her staggering as she walked to the wagon. Morgan had accompanied her, but he had not lent her a supportive hand. He sensed that Chastity had made it clear she didn't want his help. But he knew Morgan's reputation. He would not allow her to defy him for long.

If only he could be sure what Morgan was planning. . . .

Anxiety tightened inside Reed. He needed to

get Chastity away from Morgan before Morgan's patience ran out. He needed to hold her in his arms. It was his fault she had been wounded and was suffering. He would make it up to her.

And he would love her. With all his heart, he would love her.

Twilight had turned the bright sunlight of the first day on the trail into shadows. The driving had been difficult, necessitating that Morgan stay with the herd the entire day while the wagon maintained the lead with Bartell. It irritated Morgan that he had not been able to replace Bartell and ride with Chastity as he'd originally planned. The leisurely day Bartell had as a result irked him. He was determined that Bartell would not have an easy night as well.

"All right, Bartell, you take the first watch."

The look Bartell shot him did not go unnoticed. Morgan snapped, "You got any complaints?"

"No, I ain't, just as long as somebody comes out to relieve me in a few hours. I don't intend spendin' the whole night out there with the herd."

Morgan's gaze grew deadly. His voice dropped a note softer. "You'll stay with the herd as long as I tell you to. If that means the whole night, then you'd better make sure you stay awake, too. If you think I'm goin' to lose another head to the same animals that got those beeves you and Turner were supposed to bring back, you've got another think comin'. We lose another steer tonight, and it'll come out of your share."

Bartell took off his hat and slapped it down on the ground. "Well, I ain't goin' nowhere until I get somethin' to eat!"

"Make it fast, and then get out to the herd." Not waiting for a response, Morgan turned back to the wagon. He approached it slowly, frowning. He had not seen Chastity all day. His first glimpse of her had been when they halted the herd for the night and he had gone to the wagon. He had detested letting her see him covered with the dust of the trail and smelling no better than the animals they drove, but he had been desperate to see her. She had smiled weakly when he attempted to talk to her . . . a trifle too weakly for him not to feel concern.

Stopping by the campfire, Morgan picked up a plate. He motioned for Conchita to fill it, then started for the wagon.

"She says she is not hungry."

Morgan shot Conchita a deadening glance. "Did I ask you to say somethin'?" He climbed into the wagon and slid to Chastity's side. "I brought you somethin' to eat."

"I'm not hungry."

Morgan touched Chastity's wounded shoulder lightly and she withdrew instinctively from him. He frowned. "Are you in pain?"

"No."

"You're not tellin' me the truth."

333

Chastity's gaze shot up to his. "I'm all right."

"Did Conchita change your bandage?"

"It isn't necessary. The wound isn't bleeding anymore."

"Damn her! I told her to check it!" He took a breath. "I'd better look at it."

"No."

"I said—"

"I told you, I'm all right!"

"No, you're not!" Morgan barely controlled his agitation. "All right, I understand how you feel. I'll tell Conchita to do it later. But you have to eat if you expect to regain your strength. We'll be meetin' the fella who's goin' to buy the herd in a couple of days. I won't be able to get you to a doctor until after that's settled." He paused, "I don't want anythin' to happen to you, Chastity."

Chastity stared at him in silence. He saw her lips twitch as she replied, "I'll feel better if I get up and walk a little."

"No, I don't—"

"I want to walk."

If she were any other woman . . .

"All right. If that's what you want."

Morgan reached toward her, but Chastity withdrew with a stiff smile. "I think it would be better if I did as much as I can on my own."

Morgan nodded. He'd give her anything she wanted. It was a price he would have to pay to get what he wanted this time.

Morgan halted at that thought. Could it be? Was he actually accepting the need to *pay* for something he could just as easily take? Would Chastity end up making an honest man out of him?

Morgan hardly withheld a smile. The answer to those questions was simple.

Never.

Conchita stared at the wagon as Morgan disappeared inside, her face still flushed from yet another humiliating dismissal from the man who had cast her aside.

"What's the matter, Conchita?"

Conchita turned toward Bartell, who sat by the fire, plate in hand. He was smirking.

"When are you goin' to get it through your head that Morgan ain't interested in you no more? He's got himself another honey."

"No, he does not."

"Well, you got a point there. He ain't got that high-minded woman yet, but he will. Looks like there ain't nothin' he won't do to get her. I ain't never seen him so caught up in a woman before, and I ain't never seen a woman who can turn him down when he puts his mind to it." Bartell laughed. "Hell, you ought to know that well enough."

*Yes, she knew.*

Bartell scooped up the last remaining bits on his plate, then dropped the plate on the ground. He inched closer. "You're goin' to be lookin' for a new man, soon, ain't you, darlin'?"

Conchita looked at him, her lips twisting with disgust.

"I don't look good to you, do I?" An angry heat darkened Bartell's sweaty face. "I ain't pretty enough, huh? I ain't as young as Morgan is, and I don't smell as sweet."

*Culebra.*

"I guess you'll like it better goin' back to the cantina. Hell, you'd have your choice of greasers there—but you know somethin'? Every last one of them won't smell no better than me!"

"*Snake!*"

Bartell laughed out loud. Standing up slowly, he halted when Morgan stepped down from the wagon, then turned to lift Chastity to her feet beside him.

"Look at that, Conchita." Bartell's voice dropped to a whisper. "He treats her like she's made of glass. Makes you feel real good, don't it?"

Conchita straightened her back.

"How long do you think it'll take him to get her in bed? She's a good, God-fearin' woman. I figure it might even take him a week."

Conchita stood up abruptly. Shuddering with fury, she walked off into the shadows, the sound of Bartell's laughter ringing behind her.

He did not dare get any closer.

Concealed within the foliage a short distance away, Reed watched the figures moving around the fire. It had been a long, difficult day, with Chastity so close, yet just beyond his reach.

The men were eating. He had already eaten from the few stores left behind at the cabin. The need to maintain his strength was never clearer.

Movement at the rear of the wagon forced Reed to pull back. He stiffened when Morgan emerged, then lifted Chastity down.

Reed's heart began a slow pounding. She was so close . . . so close that he could see her pallor and the tremor in her limbs as she started to walk.

Morgan reached out to her.

*Don't touch her, damn it.*

Chastity waved off Morgan's help. She walked around the campfire, and Reed's stomach twisted into a tight knot of pain. She was so damned weak. Even if he could manage to get her away, she was not strong enough for them to make a run for it.

Reed clutched the rifle at his side. He was so tempted . . . but Chastity had been caught in the crossfire before. He could not chance it happening again.

Where was Morgan headed? What did he intend to do? He had been unable to overhear any discussion of their plans, but he knew that at their present rate of travel, it would be at least another day until they were out of Indian Territory. He also knew that he needed to make a move soon, or it might be too late.

Watching Chastity intently, Reed whispered into the darkness surrounding him, his voice filled with the emotion of a promise etched in his heart. "I'm coming to get you, Chastity. Don't give up, darlin'."

The absurdity of that last admonition struck

Reed abruptly. Chastity was as weak as a kitten, but she was still holding Morgan at arm's length. And she was outwitting him.

The smile that tugged at Reed's lips twisted the knife of pain within him as he rasped, "I love you, Chastity. Can you hear me, darlin'? I love you."

Chastity walked determinedly toward the campfire. She hesitated as an unexpected glow of warmth briefly filled her heart. Her throat choked tight, and she swallowed against a sudden rise of emotion. It was almost as if Reed's kiss had brushed her lips.

A responsive whisper rose within her. *I love you, Reed*.

"What's the matter, Chastity?"

Chastity was somehow unable to respond.

Mistaking her emotion for weakness, Morgan grated, "I told you that you should be resting!" Sweeping her off her feet, Morgan carried her the few steps back to the wagon and placed her inside. She saw the effort he made to control his anger when he continued, "You're tryin' to do too much too soon." When she still did not reply, he instructed harshly, "Make sure you eat before you go to sleep."

Never more grateful to see the last of him, Chastity watched as Morgan strode from her view.

# Chapter Twelve

The hot morning sun beat down on Morgan's shoulders as he looked down at the bloody carcass of the steer in front of him. He looked back up, his expression hot with anger.

"All right, Bartell, how did you let this happen?"

"The damned cat sneaked up on the quiet. I didn't know anythin' about it until this mornin'!"

"You fell asleep, didn't you?"

"No!"

Morgan glared, glancing at the nervously milling cattle nearby. "Well, we're all goin' to pay for it! Look at these beeves! They're so spooked that they're goin' to be jumpin' at every sound today!"

"It ain't my fault!"

"No, it's never your fault."

Turning away from Bartell with disgust, Morgan spurred his horse back toward camp. Reining up, he jumped from his horse and strode toward the wagon.

"Get that wagon ready to start movin', Conchita!" He flicked a disparaging glance at her as she turned toward him. "We can't waste any time. It's goin' to be a damned long day."

He approached the rear of the wagon. The attack on the herd the previous night was unexpected and annoying. He had had plans for the day ahead. With the cattle becoming trail-oriented, he had expected an easier day than the previous one, a day in which he might be able to spend time with Chastity. It was essential to gain her complete confidence, of that he was certain. She wasn't the average woman. Even wounded and grieving, she maintained an independence that kept him at his distance. He needed to bridge that distance. He was certain he could, given the time he needed—time that Bartell had stolen from him that day because of his incompetence.

Cursing the opportunity that had escaped him, Morgan turned the corner of the wagon, his agitation warming to a heat of another kind at the sight of Chastity standing inside. She was looking much stronger, and she was all woman, the reserve with which she greeted him only making him want her more. He smiled. "Are you ready to leave?"

"Yes." She paused. "How much longer do you think it'll be before we reach a town?"

"I can't really be sure," Morgan hedged. "It's accordin' to how the drivin' goes. The cattle are edgy. It might take us a little longer than I thought. Walker will be ridin' with you today." He frowned. "I'm goin' to have to stay with the herd most of the day. If I don't, it'll only take us longer."

Chastity did not reply.

"If you need anythin', Conchita will take care of it. If she doesn't, Walker will see to it that she does."

"Conchita has been very helpful."

"Yes . . . just make sure that she takes care of that bandage today." Morgan frowned, his youthful face suddenly earnest. "I don't like turnin' over your care to others, but I don't have any choice."

"I understand."

"I'll make it up to you."

"There's no need for that."

"But I will. That's a promise, Chastity."

Chastity lowered her gaze, and a hunger unlike any he had ever known gripped Morgan's innards. If he didn't leave now—

Turning away abruptly, Morgan approached Walker where he stood nearby. He warned, "Watch over that wagon with your life, you hear?"

Not waiting for Walker's response, Morgan mounted and kicked his horse into motion.

\* \* \*

Contempt closed Chastity's throat as the wagon rumbled onward.

*I'll make it up to you.*

The promise of a killer.

Chastity turned toward the driver's seat, where Conchita sat at the reins. She had never met a woman like Conchita before—young, but in some ways older than she would ever be. She wondered how many promises Morgan had made to her and then broken. She wondered if Conchita had ever truly believed them.

She supposed she would soon find out.

Chastity worked her way forward. Hesitating when she reached the driver's seat, she addressed Conchita in a voice raised over the rattling din, "Do you know where we're going, Conchita?"

Conchita's gaze remained fastened on the trail ahead. "No. Morgan does not speak in confidence to me."

Chastity ached inside at her pain. "I'm sorry, Conchita."

Conchita turned on her, eyes blazing. "Do not pity me! Better, you pity yourself!"

Chastity's throat tightened. "What are you saying?"

"I am saying nothing! It is not my business. Morgan has made that clear to me, and I have learned to listen to what Morgan says."

"Why, Conchita?" The fury that flamed to life within Chastity set her to shuddering. "Because you know Morgan isn't what he's pretending to be? Is that why? Because you know he's done terrible things?"

"So, you are not the fool you appear to be."

"No, I'm not a fool. I know that Morgan kil—"

Conchita interrupted harshly. "You *are* a fool if you say more!"

"It's the truth, isn't it?"

"The truth?" Conchita's sudden smile was hard. "I do not know the luxury of truth. To me, lies are more common than truth, and they suit just as well when one fights to survive."

"But there are some people who don't *deserve* to survive, Conchita, because they take the lives of others. Because they kill innocent people who are trying to lead decent lives. We can't let them escape to keep doing those same, terrible things over and over again!"

"It is not my concern!"

"It's everyone's concern!"

"Morgan *loved* me!"

"Morgan never loved anyone!"

"You lie!"

Shuddering so hard that she could barely speak, Chastity took a stabilizing breath. "Lies or truth, the outcome is the same. He doesn't love you now."

"Because of you!"

"No, because of *Morgan*. Because he tired of you, just as he would tire of me. But he won't get a chance to tire of me."

Conchita's dark eyes bore into hers. "Morgan always gets his way."

"No, not this time. There is only one man I love."

"He is dead."

"No, not in my heart."

Conchita laughed aloud. "It is not your heart that Morgan wants!"

A wave of weakness sweeping over her, Chastity took another fortifying breath. She grasped her locket, needing the strength it imparted, only to hear Conchita laugh again.

"A *puta's* locket."

Her gaze holding Conchita's intently, Chastity retorted, "There was no *puta* with a locket like mine. Morgan said you lied."

"I did not lie!"

Chastity's heart began a new pounding. "Where did you see this woman?"

"In the saloon where she made her living."

"Where was this saloon?"

"Not far from here." Conchita's lips tightened. "You may find her if you choose. I would give me great pleasure for you to show Morgan that all I said was true."

"Conchita . . . please. I need to know. Where was this saloon?"

"In Caldwell."

Chastity caught her breath. "Caldwell . . . Kansas?"

"Yes."

Chastity closed her eyes, the incredulity of the moment overwhelming her.

"What are you two talkin' about in there?"

Walker's shout from his position alongside

the wagon snapped Chastity's eyes open. Weakness, frustration, and the soul-draining ache within her becoming more than she could withstand, Chastity sank to her knees.

"Get back in the wagon and lie down, damn it!" His look pure panic, Walker spat, "If Morgan sees you lookin' like that, we'll all pay the piper!"

Hardly aware of Walker's words, Chastity moved back to the pallet. Her head spinning with the thought of a love lost and an opportunity that had escaped her, she lay back and closed her eyes.

A thick cloud of dust enveloped the trailing herd. Drawing up his bandanna to shield himself against it, Reed scrutinized the herd intently from his covert position beside the trail. The sun was high. The steers were uneasy. They had been trailing with loud complaints the morning long. Morgan and his men struggled to contain them, keeping to the sides of the herd where the breakaways commonly occurred. It did not take long to see that the shortage of hands was a problem that Morgan had not anticipated. Morgan's decision to neglect the drag position, sending a man back to check the rear only when occasion demanded, was a mistake that Reed was determined to turn against him.

A long night of thought and planning behind him, Reed leaned low over the saddle and rode out cautiously into the thick, grainy mist at the rear of the herd. It was approaching noon. The men were hungry, and thirst had added another edge to the cattle's irritability. He knew the time would never be more right.

Reed struck a match to the torch he had carefully prepared. It burst into flame, startling the steers nearby as he spurred his mount into a sudden forward charge. Whooping in a low voice, he dodged in and out, touching the lit torch to the heels of the uneasy beeves.

The result was instantaneous.

Frantic bellows and panicked calls picked up the heads of the cattle, spreading like wildfire in the split second before the herd moved in a sudden, frenzied surge forward.

Stampede!

"What in hell is that?"

Conchita heard it, too. She recognized the sound at the same moment as Walker, her eyes widening. The pounding hooves behind them grew closer as Walker shouted, "It's a stampede! Get this wagon out of the way, or them damned beeves are goin' to run right over it!"

Her hands trembling, Conchita whipped the team into a sudden spurt forward. She had seen a wagon such as theirs caught in a stampede. There had been little left of those within to bury.

Conchita pulled the wagon off the trail, her heart pounding as the stampeding herd came into view. The red-haired woman inched her way unsteadily forward. Her eyes widened when she saw the approaching herd. "What's happening?"

"Stampede." Conchita raised her chin, determined to control her shaking. "Something frightened the cattle. They are running."

His horse dancing nervously underneath him, Walker turned toward Conchita with a sharp command. "I'm goin' out to help with that herd before we lose half of them. You stay here, where you're safe. Don't move the wagon, understand?"

Conchita did not respond.

"Answer me, damn it, or I'll put a bullet through your heart here and now!"

Conchita's expression hardened. "I will not move the wagon."

Her gaze remained fixed as Walker disappeared into the dust.

The thunder of the stampeding herd was fading into the distance. The cloud of dust left in its wake still whirled in the sunlit air, its residue falling on the motionless wagon pulled off a safe distance from the trail.

His mount concealed in the foliage, Reed approached the wagon cautiously. He held the rifle cocked and ready, but Walker was nowhere in sight. His plan was proceeding without a hitch. Walker had heard the cattle coming and had immediately moved the wagon out of the path of the stampede. He had then ridden off to help bring the herd under control.

Reed scanned the surrounding area once

more as he reached the wagon. Walker was gone. He was in the clear.

The sound of a step!

Reed turned at the same moment a woman's voice called out with blood-chilling coldness, "Put down your gun, *señor*."

"Reed!"

Chastity wavered with shock as Reed stood tall and alive in front of her! Only minutes earlier she had watched Walker ride out of sight within the retreating herd—and had then felt the barrel of Conchita's gun in her ribs. Stunned, she had been unable to do more than follow Conchita's order to climb down from the wagon and wait silently concealed behind it. She had been confused, never expecting that when she stepped out from behind the wagon, Reed would be standing a few feet away.

Her heart thundering when the incredible blue of Reed's eyes locked with hers, Chastity started spontaneously toward him, only to feel Conchita's gun jam painfully into her back as she ordered, "Don't move!"

Reed took a step and Conchita commanded, "Stop, or I shoot!"

Reed halted abruptly.

"Drop your gun!"

Reed allowed the rifle to slip to the ground. His deep voice was a sweet music Chastity had thought never to hear again when he asked, "Are you all right, Chastity?"

"He said you were dead!" Chastity was still

reeling. "I saw the bullet hit you. I saw you fall. I believed him!"

Conchita motioned Reed forward. She stopped him when he was a few yards away. Pressing the gun more tightly into Chastity's back, Conchita addressed Reed sharply. "You are not the man of God you were believed to be, are you, *señor*?"

Reed's eyes darted to Chastity with such anguish that she trembled anew. His response was concise.

"No."

"I knew. Why are you here?"

"I came to Indian Territory to get Morgan." Chastity felt the tremor that shook Conchita as Reed continued, "I've been chasing him for a long time. I wanted to find him and bring him back to face the law . . . but I don't care about that now. I just want to get Chastity out of here before it's too late."

"You would kill Morgan?"

Reed's hard frame stiffened. "If he tried to kill me, or if he laid a hand on Chastity—yes, I would."

"I knew you were watching the wagon."

Conchita's unexpected response turned Chastity toward her with a start as Conchita continued, "You were outside camp last night. You saw Morgan and your woman walking. You were more still than the shadows." She questioned unexpectedly, "What will you do if I put this gun down?"

"I'll take Chastity out of here. We need a head

start. That's why I started the stampede, so we'd be able to get far enough ahead that Morgan couldn't catch us."

"No, the stampede will not give you enough time."

Chastity saw the tightening of Reed's expression the moment before Conchita continued, "*I* will give you the time you need."

Conchita lowered her gun. Rushing forward, Chastity managed only a few unsteady steps before Reed's arms closed around her, crushing her close. The warmth of him, the joy!

"Quickly, you must go!"

Chastity turned back toward Conchita. "You have to come with us."

"No."

"It won't be safe if Morgan thinks you helped us."

Conchita's smile was cold. "I will handle Morgan."

"But . . ."

"There is only one thing I want from you." Lifting her skirt, Conchita withdrew a knife from the sheath on her thigh. She approached Chastity, her hand so quick that Chastity did not comprehend her intent until she saw the bright lock of hair Conchita held in her hand. Making no comment, Conchita instructed, "Go."

Picking up his rifle, Reed curled his arm around Chastity's shoulder. "Let's go."

"But . . ."

Chastity's protest faded when Conchita

turned abruptly and climbed into the wagon.

Seated in front of Reed on the saddle moments later, Chastity had no further time for thought as she leaned back against the familiar warmth of Reed's chest and the horse jumped into motion.

The damned fool never should have left them alone!

Pushing his mount to the limit, Morgan raced back along the trail, retracing the path stampeding hooves had traveled only an hour earlier. Furious at the unexpected turn of events, he was still uncertain what had spooked the herd. The only thing of which he was sure was that when he had looked up to see Walker materialize in the cloud of dust behind him, Walker was closer to meeting his maker than he ever was before.

Straining his gaze into the distance, Morgan saw the outline of the wagon ahead. He released a satisfied breath. He wasn't certain what he had been expecting. He didn't trust Conchita. He had half expected her to take off with the wagon and Chastity, but he supposed she was too smart for that. She knew he would hunt her down if she did, and that she wouldn't live a second longer than it took for him to level his gun and pull the trigger.

The truth was that he was starting to feel uncomfortable with the role he was playing with Chastity. His patience was stretching thin. Too many unpredictable things were happening.

Morgan drew back on the reins as he neared the wagon, immediately alert. Something was wrong. There was no sign of movement inside.

Morgan loosened the gun in his holster. His attention acute, he urged his mount forward gradually, scrutinizing the surrounding foliage. He was within a few yards of the wagon when Conchita stepped into sight.

He dismounted beside her. "Where's Chastity?"

"She is in the wagon. She was tired and fell asleep."

"Tired, with everythin' that was goin' on?" Morgan glanced up at the wagon. "Did you check on her? Maybe she's gettin' the fever."

"No. She is sleeping."

Morgan squinted down at Conchita. There was something about the way she was looking at him. He smiled. "You wouldn't be thinkin' you could trick me, would you, Conchita?"

"Trick you, Morgan?"

Conchita took a step forward that brought her close enough that he could see the gleam of her dark hair, the mellow color of her skin, the depth of eyes so black that a man could lose himself in them. Her familiar, musky scent rose between them. He remembered the times that scent had enveloped him, when it had driven him wild with lust for her flesh.

*But those days were gone.*

Conchita grunted with surprise when he pushed her roughly aside. He started toward the wagon. He took one step up into the wagon and halted abruptly. The coverlet was drawn up over Chastity. She was so tightly enclosed in it that all that was visible was a lock of her glorious hair.

Morgan moved slowly toward her, a gradual realization dawning. Chastity was still—too still. His chest heaving, Morgan reached out to touch her hair. He gasped aloud when the lock came away in his hand.

Enraged when he ripped back the coverlet to see a mound of clothing beneath, Morgan jumped down from the wagon. His rapid advance toward Conchita halted the moment he saw her gun.

"*Puta* . . . what did you do with her?"

Conchita smiled, a glorious smile that would have dazzled any other man. "She is gone, Morgan. Her man took her away! He isn't dead, you see. He is alive and is now taking her back where you can never reach her again."

"Back to the Indian mission where he thinks he's safe, I suppose. He's a fool! I'll get her back. I'll—"

"No, *you* are the fool, Morgan." Conchita's smile turned cold. "He isn't a man of God. That was pretense! He is a man who has been chasing *you*. He came to Indian Territory to take you back to face the law. The woman came to help him."

Morgan shook his head. "No . . . I don't believe you."

"She is not your woman, Morgan." Conchita

no longer smiled. "She will *never* be your woman."

"Does it give you pleasure to say that, Conchita?" Morgan took a bold step forward. "Well, it gives me pleasure to tell you that you'll never be my woman again, either—that the sight of you makes me sick. Now, get out of my way!"

"No! Do not move, Morgan!" Conchita's finger twitched on the trigger. "You will not go after her."

"Oh, yes, I will!"

"No."

"Pull the trigger, Conchita. Go ahead!" Morgan laughed aloud. "You can't, can you? Because you still *love* me, because you still think that I may change my mind and take you back. You can't shoot me, can you?"

"Oh, yes, I can, Morgan." Conchita was trembling visibly. "I can because I have nothing left to lose. You took my hope and my life away from me when you threw away my love. I have nothing! I am nothing! I lose nothing when I—"

His hand snaking to his holster in a blurring flash, Morgan fired. Conchita's body jerked with the impact of the bullets that struck her breast. It occurred to Morgan as he watched Conchita fall to the ground that there was a look of incredulity around her eyes before they fluttered closed. That amused him. She knew him so well. He did not think he could surprise her.

That moment of amusement past, Morgan turned toward his mount. Conchita had said that Farrell had taken Chastity with him. With Chastity too weak to ride alone, they were doubtlessly both riding Simmons's horse. Riding double, they could not have gotten far.

The flaming lock of hair still in his hand, Morgan spurred his horse into motion without a backward look.

The sound of Morgan's hasty departure dwindled into silence as Conchita struggled to open her eyes. Her breathing was short. The light of day was fading. Her life was fading as well.

Conchita fought back pained tears. But her pain was not of the body. Instead, it was an anguish of the soul—for the hunger within her that had gone unsated, for love wasted and ignored, for all the dreams she had once believed in, and for the harsh reality of knowing they would never be.

Oh, Morgan . . . A sob sounded deep inside her. How she had loved him! If only he had loved her, too, she would have . . .

A rattling breath halted Conchita's silent lament. Morgan's face flashed before her, and she sought to call his name, but the sound would not emerge. The thought occurred to her, as the light rapidly waned, that a woman who was unloved really had no life at all.

She did not resist as her breathing ceased.

"Chastity, darlin' . . ."
Reed felt Chastity slump against him. They had been riding for hours along the rough trail.

355

The sun was slipping toward the horizon. He had kept the horse to a steady pace, aware that if they could manage to elude Morgan until dark, their chances of escaping him increased.

But the tension in Chastity's body had expanded more with every mile they traveled. Her wound was becoming increasingly painful. He knew she remained silent through her distress only by sheer strength of will.

"Are you all right, Chastity?"

Chastity did not respond. Instead, her head lolled back suddenly against him, and Reed was struck with a moment of pure fear.

Drawing his mount to a halt, Reed turned Chastity toward him, his heart pounding. Her complexion was so colorless that she seemed drained of life, and the fear turned to panic.

Dismounting swiftly, Reed caught her as she slid from the saddle. He carried her into the foliage and laid her on the cool ground, noting that the bandage on her shoulder was marked with fresh blood. Retrieving his canteen, he stripped off his bandanna and moistened it, then bathed her face with the cool water. Chastity opened her eyes.

"You're bleeding again."

"No." Chastity managed a smile. "I hurt myself when I jumped down from the wagon with Conchita. The wound started bleeding then, but it stopped." And at his look of concern, "I'm all right. I'm just tired."

Chastity glanced around them, appearing to realize for the first time where they were. "We can't stop, Reed. Morgan will start after us as soon as he goes back to the wagon."

Restraining her when she tried to sit up, Reed shook his head. "No, you need to rest for a little while." He stroked her cheek. He brushed her lips with his. He realized with sudden clarity that there was nothing in the world that mattered more to him then this woman he loved.

"I want to go on, Reed." Chastity struggled to sit up. She thrust away his hand when he tried to restrain her. "You know what'll happen if we stay here."

"Nothing will happen." Reed took Chastity's hand. He raised it to his lips. "We'll stay here for a half hour so you can rest, and then we'll go on."

"Reed, listen to me." Chastity's voice was weak, but familiar spirit glowed in the shimmering sparks of green in her eyes as she whispered, "If anyone had told me a few months ago that I'd be here with you now, a gunshot wound in my shoulder and a killer in pursuit, I would've told them they were insane. That insanity has become reality, Reed, but the true insanity is in the mind of the man who is following us. You know what Morgan's like. And I've come to know him, too. I saw the look in his eyes. He's a liar and a killer, and he'll do anything he needs to do to get his way. He'll be furious when he gets back to the wagon and finds me gone. I'm afraid for Conchita. I'll never comprehend how she could love him."

Chastity took a stabilizing breath, her eyes

locking with Reed's as she continued, "But I understand how she feels. When I thought I'd lost you, Reed, the world seemed to come to an end. Now that I have you back, I can't bear to lose you again. Listen to me, Reed," Chastity pleaded, "I'm tired, but with your arms around me, I'm strong. I'm not the same person I was when you walked onto the train that first day. I'm stronger. I'm wiser. I know what it means to love. And I won't let Morgan take it all away from me."

His heart so full that he was momentarily unable to speak, Reed stared at Chastity. His mind returned to the image of the woman who had approached him on the train. So prim, so proper . . . but with an inner strength and determination that would not yield. Chastity's outer appearance had changed, but the inner determination remained the same. Whatever had made him think it would fail them now?

His voice hoarse with emotion, Reed whispered, "I spent years seeking justice for a wrong that could never be righted. I came to Indian Territory believing that if I couldn't find justice, I could at least find revenge. But I found something more important." Swallowing, Reed managed words wrung from the depths of his heart. "I love you, Chastity."

His emotions held in so tight a check that he could not manage more, Reed swept Chastity up into his arms. Striding back to the gelding waiting nearby, he allowed himself only the moment it took to brush her lips with his before lifting her up onto the saddle and mounting behind her.

*The bastard . . . I'll kill him.*

Grimacing with pure malice, Morgan raced along the trail. He glanced back at the men riding behind him. It had not taken him long to return to the herd and gather his men. He had picked up Farrell's trail quickly, with little loss of time. Luck was on his side.

Conchita. He had left the Mexican whore behind him, her blood draining into the ground. He was rid of her at last. Fool that she was, she had loved him to the end.

Chastity. *Who* was she? *What* was she? The only thing of which he was certain was that whoever or whatever she was, she was his.

Farrell. The bastard was living his last day—his last *hour.* He would enjoy letting Chastity witness the end he would put to her lover's life. She would not defy him so easily then.

*Or maybe she would.*

Morgan's anticipation mounted.

A little longer. A little farther.

Morgan stiffened. There was movement on the trail ahead. A horse and rider.

Elation surged!

Morgan turned sharply to his men, shouting, "Remember—don't shoot! Farrell won't chance a gunfight with Chastity riding with him!"

A yell of pure triumph leaving his lips, Morgan urged his mount to a new surge forward.

\* \* \*

Elaine Barbieri

Hoofbeats pounded the ground behind them.

Reed looked back as his mount raced forward on the wooded trail. Sensing the trembling inside Chastity, he urged his mount to a faster pace.

The horsemen drew nearer.

They were closing in.

They were racing alongside!

"Pull up, Farrell, or I'll put a bullet through you here and now!"

Reed felt Chastity shudder at Morgan's shouted command. He could not chance her life.

Drawing his mount to a skidding halt as Morgan's men surrounded them, Reed curved his arms more tightly around Chastity.

Morgan, Walker, Bartell, Simmons—their names were burned into his mind.

"Get down, Farrell." Hatred rank in his gaze, Morgan watched as Reed dismounted. His men and he dismounting as well, he waited until they faced each other squarely before continuing, "So, you're not a parson after all. Conchita told me you came here to Indian Territory to get me." He laughed abruptly. "Don't look so surprised! You knew Conchita would be waiting for me to come back to the wagon. She pulled a gun on me, but what she really wanted was for me to take her back. I could see it in her eyes, but I told her the truth, that I was through with her. She said she would shoot me." Morgan's smile dropped away. "She never got the chance."

Chastity gasped aloud. Reed reached spontaneously for her as she swayed in the saddle.

"Don't touch her! She belongs to me, now."

Reed turned back toward Morgan with a snarl as Chastity rasped in response, "I belong to you? You're a murderer! You killed Conchita and you tried to kill Reed. Do you really think I would let you touch me?" The setting sun touched Chastity's hair, lighting it to a blazing glow that did not melt her frigid tone as she hissed, "That day will never come!"

"Do you hear her, boys?" Morgan turned briefly toward the men around him. I want you to remember what Chastity's sayin' now, so's you can remind her of it one day after she climbs out of my bed with a smile on her face."

"Bastard!" Reed lurched forward.

"Stop there!" Morgan's lips drew tight. "I don't want to kill you yet."

"Let him go, Morgan." Chastity's voice dropped to a rasping hiss.

"Are you pleading with me, Chastity?" Morgan turned toward Walker. "Get her off that horse so's I can look her in the eye." Waiting until Walker had lowered her to the ground, Morgan pressed, "Now, ask me nice, Chastity. Tell me what you'll do for me if I let Farrell go."

"Shut up, Morgan!" Reed's light eyes iced with fury. His powerful frame tensing, he looked at Chastity, standing only a few feet away. "Don't try to reason with him, Chastity. You know what he is. You said it yourself. He's a liar and a murderer."

"That's enough, Farrell!" Turning back to Chastity, Morgan abruptly smiled an appealing, boyish smile that betrayed none of the malevolence behind it as he coaxed, "Come closer, Chastity."

Chastity did not move.

Morgan's smile dropped away. "I said, come closer."

"Stay where you are, Chastity."

Morgan glanced fiercely at Reed. "Be quiet!"

"Don't go anywhere near him, Chastity." Reed looked into Chastity's eyes. He knew what was coming. He knew Morgan was waiting for just the right moment to kill him. He also knew that Morgan wanted Chastity to see him die so he could put fear into her heart.

He knew what he must do.

He took a step toward Chastity.

"Stay away from her, Farrell." Morgan advanced rapidly toward him. He raised his gun. "Take one more step and it'll be your last."

"I had enough of this, Morgan!" Speaking out unexpectedly, his wiry frame twitching with agitation, Walker spat out, "I ain't goin' to wait around all day while you get your kicks out of makin' Farrell squirm! Do what you got to do and get it over with! I want to get out of here!"

"What makes you think you can tell me what to do, Walker?" Livid, Morgan turned toward him. He leveled his gun. "I'm the boss here, remember?"

Walker refused to back down. His voice rising

# Chastity

hotly, he responded, "Maybe that's the way it was, but I'm gettin' tired—"

The angry confrontation continued, the words fading from Reed's mind as he glanced at the rifle sheathed on the saddle nearby. Walker was shouting, and the others were watching Morgan intently. He would never have a better chance.

Lurching toward the saddle, Reed grabbed for the rifle. Morgan turned to face him, raising his gun to fire just as Chastity leaped between them.

Gunfire echoed sharply!

Chastity's slim frame jerked with the rapid reports!

Reed called out her name, reaching out spontaneously to grasp Chastity close.

Clutching her against him, Reed watched, incredulity flaring as Morgan swayed, then crumpled to the ground.

Chastity turned in his arms, his shock rebounding in her slender frame as Morgan breathed a last, choked breath.

Looking up, Reed saw that Morgan's men were as incredulous as he.

Reed took a quick backward step, drawing Chastity with him as a stranger stepped out of the foliage nearby, a smoking gun in his hand. Squinting against the glare of sunset, he saw several others emerge behind him.

Indians.

The stranger approached to within a few feet of Reed. A big man dressed in buckskins, the

Elaine Barbieri

dark hair that hung loose on his shoulders held in place by an Indian headband, the fellow looked at him with green eyes that boldly declared his mixed heritage. Those eyes flicked toward Chastity at the same moment that a young woman dressed in trail clothing appeared behind the man and walked toward Chastity.

Chastity gasped as the tall, slender woman approached. A new trembling beset her that bore no relation to the furor of the previous moments as gradual realization tingled along her skin.

The woman neared, and a shaft of sunlight glinted suddenly on the heart-shaped locket she wore around her neck.

Chastity went abruptly still. She stiffened when the young woman stripped off her hat to reveal delicate features that were almost angelic in composition and gleaming blond hair worn in a long braid down her back.

A sob escaped Chastity's throat. She remembered that hair. She *knew* that face.

Somehow frozen by the import of the moment, Chastity remained immobile, her gaze intent as the young woman's face twitched, as her lips worked laboriously, as her voice emerged at last in a hoarse whisper.

"Chastity . . . is it you?"

The moment blurring in sobs of joy, Chastity reached out with trembling arms. She felt the familiar warmth of the woman's embrace close around her, holding her tight. Years of aching separation slipped away as Chastity returned her embrace, hugging her with all her strength, emotions long held in check released in choked words that flowed from her lips in disjointed phrases of loving wonder.

Drawing back at last, Chastity stared into young woman's tear-streaked face, at the clear, light eyes so similar to her mother's that they tore at her heart. She saw the tremulous smile so like her own, and she felt an affinity that the long years between could not erase.

Her breath catching in her throat, Chastity turned back toward Reed. Her voice quavering, her happiness profound, she managed an exultant rasp.

"Reed, I would like you to meet my sister. Her name is Purity."

# *Chapter Thirteen*

"Here, let me do that for you."

Reed turned Chastity toward the light, adjusting her shoulders so he might more easily see the chain of her locket that had become entangled in the bright wisps of hair at the nape of her neck. He was becoming more adept at the task. It was a practiced skill, the solitary area in which she had found him lacking.

Morning sunlight filtered through the window of the modest ranch-house bedroom. It was a comfortable room, despite its limited size. The dresser with its small mirror was adequate, and the large bed with a mattress as soft as down was divine.

A tremor of remembered rapture ran down Chastity's spine as she recalled the loving that had transpired in that bed during the dark hours of the previous night. She had given herself totally to Reed, and he had given himself to her in return, with a commitment that went beyond the ecstasy of the moment and the vows they had exchanged a week earlier. Because when all was said and done, she knew now that Reed and she were joined in ways that went beyond the spoken word. They had been singed by the flame of danger faced and conquered, they had been consumed by the fire of a mutual desire raging endlessly unbanked, and they had been fused as one by the blaze of a love so deep and true that it overwhelmed all the aching torments of the past.

Chastity looked up at Reed with a half smile. She recalled the curt, angry man who had stared at her from a bearded face that first day on the train. She recalled that she had truly believed she had never met a man as harsh and crude and totally devoid of the compassion she had sought in approaching him.

Yet, somehow, she had been unable to let him walk out of her life.

She could almost hear her dear aunts' voices now:

*"You see, Harriet, I told you! You worried too much. Chastity is a strong and intelligent woman who is capable of sage decisions. I knew she would find her way."*

*"You knew she would find her way? I'm the one who knew she would find her way! I always said*

*her independence would serve her well!"*

*"You didn't want her to travel west!"*

*"Neither did you!"*

*"You said she should never marry!"*

*"You wanted her to settle for second best!"*

*"You wanted her to work with the Bowery poor!"*

*"I did not!"*

*"You did so!"*

*"Your memory is as self-serving as always!"*

*"While you are ever obstinate!"*

She was certain her aunts' affectionate bickering would now cease. As diverse as their points of view were, the one area where they were united was in their desire for her happiness.

Other shadows of the past had also lifted. Burned into her memory was the terror that Morgan had inflicted that last day. She remembered seeing Reed reach for the rifle at the same moment that Morgan turned toward him with his gun raised and ready to fire. She had instinctively jumped between them then, and she had gone rigid at the sound of rapid gunshots.

How could she have known that the young Indian who appeared so briefly in camp when Reed and she first entered Indian Territory had recognized her locket as similar to the one worn by Pale Wolf's woman? How could she have realized that young Indian would return to his village to report back to Pale Wolf? How could she have believed that Pale Wolf would come looking for her, that he would discover where Morgan's tracks crossed theirs, find Conchita's body, and then follow Morgan's trail directly to them?

Pale Wolf—Cass Thomas—a man from two worlds, was the man Purity loved, the same man who had fired the shot that had brought Morgan down. And with that shot, Purity had been restored to her.

In retrospect, it seemed so right that fate had linked the four of them in such an unlikely way. A bond had been forged between Reed and Pale Wolf that day which would forever warm her heart.

As for herself, her wound was healed and the scar had all but faded. She was healthy and strong again.

Morgan's men were in jail. The unidentifiable stolen cattle remained on Indian land, and the reward collected for Morgan and his men had been turned over to Pale Wolf's Kiowa tribe. Reed and she felt it was a more than fair exchange for their lives.

A wire had been sent to Ed Jenkins, reporting Morgan's demise. In that way, Reed had fulfilled his promise to the man who had sought justice in the death of his only son. Chastity hoped he found peace.

The bedroom where Reed and she now stood was in the Circle C ranch house. Raised on the Circle C by Stan Corrigan after he found her lying on the riverbank that fateful day so long ago, Purity had insisted that Reed and Chastity come there to be married. Their wedding day was beautiful, the event made complete by the addition of—

"That's it. I untangled it."

Reed turned her back to face him, interrupting Chastity's wandering thoughts. He stared at her soberly as she reached up to touch his cheek. She supposed she would never become inured to the love in his eyes that melted her inside—or the realization that this man was hers, as she was his, for the rest of their lives. She slid her fingers into his heavy, sun-streaked hair, loving the feel of it against her palm as she said softly, "You look so somber, Reed."

"I was just thinking . . ." The startling blue of his eyes held hers intently, touching her heart in a way only his gaze could as he continued, "If it wasn't for that little scrap of gold you wear around your neck and what it came to symbolize for you, you might never have felt determined to leave the East and come searching for your sisters. I might never have found you on that train."

Chastity could not suppress a smile. "*I* found *you*, Reed."

"Yeah." Reed drew her closer. His expression did not change. "When I think how close we came to missing each other . . ."

"I don't let myself think about what could've been, Reed. I only let myself think about what is."

His hard body pressed tightly to hers, Reed whispered, "I love what is, Chastity. For the longest time, I didn't believe I would ever be able to say those words again. The bitterness inside me was so great that it influenced everything I did, and the way I looked at everyone I saw. It pointed me in one direction alone, but that path changed the day you walked into my life, even if I refused to admit to it. You confused me. You challenged me. You made me angrier than any woman I had ever known, and when the fever passed and my mind cleared, I still couldn't decide whether you were an angel in disguise, or if you were just a fool."

Reed paused, his light eyes searching her face, "You were so gullible . . . so trusting. I was committed to finding Morgan and I told myself that I could make good use of your trust. I deceived you inadvertently at first. I continued that deceit because it was convenient, and by the time I was ready to admit to my true feelings, it was almost too late. I want to say it all now, so there'll never be any doubt in your mind. You swept aside the shadows of the past for me. You made me realize that I needed to put the darkness to rest in order to go on."

His sweet breath warm against her lips, Reed whispered, "You made me love what 'is' again, Chastity. I love that you're my wife. I love looking at the future knowing that you'll always be there beside me. And I love even more knowing that I'll be holding you in my arms every day for the rest of my life."

Reed's mouth touched hers. His kiss deepened, separating her lips and raising a familiar wealth of emotion that sent Chastity's senses soaring. Sliding her arms around his neck, she drew him closer, feeling the need build inside him as that same need rose within her as well. The hunger, the breathlessness, the pounding of her heart that would not—

"Hey, up there. Are you coming down? We're waiting for you!"

The familiar feminine voice from below shattered the moment. Chastity felt Reed stiffen. She smiled inwardly as he drew back with obvious reluctance, his expression wry.

"It's your sister—the impatient one."

"Bossy is more the word." Chastity's smile widened with warm indulgence. "That's what happens when you're the youngest, Reed. Your sisters never forget it."

Walking down the stairs arm in arm, Chastity smiled at the dark-haired beauty waiting below.

Honesty.

Exquisite Honesty, her black hair gleaming and the sapphire blue of her eyes more brilliant than any precious jewel—she was the oldest, the prettiest, the *bossiest,* and the one who had believed most strongly of all that they would someday be together again.

Chastity's disbelief at the miraculous turn of events the day they arrived at the Circle C was with her still. The last thing either Purity or she expected when the ranch house first came into view was to see Honesty step out onto the porch. Purity and she knew at a glance that it was Honesty. Their hearts had mutually declared in that split second that it could be no one else.

She could not truly remember what happened then, except for her joyous realization, when the three of them were together again at last, that the world had come full circle and her life was complete.

In retrospect, she supposed Honesty was destined to find them. Her new husband, Wes Howell, was a tall, dark, handsome Texas Ranger who always got his man.

"It's about time you came down!" Honesty walked toward her, her radiant beauty glowing as she threw her arm around Chastity and looked up at Reed with a wink.

"I'm going to borrow your wife for a while, Reed. There's a promise I've waited a long time to keep."

"A promise?" Chastity looked at Purity, who stood a few feet away. There was no help there.

Following Honesty outside, Chastity glanced at the huge horse that stood saddled and waiting at the rail. She did not expect the tears she saw in her sisters' eyes as Honesty said, "Do you remember that day a long time ago when I took Papa's sorrel mare without his permission, and Purity and I went for that wild ride? Papa came riding after us as we raced across the prairie. He brought Purity and me back and spanked us real proper, but you were the one who cried the loudest because you had been too young to go with us. I promised you that night after we were all tucked in bed that we'd all ride together, someday—all three of us." Honesty's smile beamed. "Today's the day."

Mounted on the huge animal minutes later, Chastity looked back at the three men standing on the porch behind them. Wes shook his head with an indulgence that rarely lapsed in his dealings with his strong-minded wife. Cass's pale-eyed gaze followed them intently, and Reed's smile flashed bright and strong when Purity hooted and Honesty dug her heels into the horse's sides with a shout that startled their mount into a wild leap forward!

The wind in her face . . . her sisters' screams of delight in her ears . . . the wild and crazy joy of it as they raced across the sunswept ground!

Chastity's heart surged to bursting. In the midst of the laughter and the lighthearted cries, she suddenly smelled the scent of roses, then felt her father's smile, and she knew that her parents were finally content, now that their three dangerous virtues were together again.

Breathless and windblown, the wonder of the moment was surpassed only when the ride was over and she slid down into Reed's arms.

*I love you, Chastity.*

The words didn't need to be repeated. They were in Reed's eyes, a solemn promise for the days to come, and they were forever in her heart.

# ELAINE BARBIERI

*Dangerous Virtues:*
## Purity

*Purity, Honesty, Chastity—They were all admirable traits,
but when they came in the form of three headstrong,
spirited, sinfully lovely sisters, they were...*

## Dangerous Virtues

From the moment Purity sees the stranger's magnificent body, she feels anything but what her name implies. Who is the mysterious half-breed who has bushwhacked the trail drive she is leading? And why does she find it impossible to forget his blazing, green-eyed gaze?

Though Pale Wolf attacks her, though he is as driven to discover his brother's killer as she is to find her long-lost sisters, Purity longs to make him a part of her life, just as her waiting softness longs to welcome his perfect masculine form. There may be nothing virtuous about her intentions toward Pale Wolf, but she knows that their ultimate joining will be pure paradise.

\_\_\_4272-X                         $5.99 US/$6.99 CAN

# DANGEROUS VIRTUES:

## ELAINE BARBIERI  *Honesty*

**Honesty, Purity, Chastity—three sisters, very different women, all three possessed of an alluring beauty that made them...DANGEROUS VIRTUES**

When the covered wagon that is taking her family west capsizes in a flood-swollen river, Honesty Buchanan's life is forever changed. Raised in a bawdy Abilene saloon by its flamboyant mistress, Honesty learns to earn her keep as a card sharp, and a crooked one at that. Continually searching for her missing sisters, the raven-haired temptress finds instead the last person in the world she needs: a devastatingly handsome Texas ranger, Sinclair Archer, who is sworn to put cheats and thieves like herself behind bars. Nestled in his protective embrace, Honesty finds the love she's been desperately seeking ever since she lost her family—a love that will finally make an honest woman out of her.

_4080-8                                    $5.99 US/$6.99 CAN

# GOLDEN DREAMS

## ANNA DeFOREST

After her father's sudden death leaves her penniless, Boston-bred Kate Holden arrives in Cripple Creek anxious to start a new life, her elegant upbringing a distant memory and her dream of going to college and becoming a history professor long-forgotten. But the golden-haired Kate soon finds that the Colorado mining town is no place for a young, single woman to make a living. Then desperate circumstances force her to strike a deal with the only man who was ever able to turn her nose from a book—the dark and brooding Justin Talbott.

As skilled at passion as he is at staking a valuable claim, Justin vows he'll taste the feisty scholar's sweet lips—and teach her unschooled body the meaning of desire. But bitter from past betrayals, the wealthy claimholder wants no part of her heart. He has sworn never to let another woman close enough to hurt him—until the lonely beauty awakens a romantic side he thinks has died along with his ideals. For though bedding her has its pleasures, Justin is soon to realize that only claiming Kate's heart will fulfill their golden dreams.

_4179-0                                   $4.99 US/$5.99 CAN

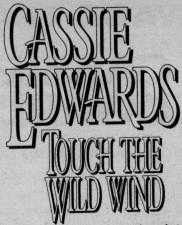

# CASSIE EDWARDS
## TOUCH THE WILD WIND

Alone and penniless, Sasha Seymour has thrown in her lot with a rough bunch, and she is bound for an even rougher destination—the Australian Outback, where she and her jackaroos hope to carve a sheep station from the vast, untamed wilderness. All that stands between her and the primitive forces of man and nature is the raw strength and courage of her partner—Ashton York. In his tawny arms she finds a haven from the raging storm, and in the tender fury of his kisses, a paradise of love.

____52211-X                                    $5.50 US/$6.50 CAN

# SAVAGE TEARS

# CASSIE EDWARDS

## Bestselling author of *Savage Longings*

Long has Marjorie Zimmerman been fascinated by the Dakota Indians of the Minnesota Territory—especially their hot-blooded chieftain. With the merest glance from his smoldering eyes, Spotted Horse can spark a firestorm of desire in the spirited settler's heart. Then he steals like a shadow in the night to rescue Marjorie from her hated stepfather, and she aches to surrender to the proud warrior body and soul. But even as they ride to safety, enemies—both Indian and white—prepare to make their passion as fleeting as the moonlight shining down from the heavens. Soon Marjorie and Spotted Horse realize that they will have to fight with all their cunning, strength, and valor, or they will end up with nothing more than savage tears.

___4281-9                                    $5.99 US/$6.99 CAN

# DELANEY'S CROSSING

# JEAN BARRETT

Virile, womanizing Cooper J. Delaney is Agatha Pennington's only hope to help lead a group of destitute women to Oregon, where the promise of a new life awaits them. He is a man as harsh and hostile as the vast wilderness—but Agatha senses a gentleness behind his hard-muscled exterior, a tenderness lurking beneath his gruff facade. Though the group battles rainstorms, renegade Indians, and raging rivers, the tall beauty's tenacity never wavers. And with each passing mile, Cooper realizes he is struggling against a maddening attraction for her and that he would journey to the ends of the earth if only to claim her untouched heart.

_4200-2                                    $5.50 US/$6.50 CAN

**TERMS of LOVE**

**SHIRL HENKE**

Cassandra Clayton can wield a blacksnake whip as well as any mule skinner and cuss as well as any Denver saloon girl. There is one thing, though, that she can't do alone—produce a male child who will inherit her freighting empire. Steve Loring, wrongly accused of murder and rescued from the hangman's noose, is just what Cass needs and with him she will produce an heir. But Steve makes it clear that silver dollars will never be enough—he wants Cass's heart and soul in the bargain.

_4201-0                                   $5.99 US/$6.99 CAN